# Gape

Aiden Truss

*Sirens Call Publications*

## Gape

**Copyright © 2013 Aiden Truss**
**Licensed to and Distributed by Sirens Call Publications [2013]**
**www.sirenscallpublications.com**

**Print Edition; First Edition**

Edited by Gloria Bobrowicz

Artwork © Dark Angel Photography
Cover Design © Sirens Call Publications

ISBN-13: 978-0615862927 (Sirens Call Publications)
ISBN-10: 0615862926

For Amanda, Aaron and Daniel.

.

# Gape

*Abashed the devil stood*
*And felt how awful goodness is*
*And saw Virtue in her shape how lovely;*
*Saw, and pined His loss.*

— Milton

# Foreword

Separated by those vast and normally insuperable gulfs of space, time and imagination, two beings sit at the crossroads of their lives - one human, and one something more than human. Both feel the weight of their existence and a solitude born of their introspection and contemplation. Both are equally lost and shackled by their seeming impotence in the face of the storm blowing around them.

Of all the different types of crises we face, it is the internal, personalised ones which hit hardest, cut the deepest and yet teach us the most valuable lessons. In that sense, it makes not one jot of difference that one of our protagonists is a female human and the other a male demon. As we shall find, near omnipotence does not denote omniscience and incapacity need not mean weakness.

Life cuts through complications – it's just that we seldom step back and allow it to take its course. We always assume that there is a point, that there is something more to it all than a series of contiguous moments, a chain of causes and effects – that there must be a cosmic narrative and a divine plan. Sometimes it's handy to know what's around the next bend in the road, but still, we must negotiate that bend and the change of direction that it brings. Whether you're a milkman or a 7th level demon, you still have to get your head around your day job and the challenges and satisfaction that it may or may not bring. In Paradise Lost, that shrewd observer of the eternal struggle, John Milton, wrote:

*The mind is its own place, and in itself,*
*Can make a Heaven of Hell, a Hell of Heaven.*

It was poetic licence – Satan never really had to jump to such conclusions, but you get the gist don't you. It's where you're at in your head that defines the world around you. For this reason, our tale is set in recognizable worlds, with familiar terms of reference. The everyday world of humanity is set in the unremarkable London suburb of Bromley. I would have used Croydon for a setting, but this might have placed us nearer to purgatory in terms of imaginative leaps. (Papers recently unearthed during Dan Brown's search through Vatican records reveal that the medieval Catholic Church considered calling the transitory state between Heaven and Hell 'Croydon', but were persuaded differently by its connotations of helplessness and despair; at least in purgatory there's the hope of something better to come!).

The universe, or cosmos as your author has chosen to describe it (paints a bigger picture than just 'universe' don't you think?), is full of different levels of life and evolution. Creatures living in dimensions unknown to traditional science co-exist in areas of space occupied by more conventional life-forms. Every so often, these planes intersect and cross over. Hence we have unexplained sightings, strange craters in the wilderness, ghosts and silly old women making a fair living at pretending to be psychics. None of which are the least bit extraordinary if you have a tiny inkling of the true nature of the cosmos. Therein lies the problem – in attempting to show the narrow scope of the human concept of the cosmos, it would be easy to overcomplicate things and to show you too much of what we all grasp to understand.

Here, Hell is exactly as you would expect it: the fantasy landscape, the salamandrine imagery, the demonic hordes, and, of course, the pointy instruments of torture. It is a recognizable construct that we have become strangely familiar with due to cultural exposure to centuries of Hellfire preaching. Our entire occidental concept of Hell seems to stem from three main sources: *The Book of Revelations* – thanks to John the

Divine's narcotic-fuelled bender while on an enforced stay on the island of Patmos nineteen centuries ago- from John Milton's *Paradise Lost*, and from Dante Alighieri's *Divine Comedy*.

These texts lead us to a perceived familiarity with the imagery of Hell – even if we just have a second-hand, post-modern understanding of the place. It's where The Devil lives and where all the bad people go when they die, isn't it? So, there are your terms of reference – I'll not try to makeover those places in your head where these people exist, I'll just use the information in your head to paint a backdrop to the drama as it unfolds. Paradoxically, you'll find that Hell is a thriving, heaving place of industry and intrigue, whereas Bromley is painted in suburban grey and not much goes on in the open, beyond shopping and washing cars. Like all suburbs, the real dramas unfold not in the streets and public spaces, but in the shadows, behind the twitching curtains and the veil of respectability.

Hell's denizens are meant to be as convincing as their human neighbours. They have personalities, ambitions and politics beyond petty evil and the acquisition of souls. Most importantly, they have a propensity for introspection and soul-searching that has been denied them since Satan's ruminations in *Paradise Lost*. Our demonic friend is as lost as any human and must find his own way out of his predicament.

Most importantly, as you will find, there is no Manichean dichotomy here – no good and evil or black and white (how boring!). There is just life in all its forms and dimensions, being played out relentlessly by characters familiar and exotic and all lost in their own way. Life doesn't present us with easy answers to our questions; this is perhaps what makes it all so interesting. As the old cliché goes, it's about the journey and not about the destination...

Aiden Truss

# I
# Hell on Earth

When theologians decided that there was such a thing as purgatory, it is almost <u>inconceivable</u> that it wasn't dreamt up while waiting in the queue to see an advisor at a job centre.

For a start, the local authorities take their people management systems straight from the deli counter at Sainsbury's. You take a ticket from a little red dispenser on the wall, then, if there is room, you take a seat or you simply wait in line. No one speaks and all eyes are fixed hypnotically on the little digital number counter on the wall. The counter is there to tick down your fate as you wait your turn for an interview with an administrative assistant.

Either side of you will be found several types of people: there are adults who are slightly strangely dressed and who barely speak a word of English, there are spotty, straight-out-of-school kids who have never had a job and are simply there to sign on to fund their tab at the local off-licence and there are the middle-aged no-hopers. These are invariably men and women who have done unskilled work all their lives – clerical jobs, minor white-collar careers, only to find themselves targeted as a 'manageable cost' and out on their ear after the last round of corporate cost cutting. Too old to start again, but too young to retire, their eyes are empty of hope and full of resignation. It's a soul-destroying moment when you find yourself among their number – one of the great unwashed and unemployed. It's as if you've had your membership of the human race suspended for the foreseeable future.

The wait seems <u>interminable,</u> but when at last the time comes, and your number is called, you feel the strange compulsion to wave your ticket above your head, just in case anyone should think that you're attempting to jump the queue. No one really pays any attention – it's just a strange impulse. It's finally time for the 'interview' in which you attempt to prove that you're actually 'actively seeking employment' and not just planning on spending the next few months at home on your arse watching *The Jeremy Kyle Show* and *Homes Under the Hammer* on TV.

I use the word 'interview' in the broadest possible sense of the word. The clerical assistant whose misfortune it is to have to deal with your case does not actually make eye contact with you – perhaps a precaution against catching the dreaded 'unemployed' disease that you are presently suffering from. You are required to fill in several forms, register your qualifications etc. and then arrange for a further interview with someone else even less interested in your well-being than the first person - but it all wastes a bit more time and money until your next 'job seekers' interview.

It was such a manifestation of purgatory into which Rose Hunter found herself one autumnal Tuesday morning in Bromley. She'd been unemployed and homeless for two years now. A succession of well-meaning social worker types had attempted to find accommodation and jobs for her up until she finally left foster care, but now she was on her own. She wasn't quite sure what she was actually doing there, but it seemed infinitely better than the cold park bench that she'd spent the last two days and nights on.

Around her, those in the queue cast sideways looks of disgust in her direction. Her clothes were greyed and shabby, she wore odd trainers and her dark hair was matted and tangled. It had been months since her last hot shower and she was giving off a lively pong. She actually had quite a pretty face, but it was hidden behind a layer of grime that coated her features in a greyish yellow, mottled effect. From a distance, she had that 'Gothic' look about her – a post-punk princess of darkness, though the up-close reality shattered the illusion.

Upon hearing her number called, she stood up and approached the small, ordered desk for her interview. At the desk, a smartly dressed and slightly plump young man carried on writing with one hand and made a 'please be seated' type of gesture with the other. The sudden infusion of body odour into his olfactory nerves caused him to grimace, gingerly sniff the air and then finally to actually look up at Rose. He reached out for a tissue from the box on the desk and covered his mouth and nose. Piggy eyes squinted at her from behind the safety of his spectacles.

"How can I help you?" he blurted out in a muffled mouthful underneath his tissue.

Rose, totally unfazed, emptied a carrier bag full of shabby scraps of paper onto the impossibly tidy desk and sat back in her chair.

"I need a job; I was told that you could help me."

At the site of the grubby infestation of paperwork now inhabiting his desk, what was left of the colour drained from the young assistant's face. He had a nice job, a nice car, a nice flat, a nice girlfriend and a nice tidy desk and now one of those nice tidy domains had been invaded, infiltrated with squalor and it was almost too much for him.

"What's all this?" he prodded a piece of paper with his clean new pencil before looking at the pencil and then throwing it into the bin by his left leg.

"It's my papers. I've kept all of them."

"What papers?"

"I'm not exactly sure. Every time I have an interview in one of these places, I get given bits of paper, so I kept them in case they were important." Contrary to the suggestion of her appearance, Rose had a quiet and refined voice – not quite estuary English, but a bit more suggestive of a 'good' upbringing and education.

The observation flickered briefly across the mind of the assistant as he surveyed the mess on his desk, looking for something that might prove useful.

"Do you have any proof of ID, proof of address, birth certificate etc.?"

Rose knew where this was going. She had no idea where her mother now lived and had none of the things that the assistant wanted to see. She was too old for a care home but her lack of a home address precluded her from getting a job. Rose was in the classic homeless catch-22 situation. She had come to the job centre in the vain hope that today she might speak to someone who might actually be able to help her – someone with a bit of understanding and compassion. With a resigned and tired sigh, she picked up the paperwork, pushed it into her bag and shoved it toward the assistant. Trying to keep some sort of dignity and to keep the tears back from her eyes, she stood and walked from the room. No one even registered her departure; all eyes remained fixed somewhere between the floor and the number counter on the wall. Her passing briefly registered in the peripheral vision of a teenager in a tracksuit sitting by the door. He had been picking his nose and was surreptitiously trying to wipe the results of his nasal excavations onto the bottom of his chair.

Rose tugged at the door handle and swept out on to the landing. Someone had left half of a cold cup of coffee on the window sill at the top of the stairs - out of habit she went to pick it up to drink it. Staring into the foam cup, the water seemed to bubble as her eyes filled with tears again. She squeezed the cup in her hand; coffee welled up and cascaded down over her knuckles and onto the white linoleum floor tiles. She let it fall and silently descended the stairs to street level.

Outside, the autumn sun was desperately trying to pierce the grey veil of the sky, but what little light got through, brought no warmth with it. Oblivious to the derisory stares of the morning shoppers, Rose crossed the market square and headed down the high street. At times like these, in the moments of quiet desperation, she always thought back to her childhood – to her hopes and dreams of how her life would unravel. Her tears were for the memory of the child she had been. She regressed and again became the innocent little girl, dressing dolls in her bedroom, wearing her mother's shoes and idolizing her father. She'd been the original 'Daddy's Girl', incapable of doing any wrong in his eyes. In the afternoon, at the nod from her mother, she'd wait by the front door for him to return home from work. At the sound of his approaching feet, she'd fling open the door and run into his arms. His face would light up every time and he'd cover her little face with kisses. Though she loved her mother, he was her whole world – her friend and her protector.

When she was six, her father had died suddenly. Only a young man, he had had a heart attack on his thirty-fifth birthday. They had all planned to go out for a meal that evening as a treat but he had never come home. Rose been left with a relative during the funeral and her tender understanding of the concept of death had not allowed the news to sink in. For weeks after the event, she'd waited patiently by the front door for the sounds that she would never hear again.

Rose's childhood idyll was consigned to photograph albums and vague memories. Her mother took to drinking soon after, and series of boyfriends had come and gone in quick succession – each seeming more lecherous than the last. Her mother's lack of discrimination went hand in hand with her decline in health and eventual 'sectioning' by the authorities. She was found to be an 'unfit' mother after the school had alerted social services, and Rose was taken into care.

For Rose, this was the real downturn in her life. Her existence took on a fragmented pattern of foster parents, respite homes and temporary placements. Her peers were other

11

children who were victims of their circumstances: kids who were abused by their parents; children who were born with addictions; petty criminals and pyromaniacs. Each child came complete with their own harrowing story – broken by forces beyond their control, and most, far beyond repair.

Rose's association with them was not good for her own development – she began to share their paranoia, their phobias, their obsessions and coping strategies. Attention came from acts of destruction, power came from inflicting fear, and love – well that came from whoever was willing to take her to bed – or into the back of a car, a field and once, even a public toilet. It wasn't the kind of liaison seen in romantic comedies and read about in chick-lit fiction, this encounter had left her with a broken jaw, several shattered teeth and an unwanted pregnancy. She'd lost the baby before she could even arrange an abortion – she was sixteen at the time.

The memory of all this was as fresh as the suburban air filling her nostrils this morning. She took a deep breath, drank in the aroma of fresh coffee from one of the identikit high street coffee shops as she passed, and looked for somewhere suitable to position herself for a spot of impromptu begging. There was nothing else to do and she might just get enough money for a hot drink and something to eat before having to find somewhere to sleep for the night. In this respect, today was no different from yesterday. Rose had no future – she only had 'now', a place to exist and survive in as best she could. She always had the option of a local charity shelter, but that was like an admission that she was finally beyond help – finally a problem rather than a person. The last minute vestiges of her pride wouldn't allow her to walk in and ask for a temporary bed.

She found a 'beggable' spot in a shop doorway near to the train station. She knew that she ran the risk of being moved on by the local constabulary, but as the shop was empty at the moment, she hoped that she'd be ignored. She knew most of the local beat police by now and they generally left her alone. She wasn't aggressive or overtly offensive, she was just untidy.

Rose sat down, arranged her bags around her and pulled out a tattered piece of cardboard, which she placed in front of her on the pavement. The card was worded with a simple request 'Spare some change please'. She sat back, rested her head against the side of the doorway and merged with the busy thoroughfare of the high street.

# II
# Hell in Hell

Hell, the real Hell, Hades, the Abyss, call it what you like, is different for everyone. There's no one describable and quantifiable place, recognizable to all of its inhabitants and new arrivals, it's an entirely unique experience for everyone unfortunate enough to find themselves taking up residency.

In human terms, our fears and expectations paint the traditional picture of Hellfire and brimstone and accommodatingly, most denizens of Hell are quite happy to maintain this façade. Given that the natives of the place are mostly demons and fallen angels (yes, that bit is true), it's actually a bit more fluid, dynamic and exciting than that. Humans express experience and define their world through language. Therefore, it could be argued that the more imaginative and descriptive a sinner you are, the more vivid and exotic your experience of Hell is. This may explain why so many politicians end up having such an interesting time there, having had the benefit of a good education.

So, to set our scene, we are in Hell and are eavesdropping on a conversation between three of its most infamous denizens – three demons; Sinn, Priest and Eldredd are arguing among themselves.

"Look who's talking, you hypocrite."

Priest shifted uncomfortably in his chair, under the incredulous gaze of his accuser.

"You love the stupid creatures, you even choose to look like one!"

"I'm a Shifter, I'd be denying my own nature if I didn't imitate others."

"But why is it always humans, especially dull-looking clerics?"

Again Priest altered his posture to a more defensive one. It was always like this, whenever he and Sinn got talking, he ended up on the receiving end of a good tongue-lashing. He was of the same rank and order, but Sinn always seemed to look down at him for some reason. Like a wicked brother, fighting off a challenge from a younger sibling. As a result of several millennia of this treatment, Priest had started to get an inferiority complex. When a seventh level demon gets an inferiority complex, humanity tends to suffer as a result.

Priest enjoyed the look and feel of a corporeal body, he enjoyed the so-called pleasures of the flesh. Though the normally amorphous, semi-formed shapes of his brethren would be considered disgusting by human terms, he used his power to make himself a bit of a looker. He enjoyed the irony of his name and his outward appearance and used the look to gain the trust of those he wished to play within the human realm. He was tall and slim with a beautiful, almost feminine face and a mop of long dark hair, bound by a silver ring, which fell nearly to his waist. The only sign of abnormality was in his eyes.

A demon sees many strange and terrible things over his lifetime, and as a result, he has no pupils in his eyes. This is sometimes not noticeable when demons take human form; unfortunately, Priest's eyes were golden in colour. As you can imagine, this was a bit of a give-away in certain circumstances. Demons can be whatever shape they want to be, but they can't change the colour of their eyes. This goes back to a long-standing agreement with God after the last war of the apocalypse.

Oh yes, there have been many wars of the apocalypse over the years. In religious terms, it's a bit like the World Cup. It comes round every few years, everyone gets excited and then forgets about it 'till the next one. This will of course disappoint those who are waiting around for the great cataclysm at the end of time. You know, the loony sects that charge up a mountain somewhere in America every so often and wait for the end and then quietly slink home when it doesn't come.

Sinn in comparison, and to his credit, made no such pretences about his unearthly origins. In fact, the reason that he had a go at Priest so often was because talking was his favourite pass-time - that and the fact that physically he was little more than a huge mouth on legs. Unfortunately, after his last promotion and metamorphosis, his eyes wound up in his throat and he had to keep talking in order to see anything. Either that or walk round with his mouth wide-open, which was not such a good idea with all the little flying creatures that seemed to inhabit Hell these days.

The two of them had been discussing current affairs and gossip in their particular circle of Hell when conversation turned to recent successful possessions and other excursions among the humans. Sinn too had a particular fondness for them, though nasty and nefarious encounters were more his bag than Priest's cruel seductions. The difference was that Sinn liked others to think that these were trivial matters that were below his rank and interest.

They were sitting on the balcony of the large Gothic edifice that Priest had created as his home. Partly modelled on Castle Dracula and partly on Brighton Pavilion, it was a black marble mixture of tall windows, jutting battlements and strange oriental domes and minarets. The golden and purple sky of Hades burned brightly overhead, creating strange reflections in the stone of the building. It appealed to Priest's aesthetic sensibilities and was in keeping with his dark adopted image.

"Lord Astolath thinks you spend too much time there as well," Sinn Continued.

"Oh he told you did he? You have the ear of one of the Arch Demons now do you?"

"I know a great many things that I don't tell you."

Priest gave in at last, shrugged and stood up to leave.

"You're boring me now, Sinn! I'm going."

"I'm just warning you of the possible consequences of your actions, Priest. Things may be changing around here very soon, and certain parties will want to know where your allegiances lie…"

Priest stopped in his tracks and looked back over his shoulder.

"What do you know?"

Sinn's skin flashed purple and rippled. His gaping maw spread in a wide grin and what would approximate a pair of shoulders shrugged in feigned nonchalance.

Eldredd suddenly decided to chime in and make a contribution to the conversation.

"Oh, some of us have been keeping an eye on things, making alliances – securing our future. One gets to hear of changes, plans and machinations."

Priest bristled.

"No games Eldredd - what specifically do you know?"

Eldredd tried his best to look magnanimous and impartial. He paced the length of the pavilion where they were sitting. He was jet black and moved with the grace of a big cat – all sinew and veiled muscle, implied ferocity and potential violence. His skin reflected his surroundings as if it were polished to a high sheen. He looked like a traditional demon from medieval art – imposing yet impish – pointed ears, horns and fiery eyes. He was an old-school demon and proud of it.

"A war is coming Priest!"

"War?"

"Even now, Lord Astolath is massing his forces to confront Lucifer – it's only a matter of time before he wages war and takes what is rightfully his."

"Rightfully his? So you're on his side then?"

Eldredd allowed himself a slight grin.

"Let's just say that I've taken note of which direction the winds of change are blowing in and I've decided to ride the most favourable currents."

Sinn snorted in agreement and both looked at Priest for his reaction.

"And you think that the Morning Star will just roll over and take this lying down! He'll crush Astolath and then he'll destroy everyone else in his revenge. There'll be nowhere safe for anyone."

Eldredd and Sinn looked at each other.

"So we can't count on your support then?"

Priest turned away from them again. In the distance, a low rumble of thunder seemed to hint at the coming unrest.

"No, I'm not taking sides – I have no allegiance to anyone but myself. I think I'll sit this one out."

"Going to crawl back to your human friends are you?" Sinn could barely disguise his disgust.

"I have some things I need to do. I'll let you and Eldredd here play at politics and war games and we'll see who comes out of all of this unscathed shall we?"

With that, Priest launched into his party trick. He spread his arms theatrically, leant back and faded out of sight of his companions.

Sinn grunted and sighed.

"Bloody show-off!"

"It's what we expected after all – I wouldn't worry about it. When the time comes, we'll make sure he does the right thing."

Aiden Truss

# III
## Priest

In cosmic terms, Priest didn't travel far. He just needed to be away from the others. Their politicking and manoeuvring had long since ceased to be of any interest to him, and the need to distance himself from the sound of their voices became a matter of urgency; it was like listening to a couple of nagging old aunts.

It's difficult to describe how he was feeling at this time, I mean, where are the terms of reference – how do you describe the mind-set of a being from a different species? Priest had enjoyed several centuries of unfettered and untrammelled licentiousness and freedom. He was also free, barring some kind of cosmic catastrophe, to do the same for the foreseeable (and unforeseeable), future. So why was he troubled? He was troubled beyond mere boredom and the limits of his non-existent conscience. But that was the long and the short of it – he was bored, big time!

He'd not thought about his destination when he'd left the others behind – he'd just willed himself to be anywhere but where he was. As a result, he found himself on the beach lining the front of a small seaside town. He wasn't exactly sure where he was, and didn't exactly care. That he had ended up on Earth spoke volumes in itself. It was the very place of his preoccupation and troubles – the realm of the shaved apes who'd caused him so much puzzlement.

It was a carbon copy, picture postcard British coastal town, the same as a thousand others with terraced, multicoloured guesthouses arranged along the coast road. It had ice cream stalls, deckchairs for hire and a ramshackle pier promising 'Amusements' and fortune telling with 'Lady Ceridwen'.

Above all, the whole place smelled of fish and chips and candy floss.

It did however seem like a good location for a spot of thinking. The beach was sandy and strewn with pebbles, shells and lengths of grey-green seaweed. The tide was creeping slowly further up the sand and, on a whim, Priest stopped, pulled off his boots and socks, rolled up his trouser legs and decided to allow the water to lap at his feet and ankles. The sand was warm and sharp between his toes and the sensation made him feel better. It made him feel connected in some way to what was going on around him. Perhaps this was the most troubling of all his problems – that he felt such a need for these transient, passing and simple pleasures. Pleasures that should have been beneath him when he had the whole of creation as his playground.

Absent-mindedly, he picked up a flat grey stone, brushed the sand from it and skimmed it out to sea. It hit wave after wave before coming into violent contact with a gull resting on the water. On the beach, Priest walked past a small child diligently patting down the sand around a fair attempt at a castle. He'd seen the man skip the stone as he'd walked past. In wonder, he'd watch the stone hit three… four… five… six times before suddenly exploding in an eruption of blood and white feathers. The child stepped backward onto his castle, compacting the miniature keep and kicking through an outer wall before turning and breaking into a desperate run to look for his parents, 'Daddy!' he whimpered as he ran.

Priest didn't notice any of this – he'd turned and walked on before seeing the result of his expert skimmer. The sound of a crying child behind him didn't do anything to distract him either and, much as in other areas of his life, he walked on oblivious to what was occurring in his wake.

Priest had spent too much time among humans. His disdain and loathing of them had, over the years, changed to a fascination and then finally a preoccupation. It wasn't enough to make mischief anymore; he wanted to get inside them and to understand them. That they led such desperate lives and yet still sought to cling onto more precious time before their death was an endless source of seductive wonder to him. None but the lucky few had any real inkling of what was to come after the transition from mortal existence, so why were people so fearful of what might happen? Humans would climb mountains, swim the vastly deep and even catapult themselves into outer space without fear. Yet, that one short step to oblivion was too much for them.

There'd been experimenters – magicians, sorcerers, witches and necromancers in the past who'd all tried to look beyond the veil into 'the undiscovered country', but none who'd returned to tell the tale. They'd failed for the simple reason that men were not meant to carry such knowledge into their world. It was a built in fail-safe, an attempt to mitigate the effects of their accidental creation. Each world was created separately; each universe was from a different design concept – a series of experiments that was meant to lead to the ultimate life form. That there was an occasional overlap was unavoidable – something as complex as an entire universe was going to have the odd irregularities and glitches. Humans were a special case, as already intimated, in that they weren't actually meant to be where they were – they were an accident. Even more reason for them to be kept confined within their own realm of existence. Still, there had been some successful and partially successful attempts to move beyond the normal confines of their world. There were rumours of some success by a man called Joshua bar-Joseph a couple of millennia ago in Palestine. He'd managed to convince quite a few people of his return from the dead, but the story was uncorroborated and probably untrue. At least Priest hadn't known anything of the story before his first encounter with Christianity. This had been the real turning point in his relationship with men. In their desperate need for fulfilment and sense of purpose they'd spent almost their entire history populating pantheons and creating deities for themselves. And, here's the rub, they were barking up the right tree, but they'd only figured out part of the picture puzzle.

Yes, there was a creator, a 'God' if you like, but he was indeed just one of many. Oh, and yes, humanity was just an accident – there was no vast eternal plan, no prophecies to be fulfilled, there was just a cock-up during the game of cosmic billiards that constituted the creation of this particular universe.

But, you try telling the average shaved ape that he's just the result of a tear in the cosmic condom, and he'll refuse point-blank to believe you. Humans have a built-in limitation in that they just can't comprehend infinity. The very idea that something may have just simply always been there, in existence, doesn't add up in the Homo Sapiens' mind-set. Men live finite lives, with defined start and end points. Everything in the human realm is a product of creation in some way – something cannot come out of nothing (it can, but human science is not sufficiently advanced to cope with this concept!) Therefore, someone must have created men, and therefore, men must by this logic serve some special purpose in the universe. Who after all would go to all the trouble of creating them just in order for them to work in banks, to have kids and then to die in care homes?

Unless of course, mankind was in fact an accident. A catalyst dropped into the primeval soup and a lucky meteorite strike was all it took. Someone had kick-started the process, but the beauty of chemistry and nature of evolution and adaptation was that you could just turn your back and let it get on with things itself. This was indeed lucky, as the creator had a pretty busy schedule at the time and could allow the Earth to run itself while he got on with other stuff.

Unless you're one of these primates who's decided to roll back centuries of progress and understanding by believing in the literal biblical view of things, you'll probably take a seat, let this sink in and deal with it in some practical way (usually by getting too drunk to make sense of anything – the usual human reaction!). The ancient Greeks long ago worked out that there was nothing to fear from death – they worked out triangles, invented philosophy and bequeathed us democratic government (Two out of three ain't bad, so you might as well go with them!). We use triangles and elect our governments, so what's the problem with death? Another trait typical of humanity – it's propensity for choosing to follow only the bits it likes and agrees with from any philosophy!

So, here we are on the beach with a barefoot demon, a crying child, a concerned father and a dead gull. The gull will now be food to every little nibbler in the sea, the child will be bought an ice cream, and the demon?

Priest had travelled between dimensions on countless occasions, was familiar with countless species, creations (and creators!), and yet was drawn by an innate compulsion to return to our particular neck of the cosmos in order to better understand the nature of humanity. Like wheels turning within wheels, his scrutiny was scrutinized from a distance by others with an interest in humanity.

Aiden Truss

# IV
# Red Rose

"Spare some change please?"

Rose was kneeling on the pavement and shouting pleadingly at the passers-by. Her tattered , stained and green combat jacket was missing half its buttons and the side of the zip was ripped. Underneath, she was dressed in a mish-mash of black and grey garments, a patchwork against the cold. She had taken her trainers off as they were a size too small and hurt her feet, which were blackened and sore-covered. To the passers-by, her age was difficult to guess; it could have been anywhere between 17 and 70 as she reached out imploringly to the indifferent lunchtime crowd rushing past.

She glanced down to wipe her misty eyes with a grubby sleeve and inadvertently let out a loud sob as she finally lost all hope of pulling herself out of the deepening mire of her situation. She couldn't get a job because she didn't have an address. The local council wouldn't house her without proof of identification or a birth certificate. She didn't have enough money to buy a copy of her birth certificate. She was sinking in bureaucratic quicksand with no route of escape.

Things had been bad before, she'd spent her fair share of time in doorways, hostels, parks and anywhere that would have her for the night. When she was younger she'd hang out in tube stations after dark and hope to find someone drunk enough to take her home 'till morning. Of course she'd have to pay the going price. After her eleventh rape and four miscarriages, she couldn't even count on a baby to get her out of the gutter. A particularly nasty infection and a radical hysterectomy had put paid to that idea. Even a good beating sounded appealing. At least someone would be aware of her existence.

The tears dried in the ducts and her vision slowly cleared to reveal a man kneeling close in front of her.

"Hello Rose," he whispered softly and smiled at her.

She stared at him hard, her memory wasn't very good these days and she hoped that the clouds of obscurity would be blown away, by the gentle breeze of recognition. A policeman... no... a priest! Yes he was a priest, a beautiful priest, kneeling in front of her smiling and knowing her.

"What's the matter?" he continued without waiting for her to say anything.

"They won't help me," and she began to cry again.

The priest moved closer and gently wrapped his arms around her shivering form and the sobbing came in hard waves, crashing against the welcoming harbour of his embrace. How long since someone had shown her this simple kindness, the acknowledgement that she was in some way worthwhile, a real person and not just a piece of flotsam drifting away from the wreckage of her life. She couldn't remember. But she felt some semblance of comfort for what seemed like the first time in her life.

The sheer effort of crying drained the last of her energy, she relaxed and slumped backward. The priest took her weight and cradled her like a baby. She looked up into his face and his golden eyes beamed down at her. She winced as if looking full into the sun and his goodness lit up the dark shadowed recesses of her heart.

"Why do you want a birth certificate my child?" He stroked her matted hair from her eyes and kissed her forehead.

"To prove I exist," she said. "They don't know I'm alive without it." She half smiled at the ridiculousness of the situation but stopped short, wondering how this person knew about her. The priest nodded knowingly and sighed. His breath was sweet on her cheek and reminded her of something from her childhood that she couldn't quite place, something comforting.

"So if you don't get your certificate, then you don't exist at all then? You weren't actually born?"

Rose laughed, "I suppose not".

"So you never lived and you've never felt pain and you've never wanted for anything?"

Her eyes welled up with tears again. "If only that were true, but then I'd never have known you. I do know you don't I?"

The priest nodded reassuringly and squeezed her gently. "I'm your friend, and I always will be, you know me alright. Let's forget about your certificate shall we. Pretend it all never happened. Your step-daddy never touched you, no men ever touched you, the world never left its cruel mark on you."

She touched his arm in wonder.

"What do you mean?"

"You can come and stay with me and I'll look after you."

"Do you live far? My feet hurt."

"No, you can see it from here."

"That's alright then, I'll come with you."

"And I'll carry you."

"And all these people who ignored me can..." She stopped in mid-sentence. They were alone in the middle of the street and it had suddenly grown dark. How long had he been here with her? Her lips struggled to form the question but she had no energy left to mouth the words.

The priest stood with her still in his arms, and began to walk slowly through the nocturnal silence. She felt vaguely aware of movement and then sweet oblivion as she lay in the arms of her Morpheus.

The morning found Rose asleep on the pavement. She sat up suddenly as a passing schoolboy kicked at her back and ran off laughing to join his waiting friends who had dared him to 'kick the tramp'.

She coughed and frowned as her normally dry mouth filled with a hot, sweet, metallic tasting liquid. She gagged as it pooled in her throat and slumped forward to try to expel whatever was stopping her from breathing. The paving stone in front of her violently changed from dirty grey to dark red and she found she couldn't inhale. Pressure started to build in her chest and behind her eyes, as she fought to stand, fought the blinding panic building in her like a volcano trying to erupt through the surface of her skin.

Life is life and no matter how deprived, she fought to cling to hers. She knew she was dying and she wanted her friend, the priest, to be with her. Or had she just dreamed of him?

The last thing she felt was the skin of her cheek against the cold wet pavement.

# V

## Saints and Fish

A troubled look briefly flew across Priest's face, then turned round, flew back and decided to settle there for a while before departing again. He hadn't been able to help himself with the homeless girl. Victims were his speciality - not creating them, but finding them and raising their hopes and expectations and just as suddenly dashing them again on the rocks of their own despair. He was a demon after all, and each troubled soul was another mark on the old celestial scorecard. God had abandoned them after all, why shouldn't he have them for his own amusement?

Once in every hundred or so years he would take a human as a lover. Male or female it didn't matter; it was all just so much flesh to him. It was something different and amusing but it would never last long. Humans seemed to spend all their lives desperately trying to have sex with each other. Anyone would do, It all boiled down to the same thing, frantic groping and grinding in the dark and then unfulfilment and emptiness. Priest didn't really see the attraction. Of course demons don't need to copulate. The continuity of their race is guaranteed by the eternal need for cosmic balance. God had all his angels and saints to help out and so the Evil one had to have his minions didn't he? You couldn't have one without the other.

Theologians and philosophers will of course argue that in this enlightened age, the devil is just some sort of anthropomorphic manifestation of ancient man's need to project his guilt away from himself. This was of course, as humans succinctly put it, 'bollocks'. There always had been a fundamental order and balance to the universe and the Supreme Being of Light needed a dark nemesis for himself.

I hear you say, 'Why would God create an evil being to create so much nastiness in the world?'. The truth is that mere mortals have such a tremendously difficult time in comprehending the concept of infinity. Being finite creatures, humans have finite vision and the thought that these beings have always existed makes for lots of head scratching and face pulling among those who deem to call themselves wise.

This latest acquisition bothered him though. This Rose was different in some strange way that he couldn't quite put his evil finger on. Her suffering had such a divine and complete purity to it. Never before had he met someone so far away from absolution in every conceivable way. In several millennia of wandering the Earth in search of mischief, he had only met one other with the same intense sadness that Rose showed him.

That man was a Franciscan monk called Anthony whom he had met in 1222 in Padua in what is now known as Italy. Priest had been stirring up the local heretics against the church just to kill some time during a particularly long and hot summer vacation on Earth. He had managed to gather about him quite a good following of disillusioned young clergymen from the local towns. They spent their days picking on lone monks and priests and nailing sacrilegious rantings to church doors, questioning things like the virgin birth and the resurrection of Christ.

One Saturday afternoon, Anthony decided to confront them in the middle of the market in the Town Square. He set up a small stage just next to the fishmonger's stall, which was a big mistake for a start. Would you like to stand there amid all that smell and listen to a monk going on about what you should and should not be doing with your life?

Anyway, you had to give the guy some credit for the effort he went to. Anthony wasn't a big guy by any means, even though he was wrapped in his thick, rough looking brown habit, you could see by his slender wrists and gaunt face. He couldn't have been more than twenty-five or twenty-six but his face was already lined with worry and his shaggy beard had flecks of grey in it. He kept his hair in the traditional pudding bowl style tonsure so favoured by the Franciscans, the one with the little bald patch in the middle. It made Priest wince to look at him as the young monk bent over in prayer. The spot was so badly sunburned that it looked like a huge glowing red spot on his head, almost as if he had been marked out for some special purpose by some divine highlighting pen.

Anthony mounted the small stage and made the sign of the cross over his small audience. Priest didn't like this bit. It unnerved him for some reason and he turned the other way, pretending not to notice, pulling his cowl up over his head. He had decided to wear his heretic costume, a long black cloak over a rich red velvet tunic, with thigh length black calf-skin boots, all set off with a large gold inverted cruciform medallion.

His new acolytes had taken to wearing similar variations on a theme of evil and stood around him arms folded with looks of defiance in the direction of the monk.

Unbeknown to Anthony, Priest had briefed his men well on the upcoming confrontation. The basic plan was that whenever Anthony mentioned the words: God, Jesus or Christ, they would all loudly shout out 'Nah nah nah' at the tops of their voices whilst sticking their fingers in their ears and jumping up and down on the spot.

It was a safe bet that these words would come up quite often so great fun would be had by all, except of course the monk.

The monk confidently spread his arms and addressed the small throng.

"Although, you see yourselves as my enemies, I welcome you as brothers in Christ."

"Nah nah nah!" Thirty or so grown men jumped up and down on the spot with their fingers in their ears.

Anthony looked uneasily at the monks on either side of him for some sort of explanation for what had just happened. They looked back at him bewilderedly for the same reason.

Priest couldn't help grinning and the others barely managed to stifle their laughs, in nervous anticipation of the next signal.

Anthony continued, "God..."

"Nah nah nah!"

Again thirty or so men jumped up and down in front of him.

The young monk struggled to keep his voice calm now.

"Jesus..."

"Nah nah nah!"

This time, the heretics couldn't help themselves. They fell about on the floor laughing and giggling.

Anthony stared at them incredulously, eyes burning with fury and one large blue vein visibly throbbing in his temple.

"What is going on here?" He looked straight at Priest, waiting for a reply.

"I'm sorry, I don't know what you mean," he replied with a mischievous twinkle in his eye.

All around, the peasants in the Market Square had stopped what they we doing to listen in on the confrontation. The entire market became suddenly quiet, traders stopped trading, customers stopped haggling, pickpockets stopped picking pockets and magicians stopped their prestidigitations.

"Do continue my friend," Priest bowed his head slightly and beckoned the monk to carry on.

"I stand here today," the heretics remained still and silent, "to try to bring about some sort of reconciliation between our two points of view."

The lack of violent reaction instilled a new confidence in him.

"For is it not true, that Christ himself..."

"Nah nah nah!" Again the heretics became restless and began jumping up and down.

"That is it!" Anthony screamed at them. "I might as well preach to these bloody fish for all the sense I'm getting out of you lot. I've had enough; the pope can hang the bloody lot of you for all I care. In fact, yes, I'm going to preach to the fish."

And that's exactly what he began to do. To spare them any discomfort, he avoided the story of the feeding of the five thousand and the eating of the loaves and fishes. He spent three hours solid going through every parable he knew until his mouth was dry and the last fish was sold.

His audience gone, he jumped down from the stage and walked through the crowd, which parted before him. The heretics had long since departed to the local inn for refreshment where they were already going over the wondrous tale of their latest heresy. But the rest of the crowd shouted his name, followed by shouts of 'Miracle' and 'Good on yer son' and 'That showed 'em'.

The miracle of the preaching to the fish became famous throughout the land and really put the formerly second rate city of Padua on the religious map. Far from making Anthony a laughing stock, he was later canonized and became St.Anthony, the patron saint of lost causes.

The heretics where all rounded up shortly after and burnt at the stake by the Catholic Inquisition. They took some comfort from the fact that their great leader would at least go with them and comfort them with some last moving words of rebellion. Funnily enough, Priest was nowhere to be seen on the day though, having somehow escaped from the dungeon during the night and fled to start some trouble elsewhere.

It wouldn't have mattered if he had stayed anyway; everyone knows that demons are fireproof.

Anyway, that was all a long time ago and if the heretics had a brain-cell between them, they wouldn't have ended up as firewood. Humans had definitely become a bit more sophisticated nowadays.

"Rose, Rose, Rose," Priest sighed to himself. The trouble was that he was actually experiencing the gnawing sensation of guilt for the first time in his long life. He prided himself that he had probably killed more people than the Spanish inquisition. He had personally lit the pyre under Joan of Arc and had even been partly responsible for the death of Thomas Becket. Nothing had ever troubled him so deeply as this before and he didn't really know how to deal with it.

The church in which he was sitting one of those ones that you see everywhere, maybe a hundred years old at most, but styled after the Victorian penchant for gothic architecture. High arched windows projected faint hues of yellow and red on the stone floor as the sun shone through the stained glass. It was cold though and reeked of that overpowering incense that the Catholic Church seems to be so fond of. Most people seemed to find it somehow reassuring, as if God actually smelled of the stuff.

In actual fact, the Supreme Being had a nice vanilla sort of fragrance about him.

Of course it was sometimes necessary to hang about in such places just to add a bit of authenticity to his disguise, but he couldn't help but find the place a bit unnerving. A bit like sitting in the other team's changing room.

He gazed up at the cruciform figure hanging above a small lace draped altar and the suffering Christ stared back at him with sad, sunken eyes.

"Don't look at me like that," he hissed at the statue.

"Hello there father." A booming Irish brogue laden voice cut through the near silence.

He turned to see a priest kneeling down behind him, his chubby, jowled cheeks stretched back in a welcoming smile.

"Um, Hello!" Priest was quickly thumbing through his mental filing cabinet of excuses to explain who he was and why he was here. He could make the real priest disappear in an instant if he so desired, but it took energy and there were always witnesses to these things. He'd made that mistake before several times; no sooner had you snapped your fingers to get rid of someone, then someone else would step out from behind a pillar, or a bush or from behind a door and raise an accusatory finger at him. That meant that someone else had to disappear and before you knew it, the constabulary was involved, which meant more work covering things up.

No he would use his superior intellect and bluff it out.

"Visiting from out of town are we?"

"Yes, I'm at a seminar in the city and thought I'd pop in for a quick pray on the way home. Anyway, nice to meet you and all that. Bye!"

Priest got up to leave but the real priest got up and blocked his exit.

"You couldn't do me a favour could you?" Without waiting for an answer he continued.

"Only I'm running the parish on my own at the moment and I've got no one to help me out with this morning's confessions."

At this, Priest lost his urge to leave so quickly; here was the chance for some fun. He eyed the other man briefly, taking in the porcine countenance of the priest in front of him. The pink cheeks and plump body definitely gave the impression of a pig in a dog collar; it was only the short grey hair that gave him away as human.

"I'd be happy to help Father," said Priest, flashing his best fake grin at the other man.

"Good on you my boy." The other priest grabbed his hand and pumped it furiously in gratitude.

"My name's O'Neill by the way."

"Gabriel," replied Priest, using the first name that came into his head.

"Grand, grand, we'll start in five minutes. I'll take confessional number one and you can have number two." With that, O'Neill waddled off towards the back of the church.

Priest's eyes followed him as headed to greet the small collection of mostly elderly penitents who had recently arrived to confess their sins. The demon licked his lips in delicious anticipation, like a hungry wolf about to descend on the waiting fold.

# VI

## Confession is Bad for the Soul

An old woman lit a small candle, placed it in the holder and knelt down stiffly to pray. As she made the sign of the cross, she shivered and turned to look at Priest full in the face, as if she knew that he wasn't quite right.

Priest looked back at her, nodded piously and stepped into the wooden confessional. It was a bit like entering an outside lavatory, with just somewhere to sit and barely enough room to stand. To one side was an opening, shaped like a small square window with a grill over it and a small red velvet curtain to one side. He sat down and waited for his first visitor. It didn't take long before he heard the door open in the cubicle on the other side of the window. It shut quietly and someone sat down and coughed as if unsure whether they were alone or not.

"Forgive me father for I have sinned, it's been three weeks since my last confession."

A surprisingly young sounding voice came through the grill at him.

"Bless you my daughter, tell me your sins," instead of Priest's voice, the girl heard Father O'Neill's voice reply.

Reassured, she continued.

"Well last Sunday, I missed mass because I told my mum that I had a stomach ache, but I didn't really, I just didn't want to miss a programme on TV, and I've been arguing a lot with my younger sister recently and...," she sounded as if she was reading from a list, "...I pulled a girl's hair at school because she upset me and..."

"Hang on a minute," he had to interrupt her, he knew exactly where this was going and he'd heard it all before.

"Did any of these terrible things that you've done feel any good to you?"

He could almost actually hear the girl frowning at the question.

"Go on, you can tell me, I won't tell your mother."

Now this appealed to her greatly, she didn't get on with her mother much at the moment.

"Well they did feel sort of good but, that's bad isn't it?"

"What do you think?"

"I don't know." Suddenly Father O'Neill didn't seem quite as boring as usual.

Priest had that feeling that a spider gets as it watches a fly struggling in its web, getting more and more entangled with every passing moment.

"None of these things are great sins my dear. You haven't killed anyone this month have you?"

The girl giggled. "No."

"Well then, I wouldn't worry too much. Your mother's got a stick up her arse anyway. God, I hate some of my parishioners."

She almost choked with surprise.

"I thought you liked my mum, you're always talking to her?"

"That's just sex I'm afraid."

"What?"

"Sex," he licked his lips and suppressed a giggle, "Sex my dear, we're all at it in secret in the church you know."

He heard the girl stand up next door.

"I don't think you're very nice Father O'Neill. I'm going home to tell my dad!"

The door opened and abruptly slammed.

Outside the small group of penitents looked up in unison to see the little girl slam the door and storm out of the church, her long red hair fanning out behind her and her freckles tightly bunched together as her faced screwed into a frown.

The muffled sound of laughter came from the confessional.

"I wonder what that was all about," One grey head said to another.

"Probably got a big penance to do, a hundred Hail Mary's or something," said another and shrugged.

Priest stopped laughing and composed himself. In a booming voice, he called out to his waiting victims.

"Roll up, roll up, next in line for confession. You've got nothing to lose but your sins!"

Another fly stepped forward and entered the web. Perhaps Father O'Neill was drunk again; it had happened several times before. Everyone knew of his secret vice, but then again, he was only human wasn't he?

The old man stepped up, opened the door and was swallowed by the darkness within.

The man sat down shakily and turned to address the small curtain between him and the priest.

"Forgive me father for I have sinned."

"Shall I draw back the curtain my son?" O'Neill's voice came quietly from the other side.

"What's that?" The old man craned his neck to hear better.

"The curtain, shall I draw it back?" Came the voice again.

"As you wish, father."

The small velvet curtain was slowly and theatrically opened to reveal what in the darkness looked like a large peach on the other side. The old man reached for his national health glasses. He put them on and realized with a shock that he was looking at father O'Neill's large, pink backside winking at him through the partition.

The old man frowned, reached into his pocket and pulled out his pipe. He prodded the large rump in front of him just to confirm that it was what he thought it was. From the other side came more raucous Irish laughter.

Too old and too tired to get excited, the old man simply got up and left.

The morning's entertainment hadn't exactly gone as Priest had thought it would. These people were too shallow and predictable to be any real diversion for him. Father O'Neill would probably be defrocked or excommunicated and several of the congregation would convert to the Church of England or Judaism or something, but these were small pointless little victories. Besides, he had other things on his mind still.

Priest decided that a little visit to his oldest friend, Mulciber, was in order. They had been friends since the middle ages, a period which most of his kind considered the Halcyon days of demon-hood, the golden era of evil. Everyone was more willing to believe in things then, the battle lines were more clearly drawn. You were for good or for bad and that was that. Of course, humans had always been pawns in one game or another. If you were on the bad side, you were offered a lifetime of wealth, power, sex or all three, and in return they signed a piece of paper giving away their souls. If you were good, you were offered a blissful eternity in heaven in reward for a good life of suffering in the service of the lord.

Men liked to think that they had free choice in these matters, the right to choose which path they took, the high ground or the low ground, but they didn't really.

It's not like everything even had to be pre-ordained with humans, they just couldn't help themselves when it came to their own self-delusion and petty needs. At least to a demon, mischief had some point in the universal balance of good and evil. Men just dressed their own impotence in the appearance of power and success over each other and then in the blink of an eye they are gone.

Mulciber had been quite infamous in those days of course. Belial, Pazuzu, Azrael, Mephistopheles and Mulciber had been the demonic equivalent of the 'Rat Pack' back in the '50's. Priest had kind of latched onto them as a younger, unofficial member, running errands and procuring victims for their entertainment. The others had treated him with typical contempt as befitted a fledgling demon of lesser rank, but Mulciber had been different and had taken him under his wing as a kind of apprentice. The older demon was not into petty evil for evil's sake and preferred to take a more philosophical look at his place in the order of things. It was from him that Priest acquired his liking for living among humans.

Like Priest, Mulciber still lived in the outlying regions of Hell, not wanting to live amongst the human madness on a permanent basis. And so it was to here that Priest headed.

# VII

## Mulciber

How do you get to Hell?

You may well ask.

Aside from the obvious route - living a life of sin and debauchery - there are many ways in to the realm of Hades. One of them is actually on the site of Stonehenge, just under the Heal Stone. One of them is in a small cupboard in the Oval room of the White House in Washington D.C. and yet another is behind the garden shed of number 22 Acacia Avenue in Wimbledon – South London.

It is easier to end up in Hell than you may think!

Priest materialised outside Mulciber's huge white art-deco mansion, with the river Styx gently lapping at the shore one side. He walked down the driveway, lined with dead trees, passing a 1920's vintage Rolls Royce parked next to a large fountain that sprayed some blood-like liquid gently into the air. He approached the imposing front door, rang the doorbell and stood back politely to wait for an answer.

A few seconds later, the door gently opened inwards to reveal the face of Crowley, (yes, *that* Crowley), Mulciber's famous butler. 'The Great Beast' himself was living out his eternity, as he had lived his life, in the service of Hell. Unfortunately for him, his hubris of calling himself 'The Great Beast' had not gone unnoticed by the real Great Beast and so he was forced to serve a five hundred year penance in domestic ancillary service before he could take his place within the unholy host.

"Is your master at home?" Priest enquired cheerfully.

Crowley stood back to let him in without saying a word.

"Thank you."

The door opened into a large hallway with a black and white checked marble floor divided down the middle by an imposing and ornate staircase. The interior of the house seemed totally at odds with the exterior, with panelled oak walls and antique furnishings adorning the rooms in view of his position at the foot of the stairs. Art Deco had given way to stylish antiquity and lavish sixteenth century sensibilities.

"My dear boy! How the *Hell* are you?"

A cheerful and very cultured English voice rang out from the upstairs balcony.

Priest looked up suddenly to see his old friend grinning down at him.

Mulciber was clearly excited to see him and quickly descended to stairs to meet his friend.

Mulciber was immaculately dressed in a smart black three-piece suit with a black collarless shirt a pair of expensive ray-ban sunglasses over his eyes. His jet-black hair was oiled and combed back and he looked every inch like a mob godfather out of one of those Scorsese movies that Priest was so fond of.

OK, so he was a demon, but Priest could still be impressed by a sharp suit, and Mulciber was a very well dressed individual. Regardless of species or universal and cosmic allegiance, he was the epitome of sartorial (and Satanic), elegance.

Following the peculiarly human trait of shaking hands in order to formally re-establish contact with his friend, Mulciber looked deep into the troubled eyes of his former protégé.

"Not just a social visit then old boy?"

Priest looked bashfully at his own feet and gave a barely perceptible nod of his head.

"How about a walk in the grounds and a chat then, eh?"

Mulciber grabbed a black overcoat from the stand by the front door and strode out into the subdued light of the early evening. Priest fell into step and followed him out in docile fashion.

They turned right at the front of the house and into the beautifully landscaped grounds. Like all great houses, it had a rose garden, a maze and a vast expanse of green, dotted with small artificial lakes and follies; temple-like structures built simply for their aesthetic effect on the surrounding countryside. It looked like a demonic copy of an earthly masterpiece by Capability Brown.

"So you've reached that crisis point in your life at last have you?"

"What do you mean?" replied Priest, a little too quickly.

"One of them has finally got under your skin and forced you to examine yourself and confront a few home truths?"

Priest held his gaze on the distant horizon and shrugged his shoulders.

Mulciber smiled and continued as if about to launch into a soliloquy.

"It's entirely expected you know; we all go through it. We all have a sudden realisation of what we are and struggle to find our place in the scheme of things. It must be something human in our lineage, or the humans must have something demonic in theirs!

"This penchant for self-examination and soul searching... it's actually quite disturbing that it matches our innate capacity for extreme acts of cruelty and self- gratification. No doubt this is all part of the divine plan and all that."

Priest stopped in his tracks and tried to look his old friend in the eye. His gaze didn't quite make it though, and came to rest somewhere in the distance, just over his left shoulder.

"I'd always been happy to wallow in my one-dimensional feelings 'til now. No-one warned me that there were actual emotions hidden away somewhere, waiting to be triggered by something."

Mulciber put a consoling hand on Priests shoulder and smiled.

"Give yourself a chance old man... you're still young yet. You'll work through it. You just have to understand that in chthonic terms, you've just scraped through adolescence and into adulthood. I felt exactly as you do and I came through it... we all do."

Priest turned his head slightly to see the older demon's eyes twinkle through the tinted lenses of his sunglasses.

"So what should I do? What's the best way to get through it?"

Mulciber smiled.

"Go back to the source of your troubles and confront it. Deal with it any way you must, but deal with it."

Somewhere nearby, a small bird started to sing.

"I told you so, I told you so," came the shrill, warbled melody.

Priest nodded in acknowledgment of what he already knew to be true. All of these alien feelings had somehow thrown him off balance and nothing seemed certain anymore. He needed water wings, something to keep him afloat while he did his pathetic doggie-paddle to stay buoyant on a churning sea of feelings, doubts and uncertainties.

"The humans call it a 'crisis of conscience' you know," said Mulciber, almost to himself as he started walking slowly off in one direction.

Knowing that his young acolyte would follow, he continued.

"The sudden realization of responsibility for your own views and actions, the idea that you might actually be accountable for what you've done and the bittersweet realization that it actually conflicts with your own needs or interests."

"So what was your crisis of conscience?" Priest stopped walking and waited for Mulciber to come to a hesitant rest as well.

Mulciber turned and looked his young friend in the eye, smiled and gave a capitulating sigh.

"You staying long?"

Priest smiled at his old friend and nodded.

"I suppose it must have been the biggest crisis of conscience of all time. I've been around a lot longer than you and experienced more than even most demons could imagine.

"Most, like their human cousins, are preoccupied with pettiness and solipsistic pursuits. Evil is a full-time career choice for them, along with all the accompanying imagery, paraphernalia and theatrical evil laughter.

"Personally, I can't help what I was born as any more than any other creature can. I can only play the cards I've been dealt, it just so happens that my particular cards allow inter-dimensional travel, shape-shifting and immortality."

Mulciber paused to make sure that Priest was still paying attention. They had wandered slowly across the lawn and found themselves by a seat carved into an imposing Roman-style archway. Both demons sat down and stared into the distance as Mulciber continued his monologue.

"Also, like humans, most demons can't get their heads around the possibility that moral absolutes exist only in the heads of the intellectually challenged. God didn't set out any laws for the universe any more than he gave the Ten Commandments to Moses. It's all mythology and supposition given longevity by the widespread lack of questioning thought.

"You see, you worry that you've been contaminated by contact with humans, but as a species, we're closer to them than any primate. The differences are purely physical; spiritually we're almost from the same metaphysical gene pool.

"You follow what I'm saying?"

Priest nodded in silent affirmation that he was paying attention.

"This is all a very long and verbose preamble to revealing that I wasn't as strong or as immune as I thought I was to having some sort of feelings. And when I did find out, I didn't know how to deal with them, they knocked me six ways from Sunday!"

"See nothing is ever as it seems, not even for those of us who think we're omniscient!"

Mulciber paused and allowed himself a wry smile.

"You've said a lot without actually telling me what happened, you are fully aware of that aren't you?" Priest looked at Mulciber and raised one eyebrow in mock accusation.

The older demon chuckled a quiet, almost musical chuckle that had both of them smiling. It had started to grow darker by now, with crepuscular shadows lengthening all around them and the breeze blew around them with increasing confidence. In the distance, the lights of the mansion were flickering on one-by-one and on the lake the geese and swans seemed to be settling in noisily for the night ahead.

"Well I don't want to make it too easy for you, to tell you what to expect. Where would the fun be in all that, what could you possibly learn from the experience?"

Priest nodded with a realization and understanding at what his only friend was saying.

"So I go back and blunder my way through it all…"

"And you'll be all the richer for it and I'll be here with a decent bottle of something when you come through on the other side."

Priest nodded and they both stood up. The two embraced and kissed like the old and dear friends that they were; the younger left the elder standing in the archway.

Mulciber watched as his former protégé crossed the lawn and headed Christ-like across the surface of the lake until he disappeared into the distance.

Mulciber turned and headed for the mansion.

"Good luck my friend."

# VIII
## Loophole

Rose awoke and tried to blink away the blurry shadows from her eyes. She felt relaxed and warm, almost as if she were floating. A cool breeze caressed her cheeks with the soft touch of a concerned mother and she nestled into it and smiled. All around her, the air was filled with the fragrance of roses and heady garden scents that reminded her of a day in the countryside that she'd once had as a child.

She still couldn't see, but slowly her vision was clearing to reveal a soft light that illuminated the area around her. Beyond that, shadows slowly moved to and fro, their sounds drowned out by the gentle, susurrant, bubbling of water running into a pool or a stream. Sitting up, she could see the outline of her hands in front of her face, but little else beyond that. With a sigh, she sank back down as the blissful feeling of tiredness flowed back into her limbs. She had no idea where she was, but somehow that didn't concern her and she allowed herself to sleep once more.

A few feet away, Priest sat with his chin in his hands and watched her breast slowly rising and falling as she slept. They were between worlds, in a little haven that he had created for himself early on in his career. It was a little bubble, a glitch, a loophole in physical law, a kink in the flow of time and space that didn't conform to any part of the geography of Heaven, Hell or Earthly existence. It let him shut out the concerns of the other planes of existence and recharge his demonic batteries so to speak. There was nothing to see or to describe there, as technically the place didn't exist. It was whatever he wanted it to be and he could always return there as he had imbued it with part of his essence. At the moment it resembled a small ornate rose garden with a rockery, 'water feature' and some nice decking that he'd seen on *Garden Force* at one end. At the other, lay a large ornate bed, covered in silk cushions and sheets. Upon this lay the reposed figure of Rose, the object of his fascination.

Technically, Rose was dead - well, physically at least. But that was a necessary part of the transition. You can't cross dimensions in human form without dire consequences too terrible to allude to here. So with this in mind, Priest had let her body die after their last meeting. To the world she was just a beggar that wouldn't be missed, another statistic, another mess for the local authorities to clean up from the doorway where she had vomited up her lungs in her final paroxysmic desperation to hold on to her miserable life. Painting the pavement had allowed her to cross over.

Despite his fascinations, Priest had no sexual feelings toward her, though the transition had done wonders for her appearance. She wasn't, however, to be one of his experiments. With the grime of the city gone, she was a raven-haired beauty with wide brown eyes and a cute little overhang to her upper lip. No, it was the suffering that had fascinated him, the human need to survive and hang on to life, no matter how deprived or depraved. Rose had fought death, had struggled to breathe and to cling on despite the realization that no one would help her. All her life had been a struggle; he knew all about her, everything she had ever done and he had seen how she had been abused through her childhood and brief adolescence. Still she had wanted to live, to face another day of the same privation and misery. And for what - to do the same thing all over again tomorrow?

What was the ingredient missing from him that drove humans on? What was the indefinable thing that drove them to cling to their miserably short lives? Lives that flew by in a heartbeat, in the blink of an eye to an immortal like him. Perhaps that was just it; the fact that they had such a short period of existence meant they kicked so hard against their doom. For most of his life, they had merely been a diversion, fish in a bowl, entertaining adornments, something to play with and then flush down the proverbial toilet once they either ceased to be of interest, or managed to break themselves in some way. This would be either as a result of one of his games, or just through simple human frailty in the face of demonic meddling. He prided himself that there was no sexual act too depraved for him, no frontier of extreme pleasure that he would not enjoy or inflict on a willing recipient. But, as a wise human had once said, 'Who wants cookies when the jar's always full?' It is easy to get bored of such things quickly. Like every human soon finds, after such intimacies, that gap between you in bed suddenly feels like a chasm. Imagine that gulf on top of the interspecies issues and you have a rough idea of the general state of confusion in Priest's head.

Rose was an altogether different enigma to him though. Was she a saint? He wasn't quite sure of her spiritual leanings, her propensities for good or for bad, but he was sure of her purity. And there is little more fascinating to a demon than innocence and purity, especially if combined in the one same handy physical package. She was a puzzle to be solved, but more than just a diversion to him, he needed to understand her and so had decided to show her something of his world. He would imbue her with some of his powers, show her the things that he had seen, and in doing so, would come to know her intimately. It was just a matter of deciding what to tell her when it was time to rouse her from her sleep. He had already gained her confidence once, but having to explain to a mortal that she had 'shuffled off her proverbial coil' and passed into a completely different plane of existence might take a little bit of subtlety. He shifted to the side of the bed, took her hand in his and softly spoke her name.

Rose awoke to find herself looking into the face of an angel. She remembered his face from the street, remembered his kindness and his promises, but couldn't remember any more than that. The clouds in her head were gradually drifting away on a calm breeze and she didn't feel troubled or confused, only intrigued at where she was. Priest was smiling at her, as if unsure of what to say next. He patted her hand absently, rose and walked to the end of the bed. Rose looked about her and tried to focus, but beyond the bed, all was misty and out of focus.

"You're alright Rose, there's no need to worry about anything anymore."

Rose smiled at him.

"I'm not worried, I trust you."

"You may not when you hear what I have to say to you…"

At this, Rose sat up, a flash of concern briefly passing over her face.

"I'm a bit confused, you said I can trust you, you were kind to me and I feel better now – what is there to worry about?"

Priest swallowed hard.

"There's no easy way to tell you this, so I'll just come out with it all. You're not actually alive anymore Rose. You're not exactly dead either. You're somewhere in-between, but you can never go back to your old life."

"I didn't have a life, remember?"

"Yes I see what you mean, but I'm not just talking about going back to the streets. I'm talking about existence, not just everyday life."

Rose's face dropped to yet another level of concerned confusion.

"But I can see you, we're talking aren't we, how can I not be alive? I don't understand."

"You will in time Rose. I'm honestly trying to avoid all the old Anne Rice vampire clichés here – you're not undead or any of that nonsense. Your physical life ended on that pavement. To all intents and purposes, and as far as anyone else knows, you died. The difference is that I never allowed the usual

54

powers the chance to get their hands on you, to decide what to do with you. I brought you here to my hiding place."

"I still don't understand."

"I'm not a priest Rose, that's just my name; it's my nom de voyage, the name I travel under. I'm not like you and let's just say that the usual physical laws and boundaries do not confine me. Your forefathers would have called me a demon, but we have a very different name for ourselves, one that we'd rather not share with others, so you may call me a demon if it will help you to get a handle on things."

Rose didn't know whether to snigger or cry out for help. Something didn't add up and she didn't know where she was, but she was no fool. She wasn't about to believe that she was in the presence of a demon just because she had woken up in a strange guy's bed. She'd been conned too many times before. There had been too many men and too many excuses, but this one was the weirdest of the lot.

"So do something magical then, if you're a demon?"

Priest turned away and tutted to himself. Maybe this was a mistake after all. Curiosity was famed for killing cats; maybe it was not above killing demons too.

"What do you want Rose, do you want me to pull a bunch of carnations out of my sleeve, do a card trick or perhaps find some water to walk on? This is real. Such petty nonsense isn't magic, its trickery and sleight of hand. It's rubbish and I'm quite frankly above it all. I'm trying to tell you that I've saved you from oblivion and I've brought you to my realm of consciousness because I find you interesting and I want to know more about you. I'm not a friendly priest, I'm not even a very nice person by human standards, but then I'm not human and so have no apologies to make. My intention was to spend some time with you, to try to understand you and perhaps to imbue you with some of my abilities, a reciprocal relationship if you like. You'd see things from my viewpoint and I'd see things from yours. I haven't yet decided what I'd like to do with the information, but then I have an eternity to decide. You, on the other hand, can grasp the hand that has been extended to you or I can send you back to a cold grave. After that, you're on your own; I'd have no say where you went after that."

Priest's shoulders slumped and the fire behind his eyes cooled somewhat, seeing the alarm behind Rose's.

"You've got a second chance at an alternative life is all I'm saying. I'm not here to be questioned any further. You can accept what I've told you or you can shut your eyes and go who knows where…"

Rose sobbed, "I want to believe you, but how can I? One minute I'm fighting for breath and the next minute I'm being told that I've been rescued by a demon. How do I know that I'm not just dreaming?"

A look of pure anger descended onto Priest's face. He lunged for her with a terrible howl and grabbed her by the throat. She felt herself launched into space, the bed faded from view and her ears were filled with a terrifying whispering which rose to a shrieking. Up, up they went, higher and faster – she felt like she was riding a comet's tail and all she could do was to go with it – to allow herself to be carried along by the priest.

She saw galaxies pregnant with stars, nebulae and clouds of cosmic dust. She reached out a hand, causing swirls and eddies in the misty fabric of the universe as they passed. Lights, lives, planets and civilizations whirled by and were snuffed out of existence, the universe played out its pageant of death and creation before her as they rushed ever onward, accelerating toward their unknown destination. She saw the arbitrariness, the indifference of the universe, the disorder and lack of a divine plan. She saw it all and through it, came to know herself, to see her place in the scheme of things. She wanted to scream with the profound realization that she was a random outcome that was a miniscule part of another random event. A chance marriage of proteins and amino acids, and the result of a cosmic ricochet and an unforeseen union of particles and subatomic strings of data. Like all humanity, she was a child of chaos theory. She had no place in the universe – she was a lucky accident, a serendipitous condensation of universal chance. She felt humbled by the realization and still they continued toward the unknown.

Priest knew exactly where they were going; he was playing catch-up with the edge of the expanding universe. He was heading for the event horizon, the boundary where the expansion had not yet reached. He would show her the secrets of the universe and then show her its limit and let its progress sweep over her and overtake her. Then, if she still needed convincing of his demonic credentials, only then would he do the trick with the carnations…

Rose drifted in and out of consciousness, but she was also beginning to understand her place in things. She looked up into the face of priest who returned her gaze knowingly. They slowed down as time struggled to keep up with them. Priest's words cut through the din.

"You have no place in the universe; it's all one huge cosmic joke. You are an accident, an experiment in a celestial laboratory, a schoolboy prank with an ocean sized test-tube and a planet sized Bunsen burner. Only, the bored schoolboy just happened to be the creator of the universe, and he's forgotten all about you."

Priest paused to let his words sink in.

"All this was to show you your place in the scheme of things. You are a speck of dust in the eye of the universe, you and all humanity, and when your time is done, you will not be missed. The universe will go on without you. Do you really think that there is a God out there who cares whether you live or die? And what if you are dreaming, how would you know it from your only perception of reality?"

Rose blinked and they were back on the bed in Priest's hideaway. She struggled to take in all she had just seen; her whistle-stop tour of creation and her new found realization that this powerful being may just be telling the truth about an indifferent God that she'd wasted her prayers on all her life.

"So what next?"

Priest smiled sweetly and touched her cheek.

"Whatever you want my dear. I've invested you with my powers for a short time. You can do whatever I can do, you can see things as I see them and if you find things confusing, you can always return here and I will be here to help you. Imagine where you wish to be, and you'll be there."

"Why are you doing this? It doesn't make sense that you'd do this to me."

"Would you rather I'd left you on the pavement as you were?"

Rose thought for a moment, remembering the sudden sensation of choking, coughing and trying to scream. It was all too much and she snapped back into the present. Anything was better than that.

Priest gently moved an errant strand of hair from her face, stood up and looked back at her from the end of the bed.

"I'll be watching you, don't worry. That's the whole point of this: I need to watch you, to understand. I don't know how it will feel – I've always been this way, but to you, it will be a strange experience until you get used to it. *If* you get used to it…"

"So I just think about where I want to be and I'll be there?"

"That's all there is to it, yes."

Rose peered at him, studying his features, looking for a sign of deceit. There was none that she could discern. What else could she do but go along with it all? She closed her eyes tight shut and thought hard.

# IX
## Coup d'État

Of course, Hell is far different than it was during biblical times.

The hierarchy has changed on numerous occasions, wars and revolutions have come and gone and very little there bares any resemblance to the descriptions that you find in those ancient leather-bound grimoires. All those sought after volumes in dusty occult bookshops are about as much use, and about as up to date as, the 1972 Chelsea Football Club yearbook. In fact, perhaps the most surprising thing of all is that Lucifer is no longer the top man, having been replaced some time ago by the demon lord Astolath.

The younger brother of the infamous Astaroth, Astolath had risen quickly through the dark ranks and had in fact killed his own brother, thus becoming the number one contender to the Infernal Throne. Of course, the throne was easy to secure, what with Lucifer's indifferent attitude to anything but the affairs of men. When Astolath finally had enough support to march upon the Citadel of Hades, it was all a bit of an anti-climax.

Standing at the head of a ten thousand strong demon army, Astolath sat regally on his skeletal horse and bellowed at the gates for Lucifer to come out to meet him. He was an imposing sight. Astolath was made for battle. With his huge muscular form and great height, even standing he dwarfed those around him. His comparatively small face peered out over the neck of a suit of red plate armour, his mouth set in a permanent rictus and his right eye continually scanning for his next victim. The other eye had been lost in battle millennia ago in an episode that had also lost him half of his right horn as well. It was the last time he had tasted any sort of defeat and he had literally been making Hell pay ever since.

After an hour or so, and just as Astolath was worked up in such a lather that he was ready to single-handedly storm the city himself, the massive gates opened slightly with a groaning metallic squeak and out walked the light-bearer himself. He was unshaved, his hair unkempt and he was slightly scruffy looking, but still, beneath it all, his beautiful blonde self. The fallen angel actually looked more like a playboy with a hangover. Since his white silk shirt was unbuttoned at the top and his sleeves were rolled up on his forearms. Black trousers and scuffed black shoes further embellished the image of someone affluent though slightly down on his luck. Seeming barely able to even summon up the energy to lift his head, he slowly approached Astolath. He actually seemed more interested in the 'nice horsey' that the demon-lord was riding than talking to Astolath himself. Without his eyes leaving the bony steed he simply asked.

"What's on your mind Astolath old man?"

Astolath snorted in disgust at the lack of fear and concern that Lucifer was showing.

"I have come for what's mine, Lightbringer!"

With that he raised his great muscular arm, pierced the air theatrically with his sword and looked to the throng behind him for a reaction. A great roaring cheer went up as the demon host made its presence known to everyone within a ten-mile radius.

Lucifer stepped back from inspecting the horse and yawned a great, sky-swallowing yawn.

"And what exactly is that?"

He made a half-hearted attempt at sounding interested, which only served to further annoy Astolath.

"Hell! I have come to take the throne of Hell from you!"

Again, a sycophantic cheer erupted from behind him. Armour rattled, demons bellowed and swords, axes and spears were defiantly raised toward Lucifer.

"Is that all... Just for a minute there, I thought you had something interesting to say."

Lucifer scratched behind his ear disappointedly, turned on his heels and started back toward the citadel.

"I suppose you'd better come in then."

Astolath gulped in surprise and looked at his second in command who merely shrugged his shoulders and looked back blankly.

"Alright then... erm that's fine." He signalled to his guards to follow him.

Astolath's two hundred strong cadre of elite demon guards quickly fell in behind his mount and marched behind him. As with the season before, and the season before that, black was the colour to be seen wearing in Hell at the time. The elite guard looked like a cobbled together collection of skeletal warriors wearing what looked like Samurai armour. Each one wore a breastplate with a highly decorative letter 'A' painted on it in red. This was quite handy really, seeing as their previous master had the same initials - they hadn't had to repaint anything after the last coup d'état.

All fell into step with Lucifer and began to close the distance between themselves and the huge city gates. During the march, Lucifer did not look back once, walking casually with his hands in his pockets and whistling some familiar-sounding show tune to himself. He had the air of a man with all the time in the world on his hands, about to take a stroll down to the paper shop on a Sunday morning, rather than hand his house over to a psychopathic warrior demon from another dimension.

Then again, we are talking about Lucifer here aren't we...?

You will be familiar with him in one or other of his guises, I'm sure. You know, he's normally depicted as the red guy with the horns and the pitchfork. Of course, this is just Judeo-Christian mythology mixed up with a trace of pagan satyr worship. For all those who've forgotten their Sunday school lessons, Lucifer was the anointed cherub, god's highest and most beautiful creation, brightest of all the angels. Lucifer also had a healthy dose of the one thing that is guaranteed to bring the greatest from their seats of power, namely, a healthy helping of pride.

Once you've reached the top, where are you going to go? There was no promotion on the cards, he'd reached the top of his salary scale, so to speak, and one person was sitting in the hot seat. Unfortunately, that person happened to be God, and we all know the kind of things that happen when you piss off the supreme deity; things tend to get broken on a cosmic scale and there are invariably tears. Lucifer's short-lived revolt ended in him shedding rivers of them.

When God smiles, it's like warm sun on your face, it's like a soothing breeze chasing the stale air from your heart, it's like the feeling of joy you experience when you hear a baby laugh for the first time, it is the same sensation that that infant feels when it looks into the loving eyes of its mother. It's a feeling that you get used to and once touched by it, you never want to be without. As punishment, Lucifer had simply been denied sight of the divine countenance. For him, Hell was like the dark side of the moon, never feeling that sunshine was his punishment for all eternity as an example to all the choirs of angels who had looked on to see what might happen when one of their number dared to rail against God.

What really grated on Lucifer was the fact that mankind, that other favoured creation had all the second-chances in the world, where he had none. Men had only to show their contrition to be granted entry into heaven, it was that simple. Why should it be so different for him?

Such, it would seem, is the relationship between fathers and sons. It's never easy to follow in the footsteps of a successful father, whether you're the son of a dustman or the first among the angels. All of this still played on the mind of the Morning Star as he led Astolath through the high wooden gates of the citadel and into the deserted courtyard of his home.

The place was a deserted ruin as far as the eye could see. From inside, the impregnable looking walls seemed cracked and in disrepair. Windows were broken, flags hung in tatters and brushwood tumbled playfully among the ruined houses of the once great city. Where there was once the sound of industry and people, there was now just the gentle whistling of the wind, punctuated by the odd corvine shriek of defiance from the numerous birds, which sat watching from every available perch. Thousands of eyes turned toward the returning Lucifer and the other unwanted guests. Lucifer reached a small doorway, entered and momentarily returned with a black coat slung over his shoulder. He pulled the door shut, reached into his pocket for the key and locked it. Then he turned back to face a bemused Astolath, who had by now alighted from his horse and stood looking at his surroundings.

"I've left all the doorknobs and light bulbs. Anything else you find, you can keep." With that, he tossed the key in the general direction of Astolath and made to leave the citadel.

"What is this?" bellowed Astolath, drawing his sword menacingly.

Without turning around, Lucifer turned his head slightly and muttered a parting shot to his uninvited guests.

"You wanted the throne, you've got it – this is all there is."

In the stunned silence, Lucifer slipped from sight.

Astolath turned to his current right hand man, the impish Helnocker. Astolath's lieutenants never lasted long, regularly being pulped for displeasing their easily displeased master. The two looked at each other and shrugged.

"After you lieutenant…"

Astolath's face stretched into a sly leer as he pointed the way forward into the city and nudged his steed forward.

# X
## Trismegistus

The huge room was lined with gilt framed portraits – old faces framed in wigs, peering sternly into the middle-distance. It was a library, with rows of book shelves stood sentry around a long, polished central table lined with high-backed chairs. The room was illuminated, but it wasn't clear exactly how. The candles in the sconces were not lit and the fireplace set into the far wall was cold and lifeless, and yet, a subtle illumination bathed everything in a soft, yellow light.

An old man hummed to himself as he wandered among the shelves. A wispy beard moved from side to side as he sucked hard on a mint imperial, the little ball of sweetness clacking against his teeth in a strange percussive accompaniment to the elusive, almost tuneless melody he emitted as he shuffled. He was attired in late 17th century dress – a blue frock coat and breeches, with his long silver hair tied back in a shabby grey bow. What really set the outfit off, was the sight of his threadbare off-white stockings, thrust into a pair of 1970s Woolworth's slippers, the ones with that nondescript tweedy pattern and rubber soles.

Hermes Trismegistus was keeper of the ancient library of the Arcanum. The Arcanum was an ancient society of knowledge gatherers and scientists. They'd been responsible for many of the most important discoveries attributed to mankind and for many of the great ancient monuments. Their influence was both widespread and profound – but Trismegistus was now the only remaining member of this ancient order. The library contained the sum of their acquired knowledge; books of ancient magic, scrolls of astrological charts, astronomical maps, tomes on the art of war, catalogues of angels and demons, long-lost sketchbooks gathered from renaissance masters and even erotic parchments from the secret Papal archives.

Trismegistus had not actually had a visitor to the library for over three hundred years but still continued to make his rounds – to take stock and even to procure new volumes which he added to the 'Just In' section by the front door. Due to the decline in both inquisitive thought and scientific advance of any real value to humanity, even the latest book was about seventy years old – a book of occult doodles by Austin Osman Spare. Spare had succeeded in devising a child's colour-by-numbers book, which if completed, would unlock a trans-dimensional portal. The designs were incredibly complicated, but such is the magic of colour-by-numbers; images that initially seemed to hint at sea-side fun and little boys flying kites actually evolved into intricate geometric forms, Enochian symbols and Egyptian death-cult summoning spells. It was a one-off edition and had yet to be placed before an unsuspecting child. Just as well, as apart from the possible dire consequences of opening a trans-dimensional portal, it would have wiped several thousand pounds from the value at the first downward stroke of a Crayola.

As the last remaining member of the Arcanum, Trismegistus saw it his duty as custodian to see the job through to the very end. Plus, it wasn't a bad place to spend all of his time. It was quiet; he kept his own hours and hadn't had to issue a late return fine since 1659.

Trismegistus ran his rheumy eyes along the top shelf of books next to him. All was in order, just as it had been the day before and the day before that. He nodded to himself and placed a tick in his ledger with a long quill pen. As you might expect, his ledger was full of ticks – as were the twelve volumes before that, all neatly lined up behind his desk in the far corner of the room.

To most of us, a heart-stopping incident would entail a car crash or maybe a comet landing or some such seismic event. Trismegistus' heart stopped at the site of a gap in his books on the next shelf. Where yesterday, there had been a vellum-bound edition of the *Tractatus Moralis de Occuli* (autographed by Peter of Limoges himself!), today there was just air – a three inch space between leathery tomes. Trismegistus gasped and winced as his ledger slipped from his grasp and landed corner first onto the big toe of his left foot. As his toe erupted in hot spasms of agony, the exquisite pain at once made him feel both queasy and yet strangely alive. The sudden introduction of stimulus and sensation into the routine and uniformity of his life brought a strange welling of energy and he leapt backward - only to ram his head into the shelf behind him. He hit it with such force that the bookshelf began to totter and rock on its ancient wooden base. As he held his head and danced pathetically on his uninjured foot, Trismegistus watched with horror as the shelf started to fall toward the next shelf. In an instant, his mind played out the carnage of his library collapsing like a set of dominoes.

For a seeming eternity, he watched the shelf swaying and picking up momentum. Incredibly, just as it reached its tipping point, it stopped and slowly returned to its upright position. His sense of relief was overwhelmed instantly by his inquisitiveness. Why hadn't it fallen?

Picking his ledger up from the floor, and forgetting his throbbing toe, he rounded the shelf to look on the other side.

"Hope I didn't startle you, Tris," laughed Priest.

Trismegistus' shoulders slumped with relief and a solitary tear set out on a lonely journey down a craggy cheek. Surprise gave way to recognition, which in turn blossomed into relieved laughter. The old man's face lit up and he extended a hand in greeting.

The solitary tear, had now been joined by others in a race down the old man's face. He sniffed and dabbed his eyes with a handkerchief, while at the same time furiously pumping Priest's hand.

"Forgive me sir; I've not had a visitor in so long…"

The words tailed off into a silent look and appraisal of his guest.

"Time has been kinder to some than to others I see!"

Priest smiled and slapped the old man amiably on the shoulder as he stepped past him and into the centre of the room. He walked around the long table and seated himself on a chair on the other side.

"I would have been in before now, but I've been a bit preoccupied."

"No mind, you're here now and I'm ready to serve. What is it that you're after, young sir?"

The irony of this was not lost on Priest. Despite all appearances, Trismegistus was actually the younger of the two. The library had certain effects, certain magical properties which had prolonged the life of the librarian (one of the perks of the job!), but he wasn't immortal and though time hadn't exactly stood still for him, it had at least agreed to slow its pace to a brisk walk instead of the one hundred meter dash that it ran for most people.

Priest considered his answer – what was he looking for? Last time he'd been here, it had just been to gather his thoughts. The seeming permanence and proximity of so much ancient knowledge had a comforting effect upon him. It was also one of the few human places where he knew that he could not be disturbed. No one knew of its location any more. Its existence was purely liminal, one of those in-between places that you'd walk straight past unless you knew it was there. From outside, it was a disused church. It could have been a Wren or a more likely a Hawksmoor, such was its mixture of styles. The deeds of the property were still in the name of the Arcanum, listed as one of their many business fronts. As a result it had not been targeted for restoration or destruction by developers. It sat there, sandwiched in between two non-descript oblong office buildings at the eastern end of the square mile. The bustling city of London roared outside the door – the storm of humanity in full force brushed past its great ruined portico. Its Corinthian pilasters had long since shed their paint and its ornate windows had been blackened and painted over during the blitz. The only people that noticed the building at all were local historians, but their investigations always hit a dead end. Its contents and purposes were safe, with its treasures, far more sacred than any tabernacle or reliquary.

Placing his palms flat on the table, Priest grimaced and shuffled awkwardly. This humanity was hard to sustain – the insecurity and lack of direction, the doubt and the misgivings about everything. He relayed his position to Trismegistus, telling him the story of Rose and his experiment.

"Does the library of the Arcanum have a self-help section?"

The attempt at levity was half-hearted and his eyes sank to the table as if weighed down by the burden of truth.

Trismegistus sighed and opened his arms, pointing to the books around him.

"You seem to be labouring under the misapprehension that you've stumbled upon a new problem sir."

Priest sank back into the soft leather of the chair, his head rested against the carved wooden cornucopia that adorned the top of the backrest.

"Men have been searching for the meaning of existence for as long as they've been capable of sentient thought. This library is testimony to that. The creation of religions, of gods, philosophy, enlightenment, magic, wars and exploration have all been used by men to make sense of the world around them. And when they couldn't make sense, they sought to impose their own order."

"So you do have the answer here then?" Priest sat up with renewed hope.

"Oh I'm not saying that I can give you any ultimate answers to ultimate questions – you're better placed and better equipped than I for that. What I can say is that here you can walk in the footsteps of those who have sought similar answers. Some have reached conclusions and others have changed the question to suit what they have found. Contemplation of the inverse is taxing to the mind. But then again, you've seen the inverse haven't you?"

"Been there, seen it, got the t-shirt!"

"I beg your pardon sir?"

Priest allowed himself a half-smile.

"Oh nothing, just something the humans say…"

Trismegistus was reminded of his throbbing toe and deferentially motioned toward a chair with a 'Do you mind if I sit down' sort of gesture.

"That's better," sighed the old librarian, wiggling his big toe under the table and trying to restore the feeling to it.

"I assume that in giving this girl some of your… erm… abilities, that you in turn have sacrificed something in order to better experience her world?"

"What do you mean?"

"Well, you wish to see the world through her eyes… and you have the ability to move beyond her world, to do things that most humans can't do."

Priest looked blankly and spread his hands, palms up in a begging gesture.

"Yes… go on!"

Trismegistus laughed and shook his head.

"In order to walk in her shoes, you're going to have to forego your powers. How else can you experience humanity without all the vulnerability and helplessness?"

Realisation hit Priest like a hammer blow. A palm struck his forehead as his stupidity became apparent. He rose to his feet, and the chair scraped backward with a slow groan that echoed around the room. He walked to the fireplace, leaning upon the mantle and peering introspectively into the non-existent flames.

"Do you have the necessary invocations here?"

"I do – as long as you're sure that you wish to proceed, I can find you what you need."

"You're one of only two people in the whole of creation that I'd trust with my essence Tris – don't let me down."

He turned to the older man.

"I'll make the preparations at once sir!"

Trismegistus slowly stood, offered a respectful bow to Priest and shuffled away, disappearing from view behind a bookcase.

Priest knew exactly what was involved and he wasn't looking forward to it. Transubstantiation meant pain beyond mere parturition – it was like giving birth to your own soul. Forces normally invoked by a skillful Master Magus wrench it from you. Having only a librarian to do the job was even less of a comfort to him. And then, once his experiment was finished, he had to trust that Tris could restore things to the way they were. This was going to be the biggest gamble of his life. He only hoped that the rewards would be worth the sacrifice.

# XI
# Machinations

Astolath, the newly installed Lord of Hell, sat on an ornate and grisly Infernal Throne at the end of what was formerly Lucifer's great chamber. The throne was embellished with skulls that seemed to move and moan in agony and torment. They were indeed souls claimed in victory over the millennia and given the final ignominy of forming a part of the chair upon which the lord of Hell sat his derrière.

The hall itself was a huge space, with a vaulted ceiling and stone walls lined with tattered and faded tapestries – images of gods and monsters locked in eternal struggle. Everything spoke of decayed refinement, once beautiful objects now left to decompose and fall apart, a parody of the splendour and extravagance of a once thriving court. All this was lost on Astolath. It was a territory to him, something to be conquered and held – a symbol of his power.

He was troubled. He had taken Lucifer's crown without a fight and now everything was just too quiet for him. Instinct told him that something was amiss, but his intellect had failed to get a grip on how events might be unraveling. Stupidly, he had allowed Lucifer to walk out of the gates and this was now troubling him. What if Lucifer changed his mind and decided to fight for his kingdom? What if he'd slipped away to raise an army and was planning to come back and lay siege to his former home? Such thoughts gave Astolath a severe case of indigestion. He eyed his courtiers - a motley collection of demons and Hell's fallen denizens, each one as degenerate and as revolting as the next. It was like looking upon an animated tableau from some medieval depiction of Hell – all horns, beards, hooves and pointy instruments of torture and war. All were eager to please and at the same time, terrified of ending up on the receiving end of one of Astolath's fits of carpet biting and incendiary rage.

"Helnocker!" he bellowed at the top of his voice. There was a frantic murmuring at the end of the hall, followed by the distant sound of shouting that echoed down long, distant corridors. Two minutes later, a panting Helnocker ran into the hall and skidded to a halt in front of the dais, which held his master.

"You called sire?"

"I did. Have your patrols returned yet?"

"Y-yes sire."

"Well?"

"There's no sign of him my lord – he's nowhere to be found."

Astolath gave a curt sigh and rose from his throne. Helnock swiveled on his one knee and turned as his master passed by. Astolath was ruthless and ambitious, but as already mentioned, he wasn't the brightest member of Hell's hierarchy. He liked to solve most problems with mindless violence; killing came as naturally to him as breathing. Mind games were a different matter. He had given Lucifer a warning of his intentions and was looking forward to a bloody siege culminating in the torture and slow death of his adversary. Lucifer had selfishly denied him all of this. For a moment he considered taking Helnocker's head – if in doubt, he liked to strike out rather than just stand there wallowing in his own mental impotence.

As he considered this, a messenger ran in with some news.

"My lord, important visitors are craving admittance to your presence."

Astolath turned suddenly and grabbed the messenger by his throat. He was a lesser demon, tall and powerfully built, intimidating in his battle armour, but next to Astolath he was like a child. The new lord of Hell held him in one giant hand

and poked at him with the index finger of the other, punctuating each word by jabbing his finger tip into the messenger's eye.

"Do-not-inter-rupt-me-when-I'm-think-ing-or–you'll-regret-it! Do-you-under-stand?"

The messenger screamed and gargled, pathetically choking on his own blood. His left eyeball was being pushed back through its socket and into his brain with each jab of the finger. Blood and whitish vitreous fluid ran down his cheek, as the soft, squidgy ball popped under pressure. The other eye rolled frantically in its socket as if looking for an independent means of escape before the last vestiges of life left his struggling body. Astolath let him go, watched his body collapse in a heap on the floor and grunted in mild surprise. For a brief moment, he looked like a clumsy and heavy-handed child who had broken a toy, or squashed a hamster. He turned his head and looked at back at Helnocker.

"What did he say... a message was it?"

Helnocker looked at the body, swallowed hard and then looked back at his master.

"Apparently, there are important visitors to see you sire."

"Humphh... I suppose you'd better show them in then!"

Several dark figures stepped forward and dragged the body out of sight as Astolath peered quizzically down at his blood-soaked index finger. Thoughtfully, he rubbed it against his thumb, looking for traces of brain and gore. Something had gotten stuck under his talon-like fingernail. This bothered him immensely. One thing he could not abide was a dirty fingernail. Using the point of a dagger, he removed the offending material, wiped the blade on his cloak and returned it to the sheath on his belt. Returning from his reverie, he straightened and strode back to his throne. There was a murmur, followed by a commotion, then finally a kerfuffle at the far end of the hall. The huge wooden doors swung open and in strode the unmistakable forms of Sinn and Eldredd.

They approached Astolath, who was doing his best to look imperious upon his throne, and bowed low in an overly theatrically manner before the dais.

"Sinn, Eldredd – the first visitors to my new court!" bellowed Astolath.

"Allow us to be the first to congratulate you on your new position, highness," offered Sinn.

Eldredd nodded in agreement and beamed at Astolath as if looking upon a bright young nephew who'd done well in the school play.

"Yes, well done – we never had any doubts you could do it!"

Astolath eyed them both suspiciously. He wasn't sure what they were up to and he didn't trust them for one moment. He did however have some strange idea that if he was to be ruler of Hell, he should at least act in some semblance of a monarchical manner – show some graciousness, make a few mighty gestures, that sort of thing. It was the stuff that his predecessor had been so good at.

"Bring chairs for our guest" he shouted at no one in particular.

Sinn and Eldredd bowed again in gratitude and sat down on the seats that had hurriedly been provided for them. Astolath's retinue had obviously not yet had time to familiarize themselves with the facilities at Lucifer's palace. Sinn was provided with what looked like a wooden bar stool and Eldredd lowered himself gingerly onto a blue and white striped deckchair. The two demons looked at each other and shrugged.

Astolath appeared not to notice the *faux pas* and continued to play the gracious lord.

"What, may I ask, is the purpose of your visit?"

Again, Sinn and Eldredd looked at each other. They'd rehearsed this moment and now it was time to begin the performance. Eldredd stood and approached the dais.

"We have certain information that will be of interest to you."

Astolath bristled with impatience, already tired of the charade.

"Well?"

Eldredd looked back at Sinn for reassurance before proceeding. Sinn reciprocated with a nod.

"We know the whereabouts of Lucifer and were confident that you'd consider this to be a matter of some importance..." Eldredd left the sentence to hang in the air, letting the import and realization sink into Astolath's thick skull. Being a very thick cranium, this took about thirty seconds.

He'd never liked Astolath. As a maker of mischief and evil, his credentials were impeccable. But, he had no subtlety, no *élan* and no class. He was a thug, pure and simple. He had the brute force, the sheer naked aggression to get things done, but now, at the apex of power, he'd just sit there until someone with an imagination pushed him in the right direction. This was an opportunity too good to miss for a couple of ambitious demons like Sinn and Eldredd. Astolath would do the dirty work for them; they'd just give the right nudges in the most advantageous directions.

Firstly, it was as important to them as it was to Astolath that Lucifer be taken out of the equation. The Morning Star was as cunning as he was unpredictable. His fall from grace had not stripped him of his great powers and his influence. If there was a chance that he might be planning a comeback, they would see to it that his options were narrowed, or even removed altogether. Secondly, they knew exactly where Lucifer had gone and why he was there.

With the decline in belief among men, Lucifer's influence in Hell had waned; conversely, his power on Earth had increased. These were godless times among men, exactly the environment in which he thrived. Unlike the Supreme Being, Lucifer didn't need the grovelling supplication, dedication and subjugation of his followers in order to survive. All he needed was for men to do what they do best – to follow their own hollow hearts and shallow, labile and capricious ambitions and to make life as unpleasant for each other as possible. A god without worshippers is nothing – he's an anachronism, a cosmic spare tyre, an embarrassing old uncle rattling round in the attic of man's imagination. He's good for the odd desperate prayer, for national anthems and for keeping men in dresses, but not for much else.

Lucifer had stepped into this vacuum and was now *de facto* ruler of the human realm. And this was why he had simply walked away from his infernal throne – he had bigger fish to fry. Eons of patient resentment at his maker had paid off and the affairs of men were now his to determine.

Why were humans so important you may ask?

Simply because of all the creations in the universe (and the universe is teeming with life, despite the solipsistic views of humanity!), humans *were* the favourites of the creator. As a result, they were the place that he could be hurt. Sure they were short-sighted, selfish and prone to delusional acts of gross stupidity and cruelty, but out of love and blind devotion, a parent will forgive even the most recalcitrant child. It was this propensity of god's to keep giving his children 'one more chance' that had landed them in the position that they were now in. Too many threats with no follow-up had reduced their fear and respect for him to a mocking and grudging acceptance that he probably wasn't even there anyway.

So, in this game of cosmic one-upmanship, humanity was the prize and Lucifer wasn't going to let a demon with a crisis of conscience upset his plans. He knew all about Priest and his fascination for a human girl. He knew that he had stopped her at the threshold of death and that he planned some sort of experiment. If this resulted in a more enlightened humanity, then his influence would weaken and all that he had so patiently waited for would be undone. Hence his sudden sabbatical to the world of men and his seeming reluctance to put up a fight with Astolath. Hell just wasn't that important to him at the moment.

Sinn and Eldredd had figured most of this out for themselves, but chose only to reveal the basic facts to Astolath, both to keep things simple and easy for him to digest mentally and to keep him from turning them both to mulch once he had decided that they were of no use to him.

"And where is the Lightbringer?" roared Astolath.

"Oh he's no threat to you at the moment my lord – he's pre-occupied with other things. But, he will return sooner or later and then you'll get your fight."

Astolath didn't know whether to laugh or to whimper. He was spoiling for a fight, but he knew he would have to wait for it. He leapt from his throne and stood menacingly over the two demons.

"No games now, just tell me where I can find him!"

Eldredd and Sinn looked at each other again. They had provoked Astolath as they knew they would and now it was time to get what they wanted from the situation.

"We have a request to make, in return for such knowledge."

"And I could kill you with one blow!" threatened the new lord of Hell.

"Yes, but then you'd never know and Lucifer would steal back and catch you off guard. You'd be far wiser to grant us our request and let us help you."

Again, they waited for the words to sink in.

The urge to kill someone was almost overpowering Astolath. He ground his teeth together and a huge vein throbbed in his domed forehead. He reached for his huge battle axe, swung it in a mighty arc and splintered his newly won throne in two. The crashing, splintering sound filled the hall and all those surrounding the dais stood back in apprehension. Any one of them could be next and they knew it.

Astolath stood panting with rage, both hands still gripped tightly on the handle of the axe. He looked around at Sinn and Eldredd and for a moment both of them thought that they'd gone too far. This was the most unreasonable of monsters they were dealing with – one possibly stupid enough to actually kill them and lose any advantage he might gain from their assistance.

Time stood still and Sinn actually considered reaching out and holding Eldredd's hand, such was his fear. This should give you a rough idea of how stupifyingly terrible Astolath was in his anger. Two major-league demons, frightening enough to look at and with a distinguished pedigree of their own in violent and evil machinations, stood practically wetting themselves in his presence.

As if someone had flicked a switch in his head, Astolath's aspect suddenly changed and he straightened and smiled a sly, wicked smile at the two trembling demons.

"Name your terms!"

Sinn shut his huge gaping maw so that no one would see the tears of relief welling in his eyes. Eldredd stepped deftly away from the spreading puddle of urine that he was standing in and approached Astolath.

"Good – I'm glad we can keep things civil. We don't want too much; we just want the Lightbringer when you've finished with him."

# XII
## Rocking the Cradle

When she opened her eyes, Rose was back at home.

It was, it seemed, as it had been before she left and she was sitting on the sofa in her mother's living room, in the small terraced house where she used to live. Around her were the familiar objects, colours, images and smells of home, the school photographs, the knickknacks and familial paraphernalia.

She stood up to look around, needing to touch something to be sure of its reality. On the dresser in the corner was a dark, carved, club-shaped wooden whale with an ivory tusk or a tooth resting in a groove on its back. It was a gift from her grandfather when he came back from Australia years ago. It was pretty grim and tacky looking, but it had held her childhood fascination. Her grandfather had told her that it was a whale's tooth and she had recalled seeing Moby Dick on the television - Gregory Peck as Captain Ahab – locked in a terrible duel with the huge white whale. To her, the tooth was a souvenir of some such titanic struggle on the antipodean waves. Rose picked up the tooth and turned it over in her hands, feeling the reassurance of its smooth coldness before returning it to the groove on the whale's back.

She felt as if she was home again – the sensations of both familiarity and unease that had marked her last years there had returned. The constant state of listening for raised voices and watching the door for a means of escape was there too. The house sounded empty, but she decided to make sure. Opening the door, she stepped into the hallway and, without entering, peered into the kitchen. People *had* been here – the dishes were still in the sink unwashed. The normal household breakfast detritus littered the small area – cereal packets, toast crumbs and coffee cups all competing for space.

Rose retreated and stepped back across the hallway to the staircase. She wanted to see her room, just to see if anyone had bothered to keep things as they were. Approaching the door, she saw it was still covered in faded posters and peeling stickers from her childhood. A pastel-coloured wooden plaque saying 'Rosemary's Room' still hung from it as an affirmation or reminder of the possession by a previous owner. Funny how she looked at the words and didn't even seem to recognize her own name. No one had called her Rosemary in years. It was like looking at someone else's name, in one of those odd times when a familiar word suddenly becomes strange with a moments idling scrutiny.

Reaching for the handle, she turned it and nervously opened the door to 'Rosemary's Room'. As she did so, it felt as if she could feel the rush of emotion and history leaving the room like escaping oxygen – as if the space had been hermetically sealed and preserved in time. Almost expecting to find someone there waiting, she stepped cautiously into the centre of the room, a pink, plush fake fur rug swallowing up her feet. There was nothing in there but ghosts and memories as for a moment she just turned round on the spot, taking in yet more familiar objects. Posters, books, dolls, wardrobe, bed covered in cuddly toys on top of a 'Sylvanian Families' duvet cover.

She sat on the bed and picked up a blue doll, which had been her favourite. Her father had brought it home for her one day. He'd sit it on the arm of his chair and make it perform to her, to her endless amusement. It had a soft body with a plastic head, painted like a clown's face – bright red nose, beaming mouth, twinkling eyes and a shock of woolen orange hair glued to the scalp. She stared into its face, struggling to stay upright against the vortex of emotions sweeping around her.

She felt for the little plastic ring on its back and pulled on it to see if it still talked.

"How're you doodly-do-do-doing?" enquired the clown in a chirpy American accent. It had a cheery, avuncular cadence that reminded her of the cowardly lion in *The Wizard of Oz*.

At the sound of the voice, her vision blurred and swam. It was a sound coming from the toy in her hands, but it emanated in a hurting, echoing resonance from across the years. A wave of unfettered and profound sadness swept its way up her body – a physical feeling of loss and helplessness that engulfed her. Before her, the doll blurred and divided into two, as heavy, impatient tears slipped their moorings in her eyes and began their solemn journey south. She pulled the doll toward her and hugged it tight, salty rain falling softly onto its hair. The pressure activated the aging voice mechanism once again.

"Well, that's a ding-dong-dandy!"

She wasn't sure how long she had been there when she heard the voice. She had curled into the fetal position and fallen asleep cradling the clown.

"Who are you?" came the voice again.

Rose looked up, trying to clear her vision, and sat bolt upright at the sight of her mother standing in the doorway with a puzzled expression on her face. She hadn't seen her for five, maybe six years. In that time, she had aged a great deal. Her brown hair was now streaked with grey, her eyes deep-set and haunted and her skin had the tell-tale yellowish tinge that betrayed her failing liver. There were some vestiges of the striking woman that she had once been, but they were only visible in flashes – little movements and shapes that revealed themselves as she spoke – desperately (so it appeared), trying to stand upright, either from shock or from inebriation.

"Mum!" the word escaped her lips without conscious thought.

Her mother stepped backward, dropping a plastic shopping bag to the floor. The bottles of vodka inside clanked together violently, but didn't smash. She put a hand to her mouth and gasped in recognition.

"Rose..." the name tailed off into numbed silence as she sank to the floor – all strength and energy drained from her limbs and she fell to her knees with a gently thud.

Rose slipped from the bed and dropped down in front of her mother. She wrapped her arms around her and buried her head in her bosom, half crying, and half laughing. All the while, her mother just knelt there, pinned down by both her daughter and by the enormity of the situation.

"I thought... I thought you were dead..."

"I'm not dead mum, I'm here, I'm back to look after you – I can look after you now."

Even as she spoke, Rose wondered at her words and at the incredible things that Priest had shown and told her. If she did have some sort of power now, then she would be able to look after her mother. There was no reason to be afraid anymore. She sat back on her heels and looked at the ravaged visage of her mother, then down at the plastic bag next to her.

"Oh mum, I've missed you, but I'm back now – we can start again... why don't you say anything?"

Her mother almost fell backwards as Rose stood and tried to pull her up.

"I thought you were dead. We never heard from you... I've grieved and got over you and now you're here and telling me that everything's OK..."

Her eyes were in a near constant state of trying to focus on her daughter, peering through a haze of vodka. As she spoke, Rose wanted to wretch, such was the stench of alcohol... and of something else that she couldn't quite place. Behind her mother, a dark shadow retreated under her sudden scrutiny. Puzzled, Rose turned back to look at the lined face, looking deep into her mother's eyes – windows that now let light into the dark recesses of her soul. Rose knew then that her mother was dying.

"Oh god – no!"

Rose clung to her again and sobbed,

"Not this… not this…"

Puzzled, her mother looked back, taking in her new appearance, trying to assess her daughter.

"What's the matter?"

"Nothing mum – I just need a cuddle."

Pathetically, her mother put an arm around her, and patted her head.

"What are we going to do with each other eh? We've got lots to talk about. You need to tell me what you've been up to."

"Let's go downstairs mum and I'll put the kettle on."

It had been some time since Rose had done anything as mundane and domestic as make a cup of tea. Almost on autopilot, she moved around the kitchen and found everything in its familiar place. Next door, her mother had gone to the toilet. Rose could hear the sound of a bottle-top being surreptitiously removed and the sound of her mother taking quiet gulps of whatever she'd hidden in the medicine cupboard. Rose stared at the floor, arms folded and waited to give her mother an accusatory look. When she finally appeared in the doorway, all her indignation had fled her and she just felt pity.

"Where's everyone else?"

"Work, school… I forget. They drift in and out; treat this place like a hotel."

"And what do you do mum… with your time I mean – you still working at the school?"

"No, not worked for two years – not since I was diagnosed…"

Rose knew the truth, but the hearing of it hurt her deeply. She wanted to be wrong about this newfound insight she felt. She could almost see the cancer spreading as she looked at her mother – the creeping metastasis, the malignancy that sought to overrun her body at every level. She was a host for the parasitic agent that would only die when she did. There was to be no happy homecoming; death had other ideas for her mother. It was his shadow that she'd glimpsed in the bedroom, and even now it was lurking over her shoulder – hanging back in the near distance reminding her of his presence.

The daughter looked at her mother and steeled herself.

"The cancer?"

Her mother pulled a chair toward her and paused as she went to sit down.

"Who told you? Is that why you came back – to bury me?"

"I didn't know mum. Not until now."

Rose sat down opposite her mother and poured tea from the pot. "I hope it's not stewed, you were a while in there…"

There was a silence as the two women looked again at each other, noting the changes and both remembering things as they once were.

"So…"

"I had to get away mum. You never understood what it was like for me."

"It was never as bad as you said. I know you never got over your dad, but you never gave me a chance to move on with my life either."

"It wasn't just Dad and you know it. I tried to tell you what was happening and you always shut me up!"

"You were lying for attention and you know it."

Rose sat back, deflated and incredulous that her mother still refused to believe what she had been through. This time however, no tears came. She clenched her fists in her lap and looked her mother straight in the eye.

"Your husband raped me and invited his friend to watch. He fucked me on that sofa and then let his friend have a go and told me that he'd hurt you and Danny if I said anything to anyone!"

By now, she was on her feet and screaming at her mother.

"I didn't know what to do but run away! When I tried to tell you, you hit me and told me not to tell lies! And, where is that son of a bitch now – I could fucking kill him for what he put me through!"

Rose leaned forward and swept the contents of the table clean across the room. Crockery exploded against the wall and painted it with steaming tea. Her mother cowered, eyes wide at the sight of her daughter's terrifying rage. The room had suddenly grown darker and Rose's eyes flamed as if she was possessed.

"I wanted things to be right between us, I wanted you to say sorry and for us to move on, but you're still in denial, aren't you!"

"Oh Rose... Rose." With the words came tears – the first real manifestation of emotion Rose had seen in her mother's face since she'd left home. She suddenly seemed to become lucid and aware of what was happening.

"I couldn't allow myself to believe it. He was good to you kids – he was good to me. I just thought that you were jealous because of your dad."

"I went to bed bleeding that night mum. You saw the stains on my bed and on my clothes and you still never believed me. You never believed me!"

Rose was clenching her teeth by now, spittle spraying the air in front of her as she spoke.

"I ran away and now things you wouldn't believe have happened to me. I've lost and aborted more children than you've had. Each one has been too much to bear – every consolation has been taken from me. I've fucked men just for somewhere to sleep and something to eat. I've begged, I've stolen and in return I've been brutalized so much that I wouldn't recognize a friendly word or a kindness for anything less than another attempt to hurt me."

The tears came again, stinging and profuse, a flood to match the stream of emotion now finding articulation in the torrent of accusations being released against her mother.

"If you'd just have admitted that it happened, I could have forgiven you and moved on."

Involuntarily, her hand smashed down upon the table, which broke and splintered, separating down the middle until there was nothing between her and her mother.

The older woman shook her head and sobbed.

"I'm so sorry, I'm so, so sorry…" Her head disappeared into her hands and her shoulders shook with the effort of crying.

Rose looked down on her, still raging and failing to contain her anger.

"It's too late mum. It's too late for us all."

She knelt in front of her mother and pulled her head toward her, whispering in her ear.

"I have a gift you know. I would have shared it with you; I would have saved you – plucked that cancer from you and made everything better."

Her mother looked up through the tears, puzzled.

"What do you mean?"

Rose put a hand on her mother's stomach and spread her fingers. As she concentrated, the tips of her fingers started to glow and vibrate softly.

"The pain… the pain is going!" said her mother.

"And I could take if all away from you if I wanted to. But I can't bring myself to forgive you mum. I'm sorry."

Rose looked into her mother's eyes and understanding passed between them.

"Can you just make it end… please?"

Rose left her hand where it was and leaned her head into her mother's lap. Both of them sobbed – one in the realization that release was moments away and the other aware that this was just the beginning of a terrible journey. Rose couldn't forgive her mother, but she could offer her a *coup de grace*. She could restore some balance to the order of things, not by taking a life in anger but by speeding her mother toward a painless end. Instinctively she knew what to do.

Without moving her head, she pushed against her mother, gently overcoming the resistance of the flesh with her fingers. Her hand slid slowly into the warmth of her mother. She found the rib cage and then the sternum before settling on the slowly beating vital muscle in her chest cavity. Delicately she moved her fingers over its surface, little electrical pulses dancing on the tips until, finally, she held it in her hand.

"I can feel your heart mum. I can't feel any love there for me – it feels hollow and empty."

Rose held on to her mother with her free hand and gripped her other tight around her heart. It tried to beat against her fingers, fighting to the last to keep life in the ailing body. Rose felt its dying pulse and felt her mother's breathing grow shallow until it finally stopped. She stayed there for nearly ten minutes, feeling the warmth of her mother's dead heart grow cooler. Eventually, she removed her hand and examined it - a bright red thing that became a fist before her and then a hand again.

"Oh god – what have I done…"

She stood and wiped her hand on a tea towel hanging near the sink. She could smell her mother's blood, awakening a sense memory of her own birth, a split second regression along the path of her life. Her mother had given her life and now she had taken her mother's. The circle of life perverted, the oroborus devoured by another serpent, turning the natural order on its head. Now she truly understood that she was outside of normal existence. Despite what Priest had said, she had taken a life and felt nothing. She was truly dead.

The brief violent communion with her mother had also revealed other things to her. She now knew that her brothers were safe. Oh, they'd be upset about their mother, but they'd get over it. She'd watch over them and see that they were OK. She also knew now where her former step-father was to be found. She had taken the first life and the first step, everything else would be easy from now on. She would set her world to rights and then go back to Priest for absolution.

Rose returned briefly to her bedroom and picked up the clown by the hand, carrying him from the house like a little girl. As she left by the front door, the clown's head smacked against the door-jam, triggering his speech mechanism once again.

"Ha Ha Ha! That's all folks!"

The door closed.

# XIII
## Temporarily Temporal?

"How the hell did you move the table Tris?"

Priest had returned to find the library floor nearly devoid of furniture, revealing a long open space in which Trismegistus obviously planned to perform the transubstantiation ritual. In the middle of the space was one high-backed wooden chair. It looked like 'Old Sparky', the infamous electric chair, with its metal rivets and leather straps. These were obviously meant for restraint and not for safety. On the flagstones surrounding the chair, a circle had been drawn in what looked like white chalk. The compass points and degrees in between were marked out with strange symbols – so esoteric that they meant almost nothing to Priest. Of course, he recognized one of them as the symbol of 'Dagon', the ancient god of the Philistines, another familiar glyph represented the planet Saturn and he was pretty sure that another character meant that a fire hydrant was nearby, but he really couldn't say for certain.

"Oh it was a fold-up job; I've got it stored flat out the back in a store room. I'll put it all back later, don't you worry."

Priest harrumphed, smiling as he mused on the idea that somewhere along the line, Trismegistus, custodian of the library of the Arcanum, may have spent time poring over an Ikea catalogue in order to furnish the place.

The librarian banished such notions from his mind.

"That table was actually designed by Pythagoras. Like all Greeks, he'd throw regular symposia for his friends, but didn't like all the space that the affair took up. Once he'd kicked the last drunken philosopher out into the street at the end of the evening, he'd fold the table up to make room for his experiments. It's been passed down to custodians of the library for thousands of years, and apart from a bit of woodworm in one leg, it's still going strong."

Stepping back to ensure that the circle had been correctly inscribed, he gestured to Priest to sit in the chair. This done, he set to fastening the straps about the demon's ankles, wrists and forehead. He then divested of his house coat and pulled on a long white talismanic shirt, covered in faded writings, symbols and what looked like equations.

"You do know that it would take more than these to hold me down don't you Tris?"

The librarian shrugged and smiled, "Feel free to test them for me sir."

Priest sighed and went to lift his right hand: it wouldn't move an inch. The same went for his left and then for his feet and head. For perhaps the first time in his long life, Priest actually felt the slight pangs of fear and panic as he actually felt helpless.

"What in the name of the Whore of Babylon have you trussed me up with?"

"Ah, the straps are made of an interesting material you see. They're not fashioned from ordinary leather, but from the skins of ancient martyrs. Christian ones are OK, but for a really strong hold, ones made from the acolytes of Baal are the best quality. A restraining spell is cast over the material during the tanning process. I believe that it's also treated by immersion in the urine of defrocked priests in order to give it that extra something special, but that may just be their marketing department trying to give it a bit of a USP. Even arcane suppliers are jumping on the advertising bandwagon now. It used to be just word-of-mouth." Trismegistus shook his head and shrugged at the passing of the old traditions before continuing.

"Needless to say, you may be able to break free after some concerted effort, but you don't have time to try and I need you to sit still while we get on with the ritual."

"It's a good job that I trust you Tris," Priest raised an eyebrow and delivered the words with the merest hint of a threat of underlying dire retribution.

"Of course, of course. Now, let us get on with it."

Trismegistus put a reassuring hand on Priest's forearm. "I'll try to make this as painless as possible, but I can't guarantee that you won't feel anything. I was going to say that you should put your right hand up if it hurts and I'll stop, but of course you can't do that can you? Perhaps you should just raise your eyebrows…"

"How about I just scream?"

"Or you could indeed just scream."

The librarian stood at the Eastern point of the circle and began to chant quietly to himself. Priest caught snatches of a strange sounding language that he didn't recognize, though he thought that he caught the name 'Anubis' in there somewhere. As the invocation continued, the light level dropped and the glyph before Trismegistus started to glow and to emit a sickly smelling yellow smoke. A warm movement of the air played across priest's face, circulating the smoke and making him blink away tears of irritation.

As his vision cleared, he saw Trismegistus step to own side. Behind him, a tall figure stepped forward. Priest now recognized Anubis, the ancient Egyptian jackal god. He now stood there like a statue, one foot in front of the other, muscled and bronzed and wearing classical Egyptian garb. In one hand he carried a staff and in the other an Ankh symbol, as if he had stepped straight out of a cartouche adorning an ancient tomb.

Anubis tilted his head slightly, looking at Priest before turning back to Trismegistus and barking something at him in a brutish version of the language that he himself had just used. The librarian replied in a brusque manner that led Priest to believe that the god of the dead had just been told to shut his mouth and to do as he was told. Next, Trismegistus moved to

Western point on the circle and this time began his incantation in yet another tongue.

This time, Priest understood the dialect. It was Enochian and contained a supplication that led him to understand that the Archangel Michael himself would soon be putting in an appearance.

Sure enough, once again the symbol began to glow and to give of a cloud of smoke. When it cleared, sure enough, God's supreme warrior stepped out from behind Trismegistus in shimmering golden armour, his silver wings stretched out behind him as if he were about to take flight. As he caught sight of Priest, he laughed and shook his head. The two of them had met before on several occasions, the last of which saw Priest on the receiving end of the Archangel's considerable wrath for attempting to steal souls that he had been conducting to heaven. That he had now been called upon to aid in Priest's transformation gave him a distinct pleasure as his former adversary would now be wondering what part he would be playing in the proceedings. This fact was not lost on Priest who turned his head to smile meekly at the archangel. He felt like a Chihuahua puppy rolling over and exposing its belly to an adult Rottweiler.

The librarian moved on to the other cardinal points of the compass and performed similar incantations. To the North he summoned Epona, the beautiful Celtic goddess of horses whose hair fell like a russet mane down over her shoulders. She was naked but for the glowing green spiral tattoos adorning her body. Epona addressed him in a guttural Gaelic greeting before taking her place.

To the South came Barnumbirr, the antipodean Morning Star who appeared in the form of a beautiful young aboriginal girl. She was covered in multi-coloured rainbow-painted dots and animal tribal markings and stood on one leg like a flamingo. She nodded to Trismegistus but paid no attention to anyone else in the room.

Trismegistus then went to each alternate point on the circle compass and uttered words over each symbol before stepping into the circle and standing next to Priest.

"We are now assembled and are at the crucial point of the ritual. I have summoned here the four psychopomps, Anubis, Michael, Epona and Barnumbirr, representing the East, West, North and South. Each are responsible for guiding souls into the afterlife in their own realms and, if they are agreeable, will between them keep guard of your essence while you are on Earth and will ensure that it is returned to you undamaged and undiminished. There will be a price to pay for its return though."

"Here it comes," thought Priest.

This wasn't any kind of duplicitousness on behalf of Tris; it was simply the way that things were done at this level of existence. Deals and transactions were the currency of the spectral realm and it was a rare day indeed that something was given away for nothing.

Trismegistus held his arms over Priest as if he were about to impart a benediction. In his right hand he held the Ankh, the symbol of his power, which glowed and thrummed with energy as he spoke.

"I who am named Thrice-Great Hermes, having the three parts of the philosophy of the whole world, priest, philosopher and king, do summon you here in attendance to do my bidding. That you will watch over the soul, the Ba, the Ka and the Akh of this being. His essence and his powers will be yours to protect and to return at the appointed time and place and on fulfilment of his promise to you."

Priest looked up in anticipation at the old man standing over him.

"Well... what's the deal?"

"You must, in your human form, ascend to the spheres. You must rise above and cast off that which has shackled you thus far."

"That was kind of the idea Tris, to find meaning and fulfilment."

Trismegistus looked around at the assembled company and smiled.

"Then half the battle is already won. But what you must do is not just for you. It must be for all. Man has lost his way and you must be the one to guide him to wisdom. Only then will your essence be returned to you. Do you consent?"

Priest thought hard. It was one thing to have a personal crisis of conscience, but another thing to have to take responsibility for others, let alone the talking apes that made up the human race. Was this worth the risk?

Also, wasn't this the kind of thing that 'the other side' were supposed to take care of – saving doomed souls and all that?

Silence hung in the room around him as the loosely assembled collection of deities and seraphim waited for an answer.

Priest examined his options.

He was utterly fed up with his existence in its current form and he knew that he couldn't go on without something new to inspire him. He had Rose, his new side project, but he couldn't truly experience her drives and motives without discarding his essence and truly becoming human for the duration. He had no choice but to go through with it. Besides, he'd been around the cosmic block a few times. How difficult could it be to set the monkeys straight on a few things? And besides, a more enlightened humanity might just provide him with more entertainment than he currently derived from them.

"How long do I have?"

"You have one cycle of the moon in which to meet the terms of the bargain, or your essence is forfeit and our friends here will be free to fight over who gets to drag you into their realm."

Priest braced himself and stared straight ahead, as if waiting for the Sword of Damocles itself to plunge down from above him.

"Just get on with it Tris."

# XIV
## Under New Management

In what looked like the guest wing of Lucifer's castle, Sinn and Eldred sat in an opulently appointed room, hung with tapestries and paintings of biblical scenes. This wasn't as strange as it might have seemed, when you took into account Lucifer's penchant for interfering with humanity.

The scenes were all those of his finest moments: the beheading of John the Baptist, the massacre of the innocents, the temptation in the wilderness, the crucifixion, and images of martyrdom being bestowed on various people in sundry acts of physical torture and deprivation.

The two demons took all this in with appreciative eyes as they sat on golden chairs on opposite sides of an ornately carved obsidian table. Eldredd's finger's traced the outline of the warped and sexually distorted human figures carved into its surface, while Sinn did what he usually did and just gaped, eyes blinking behind his impressive array of sharp teeth.

Eldredd sat forward.

"So, it's all going as planned. Astolath will go looking for Lucifer in the human domain and there'll be yet another power vacuum that we can step into. If Astolath succeeds, then we get Lucifer. If he fails, then Hell is ours to command."

"It sounds a bit too easy to me. There's bound to be something that gets in the way of things."

"Well, we don't have to sit idle waiting for Astolath's return; we can help things along ourselves."

"How do we do that?"

"Well, if Lucifer is preoccupied with the affairs of men, then we could perhaps pay a visit to Priest and make sure that he assists us in our aims."

"What can he do?"

Eldredd sat forward and changed his tone to a sinister slow articulation, as if he were addressing a complete dullard.

"Priest won't be allowed to interfere unchecked with the monkeys. Lucifer would never sit still for anything that would interfere with his own plans. We need to keep a close eye on the situation and see how we can play it to our advantage."

Sinn blinked – or rather, his mouth shut and then opened again.

"So who's going to keep an eye on things here while we're on Earth?"

"Do you ever do anything but ask questions you dolt!"

"Well, you seem to have thought this all through on your own, I just like to be kept in the loop. I'm not a junior partner in this operation you know. It was my idea to start off with."

Eldredd stood up, bristling with rage. Sinn did the same and inflated himself to double his size, a black tongue snaked its way among his huge teeth. The implied threat had the desired effect, and Eldredd sighed and sat down again.

The two of them were best friends (after an unholy and demonic fashion), but they often found themselves bickering over things. While they were both schemers, Eldredd's intelligence was of the more mercurial bent, whereas Sinn often took a while to catch up. When he did though, his strategies were usually sound.

"One of us must stay here to manage things and the other will visit Priest."

"Oh, I see. And which of us will stay and which of us will go?"

Eldredd knew exactly what he wanted to do, but he also knew that Sinn would want to do the exact opposite of what he wanted, hence his suggestion: "You stay here and manage things and I'll go to monkey world."

Sinn knew this too and so readily agreed to the proposal. What Sinn didn't know though, was that Eldredd knew that

Sinn knew this and had decided to change tack and to suggest what he really wanted in a kind of double-bluff version of reverse-psychology. But, Sinn knew this too and decided to invert the whole idea with a stratagem of his own so that Eldredd in fact suggested what he wanted. And so, with this suspicion, Eldredd countered with another volte-face of his own in order to counter the machinations of his partner in crime. Or at least that was the plan for both of them. In the event, they both lost track of what they really wanted and just ended up trying to outsmart each other for the sake of it.

Two hours later, the two of them were so confused that they just sat there staring at each other, trying to figure out what each really wanted and what to do about it.

Finally Eldredd sighed, sat back in his seat and conjured up a small flat shiny object into his hand.

"Alright, alright. Do you want heads or tails?"

Sinn made a small conjuration of his own.

"Tails, but we'll use my coin!"

\*\*\*

Downstairs in the great hall, Lord Astolath was seated at the head of the long banqueting table, making his own plans with his council of quaking advisers. He'd been at it for some time now and most of their ideas had displeased him. As usual, mindless violence ensued and the scene resembled the aftermath of an R-rated version of 'whack-a-mole' as he had set about smashing into a pulp with his massive war hammer anyone who had dared to say anything at odds with his view of the situation.

It was unfair really. He knew that they wouldn't please him and they knew that they couldn't please him but it was good form to have a retinue of advisors. It made him look more regal and important. But he only really retained them in order to have an excuse to dole out carnage. Everyone knew what was going on, but everyone was too scared to do anything about it. Besides, many thought that a quick bash over the head and rapid oblivion was eminently preferable to the terrible waiting game of serving Lord Astolath for any length of time. As a perverse result, there were always plenty of volunteers vying to become an advisor. At least your demise was quick and relatively painless in comparison with many of the other pastimes that he could devise.

There were now only six left of the original quorum of twelve. To the right of Astolath sat the permanently trembling Helnocker, surveying the detritus and remains of those who had displeased his master. Taking his life in his hands, he decided to go for broke and to venture forth an opinion on the matter. If the end were to come, at least it would be over in an instant.

"My lord, why not take matters into your own hands and pre-empt the light-bringer? Go after him yourself instead of waiting to see what his next move will be?"

Astolath glared at him, his fingers tapping the grip of his hammer in seeming contemplation before grabbing it and bringing it down hard on the head of the simpering Cacodemon sitting to Helnocker's right. Brain, pieces of skull, teeth and fleshy strips of hair-covered skin erupted and rained down on those sitting either side, resulting in a chorus of screams from the remaining advisers.

"Not a bad idea Helnocker. Send for Sinn and Eldredd. In the meantime gentlemen, take a comfort break."

With that, he rose, turned and strode from the room.

As the doors slammed shut behind him, the remaining advisors breathed a collective sigh of relief and sank into their chairs, most of them with their heads in their hands at the strain of it all.

"I can't take any more of this," piped up a minor demon from the end of the table, "If he doesn't kill me soon I'm going to kill myself!"

Helnocker nodded in understanding but didn't dare give voice to his agreement. Instead, he signaled to a guard to retrieve Sinn and Eldredd.

"I've worked some tough gigs in my time," added another.

"Tell me about it. I was once in the employ of the Witch of Endor. It was all against my will of course. She had bound me in a particularly tricky invocation and I had to do her bidding as a servant at her necromancy soirées. She'd work me to the bone providing canapés, tending the guests and then washing up afterwards. And then, she'd expect me to give her a good 'servicing' before bedtime."

The break soon turned into a group therapy session, with each traumatized demon chipping in with the low points of their employment history.

Another had been a 'fluffer' for the Marquis de Sade and yet another had nearly drowned when the Giant Gargantua took a piss on the town in which he was in possession of the local priest. The whole place was wrecked in a warm yellow deluge and he was lucky to escape. He had only done so because the priest had been in the bell tower of his church attempting to sodomize a quire boy when the torrent struck. When the town washed away, the church was the only thing left standing. To add insult to injury, the townspeople convinced themselves that it had been a miracle and it soon became a place of pilgrimage.

The unmistakable sound of Lord Astolath's ground-quaking footsteps rapidly approaching the doors brought the return of silence to the circle of wretched demons.

"Well? Where are they?" he demanded as he entered.

The sound of running and panting behind him answered his question as the guard; Sinn and Eldritch all nearly ran into the broad back of the glowering demon lord.

"Here we are your highness," gasped Eldritch as the three of them fell into the room.

"Good. Helnocker has suggested that we take your advice on what to do next with regard to Lucifer. No pressure or anything, but if I don't like your ideas, then I'm going to kill everyone in the room and possibly in the room next door as well. So off you go!"

Sinn and Eldredd stood dumbstruck for a moment before replying in unison: "He's gone after Priest!"

Astolath considered for a moment as if cogitating on the ramifications... before drawing a complete mental blank.

"What for?"

"You remember the whole Garden of Eden debacle?" said Eldredd. "You know, how Lucifer tempted the first monkeys into tasting of the metaphorical fruit of wisdom?"

"Go on..." coaxed Astolath.

"Well Priest is close to doing the same thing again... showing men the path to knowledge that they shouldn't possess. The Lightbringer has got wind of this and wants to make sure that his meddling doesn't go too far and initiate another war."

"How do you know this?"

"Let's just say that we know Priest and we also know for certain he and the Lightbringer are on a collision course. They have a conflict of interests you might say."

"So what do I do?"

"You follow them both; use Priest to lure the Lightbringer into a trap and then you give him to us."

Astolath smiled at the plan. It wasn't too complicated and with any luck he'd get to kill absolutely everyone involved at the end of it. Why should these two ambitious fools have Lucifer at their mercy when he could get rid of the lot of them at one fell stroke? He would look for Lucifer in the human realm and would take a few of his most trusted – or least incompetent - lieutenants with him. He couldn't risk losing his new dominion by taking his entire army with him, and so he was going to do things the old-fashioned way: he'd travel to the human realm and beat, bludgeon and black magic his way until he got what he wanted.

Hell's most savage demon turned to two of Hell's most scheming and nodded his assent, his mouth spreading in a sinisterly toothy grin.

"It's a good plan. We leave immediately!"

Aiden Truss

# XV
## By Any Other Name

Rose found herself back in Priest's hideaway, back on the bed in which she'd first awoken to his revelations about her new condition. She didn't know how she'd arrived there and the last thing that she remembered was being with her mother. She raised a hand toward her face but there was no trace of blood.

Had she dreamt it all?

Looking around, she wondered whether in fact it was a dream within a dream. She was in the same place as before, but Priest was nowhere to be seen. The same heady, cool, floral scent filled the air and she had to fight the urge to fall back into a deep slumber.

Slipping from the bed, she walked barefoot across the floor towards a gentle spring, which was emptying into a small pool. Sitting down at the edge, she glanced into the iridescent water-like liquid and saw her new appearance for the first time. She'd often caught her dishevelled form in shop windows but the face that stared back now shocked her. It was her, but it wasn't her. It seemed that she'd undergone some sort of supernatural makeover and it took her time to adjust to the face staring back at her. It was only then that she looked at the rest: she examined her hands and arms for non-existent bruises and cuts, and did the same to her legs. Reaching under her dress, she felt the lack of scarring on her belly and her breasts and then stopped still in confusion and panic. As her fingers probed, she realized that she had no heartbeat. She used both hands to search for one, but still it remained silent. The panic was still there, but it felt different with no heart to pound out a warning in her chest. She instead felt a sort of drowning sensation, as if everything strange around her was about to swallow her up into its mysteries.

Rose lay back and tried to steady her feelings, like a drunk clinging onto the pavement to avoid the world spinning. What had Priest said to her about her new condition – that she was dead and yet not dead?

So what was she? And, had the episode with her mother really happened?

She turned onto her side and let an arm dangle into the pool, feeling its cool water caress her hand. She cupped it and it run through her fingers. The feel of it made her want to discard her clothes and jump in over her head to wash away her confusion, but looking into its depths, she saw drifting images of scenes from her life that instead made her sit up to watch her memories swirl, coalesce and tear apart in fleeting instants of recall. Yes, the visit to her mother was there as well. She saw the conversation, the argument, the final *coup de grace* and her own desolate emptiness at what she had done.

It *had* all happened.

Rose stood again and wandered through the garden in a reverie, trying to piece together how she had done what she'd done. She remembered thinking about her mother and her home and then she just seemed to be there. Was it that easy? Could she just imagine where she wanted to be and have it happen?

It all seemed a little too much like a fairy story from when she was little. Or one of those fantasies she'd had when lying in a cold doorway, of a genie appearing and offering her three wishes. Of course, she'd ask to be rich and to be beautiful, but she'd always save the third wish to ask for any future wish to come true whenever she wanted it. This is what everyone secretly wishes for surely?

Being a deep thinker, her fantasy then invariably developed into a philosophical discussion with the genie (who always looked like the blue genie from Disney's Aladdin cartoon movie, and always had Robin William's voice). She needed to know whether she was in fact allowed her third wish or whether this was cheating some magical rule. Also, she was all too aware of the old maxim about being careful what you wish for. What if she wished for something on a whim that she regretted later? In such a situation, could you wish you were dead and then actually kill yourself or did genie lore (and law), have safeguards against such things? Her mind was spinning with questions and she wanted Priest to answer them.

Looking around, she thought of calling out his name, but somehow knew that he wasn't near. Somehow though, she knew that she would be able to find him. This place was saturated with his presence, like a magical scent. Every inch of it sang of Priest and gave her the courage to trust her instincts and to reach out for him. Spreading her arms wide, she closed her eyes and invoked his powers, conjuring up his face in her mind and moving toward him.

*** 

Priest was in darkness.

Around him, the noise had ceased and the bonds around his arms, legs and head had been removed. The long table had returned and he sat at one end, while Trismegistus sat at the other, seemingly waiting for him to return to consciousness. The old man smiled at seeing him stir and waken.

"Ah, you're awake," he rose and approached Priest, examining his appearance much like a doctor, looking for signs of trauma. "You seem to have come through it all unscathed. How do you feel?"

"Like I've just been dropped from the top of a mountain onto my head," replied Priest.

"That's only to be expected. Your essence and your form have parted ways after all. I underwent the procedure myself centuries ago and it took me three weeks to recover from the experience."

"You underwent it as well? You never told me about that."

Trismegistus shrugged his shoulders.

"I wasn't always a librarian you know. I had a life before this one and I try not to think about it too often."

"So those rumours were true about you?"

"Rumours…?"

"The strange disappearance of Thoth all that time ago and your sudden appearance."

"I did indeed go by that name once. Out of necessity though, I chose to discard my powers, to walk among men and to try to impart wisdom to them. I speak of wisdom and learning that was ancient even in ancient times. My work has been forgotten by all but the very few and now I look after this depository of arcane knowledge. But I am content."

"It's hard enough to be a demon; I imagine that being a god is much worse. All that power reliant on the caprice of men."

"Indeed. Nowadays with the whole social media it's a bit easier, but in those days I stood no chance once the whole Jesus thing took off. Who saw that meme coming?" Trismegistus gave a rye harrumph and tutted with a shake of his head.

"Give me the Corpus Hermeticum or The Kybalion over the Bible any day Tris. I can't remember how many times I've read them both!" smiled Priest.

"You are very kind to say so sir. But as I said, that was another life."

Priest looked around him before attempting to stand on shaky legs.

"So what now?"

Trismegistus rose to his assistance and steadied him.

"Well, for a start, you'll probably need to rest further before you attempt to go anywhere. You've only been out for two days and no longer have your cast iron demonic constitution."

"You're telling me. I've never been drunk before, but I imagine that this is what the day after feels like." Priest sat down again quickly and held his head in his hands.

"Once you're feeling better, we can go over what you can and cannot do now and discuss the strengths... and the limitations of your new existence."

"I can't wait. In the meantime, just point me at whatever passes for a bed around here."

Aiden Truss

# XVI
## Wakey, Wakey!

Priest came to with the touch of gentle breathing on his cheek.

When he opened his eyes, he was staring into the eyes of Rose, she was cradling him now and looking down on him as if she were about to suckle him from her breast.

"Where am I?" he began.

"For a demon, you do talk in clichés don't you? Everyone who ever walks up in a movie says 'Where am I?'."

Rose smiled at him and shifted to allow him to sit up.

Priest looked around and let the familiarity of his surroundings creep into his consciousness.

"Did you bring me here?"

"It seemed the right thing to do. Besides, you didn't look very happy where you were. What happened to you?"

"That's a long story."

"I've got nowhere else to go at the moment."

"Very well. I'm trying an experiment."

"What sort of experiment?"

"I've divested myself of my powers for a time."

"Why the hell would you do that?" whispered Rose, puzzled.

Priest swung his legs over the side of the bed with the intention of trying them out again to see if they worked properly this time. After hopping gingerly to his feet, he decided that indeed they did seem to be obeying him and so found that he was free to pace the garden dramatically as he allowed Rose to hear as much of the tale as he was prepared to tell.

"Do you know how long a demon lives Rose?" without stopping for an answer, he continued, "An awfully long time. That's how long.

"I've been around for longer than you can fathom – though not as long as some of my kind – and have almost reached the point where I'm actually bored. Yes, as amazing as that may seem, with the cosmos and all of time as my playground, I've run out of things to do. That's the problem with near omnipotence: the gloss wears off after a while and you find yourself doing anything for a new distraction. That's why so many demons are addicted to chaos and evil. They slowly go off their heads and are driven mad by ennui.

"I on the other hand have decided that I'm going to take a walk around in human shoes for a time in order to see if I can arrest the encroaching tedium. This will avoid actually having to go the way of a lot of old demons and have myself exorcised out of an Irish schoolgirl by a whisky-soaked pederast in order to find peaceful oblivion."

"Let me get this straight. You're actually tired of being alive?"

"That's almost exactly correct. I've had enough. I'm bored shitless. I've watched the paint of life dry for so long that it's now flaked and peeling and ready for another coat of tedium."

"Can't you take a holiday or something?"

"Interesting that you should say that. I mean, there is nowhere that I haven't seen already. The Cote d'Azur or Highlands of Scotland are pretty, but nothing compared to watching newborn stars emerge from a stellar nursery or seeing the triple moons rising over the decaying souls in the Canyon of Grief on a fresh autumn day in Pandemonium City. But, now I can take in these sights through different eyes. Hence my transition to a nearly human form."

Rose had taken to pacing alongside him but stopped at this revelation.

"So you have none of your powers anymore?"

"Well... I have a few, but for the most part I'm as fragile and breakable as any human. Tris is supposed to be filling me in on all the pros and cons of my new existence, so I'll need to get back to him soon."

"He was the old man who was looking after you?"

"That's right, only he's not just any old man. I've known him for centuries and only just found out that he used to be a god, but chose an alternative profession when he started to lose his following. It seems that rather than waiting for the inevitable end, he bowed out while the going was still good and as such is still very much alive and kicking. Some of the ancient gods just didn't know when to hang up their boots and eked away at such an ignominious existence. The lucky ones faded quietly into myth, but others ended up as Dungeons and Dragons characters. Very embarrassing."

Rose smiled at this idea.

"You mean that if being remembered by schoolboys is the only way that they are remembered then that's what they continue as?"

"Exactly. What's a god without followers?"

"So what about the big God?"

"Which one?"

"The big God that everyone knows!"

"There's no such deity. No such thing."

"But there must be."

"Oh, there is a creator of the universe, or rather, there are many creators of the many universes, but they are nothing to do with Christianity or Islam or Scientology or any other silly belief. The particular creator responsible for your universe would be amused with the notion of all the silly rules that you people follow. That is, if he had any inclination to take any further interest in you."

"So he doesn't care?"

"He never claimed that he did. You lot made up all that stuff about the 'heavenly father'."

"You said that before, that he'd forgotten about us…"

"In all of creation, humans are kind of 'special'," Priest made the speech marks gesture with his fingers in the air, "insofar as you were an accident, something that wasn't meant to happen. For this reason, the creator did pay you special attention for a long time. But this was only because you were a glitch, an anomaly, an unintended result. You were an object of study, something under the cosmic microscope. Once it was decided that you weren't likely to develop into anything special, you became yesterday's news."

Rose had by now stopped mirroring his pacing and had sat herself down resignedly on the grass, digesting fully the implications of what she was being told.

"So all the times that I prayed for help, there was no one there listening?"

Priest stopped.

"Nope. Depressing isn't it?"

He said it so matter-of-factly that Rose felt a wave of sudden anger at him.

"How can you be so callous?"

"Hey, I'm not responsible for what humans choose to believe. It's you lot that choose to complicate your lives."

"But what is life without hope?"

"It's exactly what you make it. The cosmos doesn't owe you any comfort."

Priest waved his hands despairingly.

"Now, I have things to do, would you kindly take me back to Tris?"

"And what do I do while you're gone?"

"Whatever you want! I've given you my powers and you may use them in any way you want until I need them back."

"What happens when you need them back?"

Priest paused awkwardly.

"Errm, I've not considered that far. We'll talk about that later."

"We'll talk about it now." Rose was glaring, her eyes flamed orange and red and the calm of the loophole was shattered by the growing howl of a chill wind that blew about them.

Priest took a step toward her in a fit of anger of his own.

"You dare to tell me what to do?" he screamed, "I could turn you inside out and send you back to rot where I found you!"

"And how will you do that?"

Priest raised his hands to perform a conjuration but ended up just looking like a strange mime artist as he swatted the air like a demented orchestra conductor. It took a full minute before the realization hit him that he wasn't actually performing any magic, but just making a fool of himself.

"Ahh... erm..."

Rose collapsed backward in a fit of laughter at the look on his face.

"That was most impressive!"

Priest's anger evaporated only to be replaced by a feeling of what he assumed was embarrassment. He'd never felt it before, but he could feel his face burning and the sudden urge to run away as far as he could and to hide his head under something. This feeling was then replaced with another that stretched his face into a goofy grin which he didn't like either.

"That should have summoned my cousin, Azagthoth, to drag you away to his lair to be consumed alive after being slowly cooked and flayed over a pit of molten lava. He usually saves the heart for last and eats it in front of you with a bowl of chocolate custard."

"Instead, you pulled off some pretty freaky dance moves."

Rose giggled again, holding her sides as if they were about to burst.

The former demon sat down next to her and sighed.

"This is going to take some getting used to. Please take me back to Tris and I promise that I'll answer your other questions."

"Ok. Shall I do it with or without the dancing?"

# XVII
## Welcome to Earth

The Arch Demon Astolath stepped out onto the street and looked around him. To passers-by using the busy London thoroughfare, he was a big guy in a suit - a very big guy. Even in disguise, Astolath had found it difficult to hide his bulk and his muscular frame strained against the black three-piece that he was wearing. His bald head glinted in the morning sun as he surveyed the scene through his rather snazzy-looking sun glasses and grinned. There was so much humanity around him, completely unaware of who was in their midst.

He'd made the trip to Earth along with Eldredd and two of his subalterns, Moloch and Abraxas. The idea was that they'd arrive in human form and in formal garb, but something had gone slightly wrong on the journey. Not all demons are shifters by nature. While some develop the knack over time, others have to rely on more experienced practitioners in order to help complete their transitions. But, whereas Moloch and Abraxas literally followed suit and appeared much like Astolath, Eldredd's transition had not gone according to plan. He stood on the pavement next to three of them in the form of a young female brunette in a short red dress and high heels, all set off with an expensive looking handbag.

"I don't like this Astolath. Can I go back and change?"

"No!" bellowed the Arch Demon. "If anyone asks, you're my wife," he chuckled gruffly and gave his most salacious leer.

Eldredd had used every piece of trickery, coercion and sophistry at his disposal in order to convince Sinn that he should be the one to go with Astolath and now, here he was about to embark on his mission as a puny human female. As if the shame and ignominy of his appearance were not enough, the high heels were killing him and he'd already had wolf-whistles from two builders in the front of a lorry that had just driven past.

The whole idea of a disguise was not to fool the humans, who were largely irrelevant, but to give them the jump on Lucifer when they found him. It would not do to make a scene that might alert him to their presence. And so, to all intents and purposes, they were now a rich businessman, his trophy wife and their two minders. Helnocker had arranged the details of the alteration for the journey in collaboration with Sinn, who had sneakily arranged for Eldredd's new persona to end up in its current fetching form. It was a small act of revenge for being left behind, but at that moment, somewhere in the depths of Lucifer's castle, that great wide mouth was shaking the chandeliers with howls of evil mirth.

The strange party checked into a hotel near to one of the big train termini at the centre of town. It wasn't exactly five star quality, but it would suffice as a base of operations. Word had reached Helnocker that Priest had been to visit the Arcanum library and so he had made sure that Astolath found his way to the vicinity in case Lucifer should follow him there. The lugubrious hotel staff had paid them little enough attention other than to note that they paid their bill up front in crisp new fifty pound notes – notes which even now were probably reverting to their true form and decaying into the black chthonic mulch that they'd been forged from. But, who would be able to blame the new visitors, especially ones who were so intimidating in appearance? The brunette in the party looked nice though.

Now on the streets, Astolath strode purposefully in the direction of the old financial district of the city where the library was to be found. In the near distance he could see the spire of the old church jutting up above the surrounding office blocks.

"We'll head for the Arcanum and see what they have to tell us."

"Yes my lord," barked the two hellish bodyguards in unison.

Around them, the bustle of the city went on uninterested in yet another group of suits in their midst. Astolath quickly became puzzled by the strange phenomenon of people walking into him as if he wasn't there. He'd been told that if he bumped into anybody, the correct response in order to avoid raising suspicion was to quickly say 'Oops' and then 'sorry' before smiling politely and then moving on without another word. He'd managed this quite successfully on the first two occasions that he'd come into contact with a human – and had even felt quite pleased with himself at his seeming ability to assimilate with his surroundings.

On the third occasion though, his ire was invoked beyond all reason or restraint. These people kept walking into him head first, while peering into small black devices that they carried in their hands. They appeared to be preoccupied with manipulating something with their thumbs, almost as if they were in an act of devotion. This meant that they paid no attention to anything else around them. Everywhere he looked, people had the same fugue-like look on their faces.

This time, he just stopped still and allowed the zombie-like pedestrian to walk into him head-on.

"Oops, sorry," said the young man in the suit and went to walk around him.

Astolath grinned and grabbed the man by his throat as if he were about to throttle the life out of him there and then. Looking about him, he saw a sign for 'Hanging Sword Alley' in between two buildings and darted into its shadows while bodily carrying his victim.

"Oops, sorry," grinned Astolath, pinning the man against an air-conditioning unit with his Italian leather shod-feet dancing in the air as he tried desperately to escape.

"W-what d-do you w-want?" gasped the man.

"I want you puny little monkeys to stop walking into me. What are these things that so occupy you?"

Astolath was still holding him in one huge hand and used the other to reach for what the man was holding. Even in the desperate struggle for survival and the attempt to breath, he still clasped his mobile phone tightly.

"I-t's a phone," he rasped in a choking whisper.

Astolath took it from him and examined it. The display was blue and white and said 'FaceFriend' at the top. Underneath was a picture of his victim – whose name apparently was Milford King - in what looked like a bar, obviously inebriated and surrounded by other grinning inebriates. Underneath were the words, "OMG, wot a night. Am so late for work now!" Below this was a thumbs-up symbol indicating that eighteen other people liked these words.

"What does this mean?" Astolath looked back at Milford for an explanation, but by this time he had lost consciousness. The Arch Demon cast him casually aside to examine the phone further.

A little later, Milford King's latest status update appeared on FaceFriend. It showed a photograph of Astolath grinning into the camera with the words underneath, "OMG, wot a morning!"

A little later still, the City of London coroner had one of the most interesting cases of his career. That morning, office workers had stumbled across the body of a smartly dressed young man in an alley behind Fleet Street. The cause of death seemed to be very straight forward as evidenced by the bruising around the victim's throat, the crushed windpipe, red neck and face, the bulging eyes and the extended tongue. The hyoid bone, he noted, and the thyroid cartilage were also broken.

What was more puzzling though was that further examination that revealed a mobile phone wedged into the rectal cavity of the victim.

# XVIII
## Library Returns

Hermes Trismegistus was waiting at the table for Priest's return. He'd not been present when he'd disappeared, but knew that it was only a matter of time before he returned. There was too much that he needed to be told, more information needed for the next step on his journey.

As he sat twisting the various gold and silver jewelled rings on his gnarled old fingers, he realized that he was being watched.

Turning about to face what he expected would be Priest standing there; he was surprised to see the dapper appearance of a man standing there in the shadows. As he stepped forward, it became clear that he was wearing an immaculate double-breasted suit and black and white wingtips, one hand holding a silver-topped cane and a huge grin beaming out from behind his sun glasses.

"Mulciber?"

"Hermes Trismegistus! Or can I just call you Hermes?"

Trismegistus turned and made to stand.

"My name is unimportant. How may I serve you?"

Mulciber nodded and his grin seemed to stretch even further.

"Oh, don't get up old fellow, I just wanted to check up on my friend the Priest and see what he's been up to…"

"I don't know what you mean."

"You know exactly what I mean. I can still smell the ichor and brimstone in the air. You've been playing at invocation recently and I want to know what for."

As he spoke, Mulciber crossed the room and leaned against the huge stone fireplace. He leaned his cane against one of the ornamental dragons that sat at either side and with a subtle wave of his fingers, a roaring fire leapt into life in the grate.

"Ah, that's better. It's cold in here."

Trismegistus had never met Mulciber, but knew him by reputation. He'd heard of his exploits in the middle ages and that he was largely responsible for the whole preoccupation of the medieval mind with devils and demons, such was his penchant for appearing before humans and for inflicting acts of treachery and cruelty upon them. He also knew that Priest had been involved with him at one stage, but wasn't sure to what degree.

He decided to play it safe.

"I've been giving my assistance to Priest on some matters of research in which he was interested... nothing more"

"I can smell a lie a mile away old man and right now you reek. Not very noble of the 'Thrice Great One' eh?"

Trismegistus' mouth gaped at the realization that Mulciber knew his true identity.

"Yes, I know who you are. You're the fallen god aren't you; the one who took the coward's way out and decided to hide among your books instead of fighting your corner. I also know how you managed to cast off your former essence and to achieve your current form with the help of some of the heavenly heavyweights." He paused to let the revelation sink in. "Did you help Priest to achieve the same thing?"

The librarian swallowed hard and dug deep for something with which to fight off his demon interrogator. He knew both how persuasive Mulciber could be and how low he could stoop in order to achieve his ends. Reaching into his cavernous pockets, Trismegistus felt the shape of the golden Ankh which had once been the symbol of his power. He gripped it in his hand and slowly brought it up to the table, hiding it in his closed hands.

"I really wish that I could be of help sir. Perhaps I can interest you in an ancient volume of something, or a tour of our library here?"

There may be a word for what happened next to Mulciber's formerly charming demeanour, but if so, it has yet to be discovered. Simultaneously it seemed that every muscle in his body tautened and a terrifying rictus suddenly replaced his smile. He looked as if he were about to fall victim to a grand mal epileptic seizure as he stood to attention and began to shake violently on the spot.

The flames in the fireplace leapt out from among the stones and enveloped him in their golden, licking embrace and tore his suit from him. They crawled all over him as if they were alive and started to burn the very skin from his body, revealing the truth of him beneath. In seconds the real Mulciber was exposed to the librarian and a terrifying sight he was, or would have been for any mortal looking on. Trismegistus on the other hand had been around the cosmic block a few times and had dealt with demons before.

Mulciber, being one of the great classical demons, had an imposing physique made up of dark green-scaled skin and knotted muscle. His legs were covered in tufted brown hair and ended in golden hooves. Atop his head sat an impressive pair of huge horns, one erect at a forty-five degrees and the other curled into a spiral before correcting itself to the same angle. Behind him, his huge blue wings unfolded and spread out as if he were about to take flight. The only innocuous feature in this archetypal image of a demon was the pair of rather swish sunglasses that he was still wearing and which hid his furiously burning eyes from view.

Trismegistus rose slowly from his chair.

"I take it that that is a 'no' then?"

Mulciber leapt onto the table and bellowed at the top of his considerable voice, "Ridiculous creature. Do you think that I have time to play games here? I know that Priest has been here and that you have aided him and I want to know where he is. Now!"

The librarian stood his ground and held the Ankh aloft in front of him, wielding it as if he were Van Helsing holding a crucifix before Count Dracula.

"I'll never reveal to you what has passed and I still have one last shot of the old magic left. Now demon, begone!"

At this, the Ankh flashed brightly, emitting a blinding beam of light, which struck Mulciber full in the chest. The demon flinched and waited for the Ankh to do whatever it was going to do… which after a few seconds appeared to be absolutely nothing.

Trismegistus looked at the symbol clutched tightly in his hand and frowned. As he did so, the light blinked twice and then faded before disappearing completely.

"Bugger!"

He looked at the Ankh before shaking it and banging it on the table top before trying again to use its power on the demon. It was no use. He'd held onto it for the last thousand or so years without using it and now two uses in a week had polished it off. Whatever residual power it carried was now spent or had leaked into the ether.

Mulciber laughed a piteously mocking laugh at the old man as he stepped toward him and lifted him off his feet and into the air.

"No more chances my thrice great friend. Your tenure as librarian is at an end. From now on you'll be known as 'Thrice dead!'"

With that he grasped Trismegistus in one hand by his wispy silver hair before violently ramming his other hand into the old man's mouth. Once his fingers found the back of his throat, he twisted his wrist and forced it downward, pushing through the resistance of muscle, bone and cartilage and until he was almost up to his shoulder in the twitching librarian. As he reached something warm and squishy in the abdominal area he stopped, grabbed a handful of what he found and then reversed his arm, pulling hard.

Still conscious, Trismegistus watched in surprise as his attacker's arm emerged from his mouth followed by what looked at first like a string of sausages. Even then, his intellectual curiosity kicked in to inform him that he was indeed being disemboweled and that these were not in fact sausages but his intestines that were emerging from his mouth. This made sense as he'd not in fact ingested sausages for some time and their presence would have been strangely anomalous.

The relief that these were in fact his intestines emerging was quickly replaced by the realization these were in fact his intestines emerging and he tried to emit a desperate scream, which in turn was stifled by the presence of his own viscera blocking his throat. As the last few inches of bowel emerged, Mulciber gave an almost gentle pull to separate the guts from whatever tethered them to the old man's innards and threw the whole red sticky mess into the fire, where they started to sizzle and pop as they hit the grate.

As Trismegistus lost consciousness - scientist to the last - he made a brief mental note that the searing offal smelled more like steak and kidney pie than sausages.

Mulciber allowed his victim to fall in a heap where he was, before jumping nimbly down from the table and retrieving the Ankh from the dead grasp of the old librarian. As he did so, he heard footsteps approaching from the next room and with a violent shrug, returned to his previous besuited human form.

"Mulciber!" shouted Priest in surprise before looking down at the crumpled form of his old friend.

"Priest. Thank Hell you're here. I've just arrived myself and found old Hermes in this dreadful state."

Priest raced over to the old librarian and fell on the floor next to him but could find no sign of life. Tris' mouth was ringed with blood, almost as if he was wearing lipstick, but other than that, he seemed to be in one piece and it wasn't immediately obvious how he had died.

"Who has done this?" he rasped at Mulciber.

"Steady on old man! As I said, I just arrived and found him like this. He was on his last legs and said something about telling you to carry on with what you were doing. What did he mean?"

Priest looked up at the elder demon and frowned.

"He told you what we'd done?"

"Of course he did. He knew that we were old friends and I think that he wanted me to help you in some way."

Scanning the glass covering Mulciber's eyes, Priest tried to discern the truth of what had happened. While he had no reason to doubt Mulciber, he had no reason to believe that Tris would impart knowledge of the ritual to anyone else either. The old man had been fastidiously discrete in all of his past dealings.

Something wasn't quite right.

Priest turned back to his dead friend and gently started to go through his pockets.

"What are you doing?"

"I'm looking for the Ankh."

"The Ankh?"

"You know – the ancient Egyptian symbol for life. It was very important to the old man and I'd like to keep it."

"I can't recall seeing an Ankh anywhere." Mulciber backed away and turned around as if scanning the room for such an object.

Finding nothing, Priest stood and turned to Mulciber.

"It has to be here somewhere… unless… unless someone killed the old man for it."

Priest looked his friend right in the sunglasses again as he said this, searching for some sort of reaction. Right now, he didn't know who to trust. All he could think was that he now wasn't going to receive any guidance as to what he had to do and that if he in fact did succeed, then there was no guarantee that anyone else could perform the ritual to return him to his original form.

The strange tightening feeling in his chest was panic, but having never felt it before, Priest didn't know what was happening to him. He lurched as the room started to spin before doubling up and vomiting all over Mulciber's impressive and no doubt expensive shoes.

"What's happening to me Mulciber?" he gasped, wiping green bile from his lips with the back of his hand and inspecting it as if it were something alien.

"I've seen humans do this often. It's what happens when they're deeply afraid. I assume that it will wear off in a while when you've calmed down."

Mulciber knelt sympathetically next to Priest and continued.

"So it's true then. You did make the transition?"

Priest nodded slowly with his eyes shut tight, desperately attempting to stem another bout of retching spasms and failing utterly as he was sick yet again. This time he thoughtfully managed to avoid his friend's shoes.

"Tris helped me. I needed to find out what it was like to be human. I'm learning lots already. Mostly it hurts and feels uncomfortable."

At that moment, he realized that someone else had entered the room with them. Just beyond Mulciber, the morose Crowley had appeared and announced, as if to no one in particular, "You are required back at the house sir!"

Mulciber shook his head and tutted.

"I'm sorry my friend but I must leave you for now. I have some other urgent business to take care of."

He left Priest where he was and joined his butler by the door where they both faded from view without a backward glance.

Finding his feet again, Priest lifted Trismegistus from the floor and laid him out respectfully on the long table. What was he meant to do with the body? This was something else with which he'd never had to deal with before.

He decided to search the library as best he could to see if he could locate the Ankh, but he knew deep inside that he wasn't going to find it. But it would give him something to do while he decided where to go next, and he might just find a useful tome or two that might give him a hint.

# XIX
## Sins of the Step-Father

The job centre was ticking over with a steady stream of, if not the usual suspects, then the usual type of suspects. At home among the transient and lost souls in the waiting area sat one individual in particular that 'we need to focus upon for the moment, unfortunately.

Karl Grieves was back for his fortnightly interview. He had to report in order to convince the staff that he was 'actively seeking work' in order to continue receiving the various benefits and allowances he had been claiming since he had lost his job. He'd worked as a scaffolder and had suffered a minor accident that he'd managed to string out into a claim against the company and then a long tenure on sickness benefit. Between the payout from the company and the various forms of government supplied funds, he had a comfortable income and managed to live in a very comfortable fashion.

He wasn't stupid enough to flaunt his good fortune though, and always attended these interviews in a pair of old jeans, tee-shirt and beat up old trainers. He'd also make sure that he didn't shave for a day or two beforehand to give him a more convincingly disheveled look.

These visits were usually routine. Having as he did a doctor's certificate, the staff didn't tend to question him in too much detail. It was just too much effort and trouble to dig up the dirt on people unless one of the regular politically-motivated clampdowns was in force and the local unemployment figures needed massaging. All he needed to do was to keep his appointments, keep an eye on the paperwork and affect a slight limp in his right leg whenever he went out of his flat.

This week had been slightly more interesting for him though, as just a few days before, he'd seen his step-daughter coming out of this very building. She'd dropped off his radar for the last couple of years and her appearance had been a bit of a shock to him. Looking at her gaunt figure he couldn't help remembering the fuller frame that she'd once had and that he'd taken so much pleasure in. It had been a golden time for him when he'd first met Rose's mother. He had somewhere to live, had someone to wait on him hand and foot, and someone who was so needy that she didn't dare rock the boat when she developed suspicions that she had been sharing him with her own daughter.

It hadn't been the first time and he knew exactly the type to go for. Someone the wrong side of forty, not unattractive but starting to lose her looks and who would be grateful of the attention. This type usually came with a kid or two as baggage but if it was a nubile young daughter then he wasn't going to complain. He'd charm them both for his own perverse ends and then just walk away if the questions got to be too difficult.

Karl followed Rose for a few hundred yards before seeing her slump into the doorway of a derelict shop and he sat watching her for a while. It even crossed his mind to go up to her to offer her some help. Who knew, perhaps out of gratitude she'd offer him some of the old good times?

But his courage had failed him and his libido had been overwhelmed by his cowardice. He wasn't going to risk making a scene in the middle of the busy high street if she turned on him. He'd wait until after dark and go back later on once the pedestrian traffic had thinned out.

Only when he went back, she was gone.

*\*\**

Arriving home a few days later, after his visit to the job centre, he unlocked the door to his flat, his government subsidised little kingdom, and headed for the fridge and his second beer of the morning. The flat had belonged to another girlfriend who'd moved out six months ago. He'd not had to worry about picking up the rent and had just completed another application form to get it paid for him.

He also liked the proximity to the local pub, which was one of a soulless chain normally frequented by old men. Most towns have them now, full of old codgers who spent their retirement trying to break the record for nursing their one solitary pint of the day for as long as possible. It was called 'The Wrong 'Un' but the locals called it 'the funeral parlour', such was its reputation for fun. Karl loved it though as it allowed him to drink as much cheap beer as he could and to pick up the odd grateful middle-aged female out for a quiet drink with a friend.

Drinking straight from the can, he kicked off his trainers, walked into the living room and dropped onto the sofa before reaching for the remote control for his giant sixty inch TV. The Channel Four racing programme was just about to start and he'd placed a few bets that morning that he was eager to check up on. Putting his feet up onto the coffee table in front of him, he settled down for a morning's drinking and racing before returning to the pub for a pie and another few pints before scoping out what he thought the evening might bring. There was a small cabal of similar social scroungers who he knew would all be in place by about seven o'clock and he knew that he could always see out the evening with them until chucking out time.

After the second race had come up empty for him, he got another beer and tried to settle back into the sofa, but couldn't quite get comfortable. Twisting this way and that and adjusting cushions didn't seem to relief the situation and nor did switching from one end to the other. At length he decided to stand up and pull everything off in order to see what was causing his discomfort.

He grabbed one of the large back cushions, meaning to look behind it but as he did so, his hand was grabbed violently by something.

"Shit!" he squealed, almost expecting to find a large spider or something, but we then yanked forward as he tried to pull away. Something had him in a grip like a vice and was pulling him into the sofa. He tried to brace himself with his foot against the front of the furniture but it was no use and he soon found his face pressed in against the fabric of the sofa.

He was suffocating slowly and could do nothing to resist the relentless pull of whatever it was that had hold of him. Even as he struggled, he knew that there was no way that anything could be doing this. Behind the sofa was a solid brick wall, but if this continued then he'd be dragged through that as well. But no, he was still moving further into the sofa and darkness was engulfing him inch by inch.

As the blackness became absolute and he felt as if his lungs would explode from the lack of oxygen, he fell forward into nothingness and landed with a heavy thump against what felt like a concrete floor. In doing so, he felt his nose pop as it broke and several of his front teeth crack under the impact as they forced their way through his top lip.

He squealed in pain and tried to emit a loud exclamation of "bollocks!" but with the state of his mouth, it came out as a "bowwockth!" which echoed about the dark space around him. Blood and spittle dripped down his chin and as he tried to get up, he heard it drip, drip onto the floor. Unthinkingly, he brought his sleeve up to wipe his face but this just served to pull his lip open further and to brush against the newly exposed pulp of his incisors. This elicited another "bowwockth!" followed by a pathetic "Jeethuth quithe!"

\*\*\*

After the painless and simple process of transporting Priest to the Arcanum with the merest hint of a flick of a whim, Rose decided that she needed to pay another visit to her family before she could move on with her new life. She needed some sort of closure to the 'relationship' with her step-father. She was starting to get the hang of her new abilities and had decided to be a bit more creative when tackling Karl. She was going to make things exactly as they had been in her fantasies when she'd imagined getting back at him.

At first she'd just wanted to kill him. A bullet to the head from out of nowhere would be sufficient. But then she had decided that this wasn't comprehensive enough. There had to be a reckoning but she had to make him see how he had made her feel. This then had to be followed by a great deal of pain and bloody retaliation, preferably of a nature that reflected the sexual nature of his crimes.

She'd played out various scenarios in her head – mostly informed by horror movies. They showed torture sessions in abandoned warehouses, dark cellars with an assortment of noisy power tools, and secluded cabins in the woods with carelessly abandoned wood axes lying around. Some were set in a gory Christmas or Halloween setting complete with menacingly masked assailants looking to exact terrible revenge. Perhaps she'd stage a succession of grim tableaus like one of those cheesy horror anthologies from the nineteen seventies. Only instead of having separate characters in each segment, she'd have Karl stumble helplessly from each one to the next, with his fate culminating in a final decisively and terminally grisly dénouement.

In the end, she'd gone for a bit of everything: a macabre mélange of misery would await her tormentor - hence the theatrics with the sofa. It seemed to her that it was something that might have come straight out of one of the Nightmare on Elm Street movies that she had loved when she was younger. Freddy Kruger was always popping in and out of walls or furniture and dragging his victims to an elaborate and Grand Guignol dispatching.

The place in which Karl now found himself was just the first step on his personal path to oblivion. That he'd managed to damage himself as he arrived was an added bonus for Rose, who was all too happy to see the suffering get off to a flying start. As she was improvising this event though, she wasn't quite sure at which point to put in an appearance. Should she just watch in the wings as he stumbled from misery to misery before a great reveal at the end, or should she let him know up front that she was the cause of his messy downfall?

For now, she decided that she was content to just watch things play out and to see where they went.

Karl, on the other hand, didn't know what to think. He was standing now and blindly waving his hands about in an attempt to make sense of his surroundings or at least to find out where the walls were. So far he'd not found anything and the unevenness of the floor also made him suspect that the next step might result in a painful fall into another hole.

"Hello! Ith anybothy there?" he lisped loudly through the broken wreckage of his mouth. Again he just heard the faint echo of his own voice as if he were in the middle of a huge cavern. If there were any faint light to be found, his eyes might have adjusted to it by now, but still he was swimming in darkness. He thought he could see the odd flash of light in his periphery but each time that he tried to follow its source he quickly realised that it was probably just his imagination playing games with him.

In frustration and fear, he eventually just gave up and sat down on the floor and decided not to move any further until he could somehow get his bearings. It was at this point that he remembered he had a lighter in his pocket. Cursing and dribbling he reached into his jeans and pulled it out. As the striker made contact with the flint and it burst into life he immediately regretted his actions.

Staring back at him suddenly was a grotesque, bloodied face etched with sheer terror. It looked at him, without blinking, before opening its mouth wide in a scream of agony and horror. Hearing the sound originate in his own gargling throat, Karl came to a sudden panicked realization that he was staring into his own face. Before him was a mirror that reflected both him and the glowing lighter which guttered as his breath came hard and fast.

He let the light go out and sat there panting with his eyes shut tight.

After several minutes he allowed himself to look around again into the darkness. Reaching out in front of him, he couldn't feel the glass surface of the mirror. It seemed to have disappeared. But this time, he could definitely see a light in the distance. Clinging to the hope of escape he scrambled headlong toward it ignoring the fear of falling that had previously gripped him. Arriving at where the light should have been, it now seemed to him to be further away, as if it had been moving as he had and maintained its distance from him. Desperate to clutch at any shred of hope, no matter how tattered, he continued to run as fast as his shaking legs would carry him, before finally catching his foot on something and falling heavily again in a heap upon the ground.

"Aaargh!" this time the scream was in frustration and not in pain. He didn't know how long he'd been flailing his way around this dark labyrinth but his fear was now being replaced with anger.

"Where the thodding hell am I?" he yelled as loud as he could, spinning around in a small circle as he did so.

Then the voice came.

"You're right where I want you Karl."

Rose had enough of watching and decided to make her grand entrance into the unfolding nightmare.

"Whoth that?"

"You don't recognize my voice?"

Karl was bent double, holding his knees and fighting for air. He was also trying to figure out where the voice was coming from and who it belonged to.

"Thtop the game. I give up – who ith it?"

"I'm disappointed Karl. You always told me how special I was to you."

"Rothe?"

"It's normally pronounced 'ROSE', but I'll let you off as you're in such bad shape."

"Thank god – help me out of here!"

"Uh, uh Karly boy, we're just getting started." He could hear the malicious smile in her voice as she continued, "I've got a full afternoon's entertainment planned for you and we can carry it on into the evening and the night beyond that if needs be. It all depends on how long you last the course."

"Where are you Rothe? Can't we talk about thingth?"

"Oh we're going to talk about things alright. And we are going to cry about things and then maybe even scream and shout about them. But you're going to be doing most of the listening as I've got a few things to get off my chest and a few bones to pick of yours."

"I alwayth loved you Rothe, you know that."

Rose chuckled with vicious laughter laced with sharp and icy contempt.

"You loved me?" she frowned as she summoned up a small tornado of furious wind that almost buffeted Karl from his feet.

"In my own way," he offered pitifully.

"Rape is not love! Beating is not love! Lying and betrayal is not love!"

This time he was thrown to the floor by the sheer fury that bore her words to him. Each syllable felt like a slap to the face and he reeled under the savagery of the blows and he ended up curled in a fetal ball on the hard ground.

"No more. Please!" he whimpered.

"No more? We're just getting started." Rose spat the words at the vulnerable, shaking form on the floor.

Aiden Truss

# XX
## Closed Encounters

Astolath stood outside the spired church with his small band of companions and sniffed the air in a deep and inquisitive sniff. This had to be the correct building: he could smell the faint trace of demonic presences along an underlying scent of recently used magic. At a curt nod from his large, domed and shiny head, Moloch and Abraxas took their cue to step forward and approach the large wooden doors.

The doors, which sat in an ornate gothic arch, were covered in graffiti, posters and old flyers which flapped back and forth in the breeze. Nowhere did there seem to be a handle, a knob or even a keyhole by which to gain entrance. The two demons wasted no time in shredding the collection of posters in order to get at anything that might be behind them and provide a clue as to how they might gain access. All the time they did this, they were acutely aware of Astolath's eyes burning into their backs and his microscopically short temper.

Giving up at last, they gave each other a quick and nervous look before turning back to their boss. Abraxas summoned up slightly more courage than his partner and dared to speak out.

"There doesn't seem to be a way to gain access my lord."

Astolath eyed him through his sunglasses for a moment, weighing up whether to pulp him on the spot before finally (and reluctantly), deciding against it.

"See if there is a back entrance. Go now!" he barked.

Eldredd took this opportunity to suggest a means of getting off his feet for a few minutes. Looking across the street he spotted a small, greasy spoon-style café with steamed up windows with 'Regency Café' stenciled across them in large red letters.

"If we are to blend in with the humans, might we not do as they do my lord and follow one of their customs as we wait for the others to find a way in?"

"What do you mean?"

"About this time of the day, most of the humans indulge in what they call 'breakfast'. It involves eating and drinking and there is an establishment over there that would allow us to partake."

Other than killing, raping and destroying things in general, eating was one of Astolath's favourite pastimes. As such, he was agreeable to the suggestion.

"Very well. Lead the way."

Crossing the busy street with complete disregard for the traffic, the two of them made their way to the café. They were almost across the road when a black taxi roared to a stop with its brakes screaming from the effort of stopping.

An angry head appeared out of the driver's window and bellowed in harsh cockney at the two of them.

"Why don't you two watch where you're bleedin' goin' you idiots?"

This sudden outburst stopped Astolath and Eldredd in their tracks. Eldredd cursed to himself and sought to restrain the inevitable actions of his new master and, remembering his current appearance, he made an attempt to play upon it. Placing himself in between Astolath and the angry cabbie, he sashayed over and offered what he hoped was his most feminine and alluring apology.

"I'm so sorry daahling. It was entirely my fault." As he said this, he fluttered his eyelids for effect and put his hands on his hips to flout his impressive pair of breasts.

The cabbie stood no chance.

"Errm, that's alright love. Just watch where you're going next time eh?"

"Of course," pouted Eldredd. "Thank you so much."

With that, he grabbed Astolath's arm and pulled him toward the curb.

"I was going to kill him for his insolence, Eldredd."

"I know my lord. That is why I acted as I did. Please forgive me, but we still need to be as discreet as possible."

Astolath thought for a moment before shrugging. It was hard not killing anything or anyone for any prolonged length of time but even he saw the necessity of keeping the blood to a minimum for the time being.

"Very well. Let us do this breakfast thing."

Eldredd sighed with relief and led on toward the door of the café.

\*\*\*

Al, or 'Big Al' to most of his clientele, wasn't exactly rushed off his feet. The early morning crowd of builders and office types had been and gone like a plague of locusts and devoured copious mugs of tea and coffee, a mountain of bacon, eggs and sausages and enough toast to pave a small country. Now it was the mid-morning lull with just a couple of customers – a young guy who was nervously sipping a latte as if he was waiting for an interview and an old woman who was feeding bits of a chocolate muffin to a toy dog that had its head protruding from a bag hung over her shoulder. Al watched her speaking to it and shook his head in amused bafflement. His thoughts were interrupted by the sight of the gorgeous brunette and the bald gorilla in a suit that entered at that moment.

Wiping his hands on his apron, he pulled out his small notepad, ready to take their order. Smiling in greeting, he called out cheerfully, "Anywhere you like love!" He then watched as both new entrants surveyed the tables around them, taking an agonizingly long time to decide where to park themselves. Eventually they settled on the farthest corner from the counter and most secluded table in the place. The woman sat down immediately but the big guy took up so much space that he ended up pushing the adjacent table back about three feet in order to accommodate his bulk at the table they had chosen. He wasn't fat, he was just enormous. Al found himself wondered where the hell a bloke like that managed to buy his suits.

Astolath groaned at Eldred, "Well? What do we do now?"

"You look at this," said Eldredd handing him a laminated menu card, "and you choose what you want to eat and to drink."

The new Lord of Hell and the supreme Arch Demon perused the menu. He wasn't sure what 'chips' were and he wasn't sure about 'salad' either. He did recognize most of the meat-based meals though and so decided that he might have an 'All-day Jumbo Breakfast'. In fact, he might order two or three of them.

Eldredd had no real appetite, but was happy just to kick off his heels under the table and to flex and stretch his gorgeously pedicured and red-nailed toes.

After a few minutes, the man behind the counter approached them with a smile on his whiskery, semi-bearded face. He might have been quite a big guy in human terms, with broad shoulders and muscular tattooed arms, but as he approached Astolath, his stature seemed to diminish. So much so that when he arrived at their table he looked like a little boy.

"What would you like, folks?" he asked amiably.

Without looking up, Astolath declared his desire for three All-day Jumbo Breakfasts.

"Three?" Al echoed uncertainly. "You're a big bloke, but even you might struggle with three. It does come with tea and toast as well, you know?"

Eldredd interjected before Astolath could bellow anything.

"My husband has a very healthy appetite." And hit Al with his best smile.

"Whatever you say love! And for you...?"

As he asked, he stole a glance at Eldredd and thought naughty thoughts about what he'd like to do to this woman if only she didn't have such a juggernaut of an old man.

"I'll just have a cup of tea please."

"No problem," he said as he jotted it down on his pad, "Be back in a mo with your drinks." He finished up with a theatrical wink and a wiggle of his eyebrows at Eldredd before retreating out of sight to the kitchen.

Once there, he prepared the tea cups and threw bacon, eggs, sausages, mushrooms, tomatoes, baked beans, black pudding and toast into their various preparations, making sure to triple the portions that he usually made. As he moved about, he glanced over the counter from time to time to get a glimpse of those spectacular legs again. Ooh, what he could do to her!

As the eggs popped and the bacon sizzled, he daydreamed of what might happen if she walked in again tomorrow on her own, the café empty but for the two of them. He saw them naked on top of one of the tables, abandoning themselves to wanton passion and rolling around the floor covered in ketchup and mayonnaise. But the toast popping up out of the toaster dispelled his fantasy and he began to pour the tea and finish getting everything onto the three plates. He took four cups of tea to his visitors before returning to fetch the food.

When he returned with the tray, all of the tea had gone. He looked around to see where it had been thrown, but all he saw were Astolath and Eldredd sitting there innocently.

"What happened to the tea?"

"We drank it," said Eldredd. "It was very nice."

Astolath made an effort to join in with the charade.

"Yes, very nice. Four more cups please!"

Al put three All-day Jumbo Breakfasts in front of the big man, which were followed by a plate heavily laden with toast.

"Any ketchup?" he addressed the question to Astolath but looked at Eldredd as he did so.

"What is ketchup?" asked the giant.

147

"You know, tomato sauce…"

Astolath shook his head. "No tomato sauce. The meat will suffice thank you." And he set about impaling as much on his fork as possible before filling his considerable mouth with it.

Al looked away in barely disguised disgust and promised to return shortly with more tea.

As he walked away, Astolath peered after him and harrumphed. "That human desires you."

"Don't you think I know that? Did you pick up on what he was thinking about before he returned?"

"Have you never had a human in that way?"

"Never. Priest is the one fascinated by humans, not me."

Enjoying his food more than he expected had put Astolath into a fair semblance of what might be called a good mood.

"I think that you should follow him and do what he wants," smiled the Arch Demon.

Eldredd went rigid with surprise and anger.

"My lord, I'm here to assist you to apprehend the Lightbringer, not to provide you with entertainment!"

Astolath continued to smile a wicked smile. "You, my dear, are here to do my bidding and if I tell you to make the beast with two backs with a human you will do it." The pronouncement was ended with the delivery of another huge forkful of food into his eagerly gaping maw.

Eldredd stared into his own reflection in Astolath's glasses and tried to peer past it to look for a hint of a joke or an indication that the great demon had made a rare jest, but there was nothing there to allay his fears. He gulped hard and was about to risk a protest when the door opened and Moloch and Abraxas appeared.

"We've found the way in my lord."

Astolath was still gorging himself but now put down his fork and wiped his mouth on the back of his hand, before remembering himself and wiping it clean with a paper napkin.

The food was good, but it was entirely secondary to what he had come here to do.

"Good. Take me to it."

Eldredd stood to leave with him just as Al returned with a tray full of mugs of tea.

"We've changed our mind. We're leaving," he explained. "What do we owe you for our food?"

"Nonsense my dear," barked Astolath, "You stay here and come to some accommodation with our friend over the price of our delicious repast." At this, he gave Al the same wink and raise of the eyebrows that he'd unknowingly given Eldredd earlier. Al looked at him then at Eldredd and smiled salaciously. He followed the three demons to the door, bid them "have a good one" and then called to his other customers that he had to close early for personal reasons. The main reason was pushing impatiently at the crotch of his trousers as he impatiently ushered them out the door before flicking around the open/closed sign to prevent any unwanted disturbances. Then, he turned back to the sumptuous brunette sitting at the table.

"So, what did you have in mind?"

Eldredd felt betrayed and angry but at least here there was a way to vent some of his frustration.

"Isn't there somewhere more private that we can go to? It all feels a bit exposed with these big windows."

Al grinned.

"I've got a room out the back. It's a store room but I'm sure that we can make it comfortable." Eldredd gave what he hoped was a coquettish giggle, fluttered his eyelashes again and stood up. "Lead the way."

***

It was a strange week for the City of London coroner and he was beginning to wonder if he didn't have a new type of serial killer on his hands such was the similar modus operandi that seemed to have been employed on his two most recent examinations. This one also had been obviously murdered, this time by having his neck broken. He was an otherwise healthy and quite athletic male in his late twenties whose head appeared to have been turned around three hundred and sixty degrees, killing him almost instantly.

What really raised his suspicions though, was that the examination had found yet another foreign object lodged in a victim's rectum. This time it was a small glass bottle of tomato ketchup.

# XXI
## Anybody Home?

The church into which the demonic duo was trying to gain access was guarded by a simple spell which caused those passing by to ignore it once they had given it a fleeting glance. Of course, this didn't work on demons and Moloch and Abraxas simply stuck at it until they found what they were looking for.

The rear of the church was to be found a couple of streets away backing onto a brownfield site, a patch of waste ground that seemed to have escaped the attention of city developers in the same way that the church had strangely escaped the attention of most people in it vicinity. Following a high wooden fence along its length, and finding no way in, they decided that with no one else around it was safe to actually use some of their natural skills and bounded easily over the top.

Once inside it became quickly apparent that the church had a false front and that here was the real entrance. Passing through the narthex, they found themselves beneath a large circular stained glass window was a small set of unimpressive double doors. Moloch and Abraxas took a door each and simply kicked hard. Once inside they surveyed their surroundings.

Behind them, the window revealed glowing scenes of obscure meaning, with strange creatures in alien landscapes. It had actually been designed by William Blake – a part-time magician and alchemist – who had once frequented the library. The centrepiece depicted the bearded Urizen reaching down out of a full moon to plant a pair of compasses on the earth below. This little tidbit of information was lost on the two intruders though, whose usual interest in windows extended only as to whether they could smash them or not.

Proceeding down the main aisle of the church they noted that the pews had been removed in favour of reading desks in neat rows complete with green lamps. All along the sides there were bookshelves lining the white walls where the Stations of the Cross might usually have been on display.

Where the altar should have been there was instead a carpeted area with comfy looking chairs and sofas next to what looked like the information desk in any library or bookshop. At one side of this area, where the lectern usually stood, was instead a helical staircase enclosed in an ornate brass banister rail which seemed to lead up into the spired tower above from where they could hear faint noises as if someone were moving about furtively.

Eyeing the ceiling above them and satisfied with making it thus far, the two demons decided to return to Lord Astolath and report back with their success.

***

Unaware that there were visitors downstairs, Priest continued looking through the bookshelves, rifling through drawers and rummaging through filing cabinets in search of the Ankh. He guessed that he'd been at it for about an hour now and, not having any of his former powers at his disposal, guessed that it would take a few hours more to completely go through everything. His gut also told him that the Ankh indeed had been the reason that Tris had been killed and that it was probably pointless to look for it any further.

Climbing the helical staircase to the floor above, he came across another room filled with books almost identical to the one that he had just left. The difference was that in one corner was a small cell-like room that extended out into the space occupied by the shelves. Approaching it, Priest tried the door and found it unlocked. As he entered, the room lit up gently as if some sensor had detected his presence. The small chamber contained a small bed, a pedestal with a water bowl, an old wooden trunk and a small bookshelf containing half a dozen or some ancient-looking tomes. Was this Tris' bedtime reading material?

Priest could just about read the titles in the gloom, but decided to pick out the one volume with a bookmark protruding from the top of the spine. Taking the leather bound volume into the library area; he placed it upon the table and sat down.

Straight away he realized that he'd lucked onto something useful when the embossed design on the cover was made up of a circle with the same symbols that he had seen when Tris had performed the transformation ritual. Opening the book, he removed the bookmark, a strangely anomalous object. It was red-tanned leather, but very new and was covered in a gold embossed seaside scene with 'Didn't we have a luverly time the day we went to Margate!' written underneath. Tossing it to one side, Priest proceeded to peruse the diagram-filled text. The book was undoubtedly describing the ritual but he couldn't make head or tale of it. The language in which it was written was completely alien to him. He knew more languages than most people could ever hope to learn in the average lifetime, but he could find no purchase on the strange symbols that he saw before him. In frustration, he slammed the book shut, tucked it under his arm and returned to the staircase to descend to the room below.

Returning to Tris, he looked down on the reposed form of his old friend and felt the strange stirrings of yet another new feeling. As he stood there, the old man blurred before him and Priests' eyes misted up with tears. He put a finger to his eye to examine it and as the tip brushed the bottom lid, it overran with a solitary tear which escaped quickly down his cheek before settling on the underside of his chin. In a moment it was joined by another and another until his face felt wet and his nose started to run.

Inside, he felt as if he were melting.

Priest made a mental note to ask Rose about this strange feeling later, but his brief moment of puzzled introspection was interrupted by a crashing sound from downstairs.

Had the killer returned?

Marching toward the stairs, Priest was determined to use his powers to punish whoever had killed Tris. He puffed out his chest and was about to summon up an enormous ball of flame to cast down the steps when he realized that he couldn't do that anymore. He realized this just as he glanced downward to see Moloch and Abraxas climbing swiftly up toward him. The feeling of panic returned as Priest realized that this was the only way in or out of the tower and that if he attempted to head upward to a higher floor then they'd see him, or at the very least, feel his steps vibrating through the staircase. All he could do for now was to find somewhere to hide.

*** 

Within moments, Moloch and Abraxas stepped into the room, followed closely by Astolath. They trooped along the rows of book shelves, seemingly uninterested in their contents, but stopped when they reached where the body had been lain out.

Astolath looked at the empty table and sniffed the air. Someone had definitely been here recently.

"Look upstairs and bring me anyone you find."

"Yes my lord," snapped the two hench demons and raced each other from his presence.

The Arch Demon looked about him, taking in the place. He had no time for books or learning. Whatever he needed he simply took, or he got someone else to take for him. His magic was the destructive kind and not the creative – unless you counted sowing chaos and destruction as a creative act. As such, the whole notion of a library left him distinctly unimpressed and he counted the minutes until he could destroy the whole place.

Moloch and Abraxas returned breathlessly and stood to attention before him.

"There's no one here my lord."

Astolath nodded and smiled. "They've been here and they've gone. Destroy the library. If there is anyone hiding it will flush them out. If someone's planning to return, they'll have nothing to return to."

With that he walked toward the stairs. At the last moment though, he couldn't resist what had been on his mind since he had arrived and pushed hard against the nearest bookshelf, sending it crashing down onto its neighbour and watching with satisfaction as this then cascaded onto the next in line. The noise was deafening as the whole room seemed to collapse in slow motion.

Astolath was still chuckling at his act of destruction as he ascended the stairs.

\*\*\*

Priest had been in uncomfortable situations before but had never been stuck inside a fireplace with a corpse – let alone the corpse of a friend. Though he hadn't yet started to ripen, Tris had been decidedly uncooperative in his deceased state and wouldn't stay in the same position without gravity working upon him and trying to pull him out into plain sight. To make things worse, the method of Tris' destruction had become apparent once Priest had trodden on something squelchy and realized that he was ankle-deep in his friend's viscera.

What initially seemed like an ideal hidey hole had turned out to be anything but. The fireplace was another magical conceit and didn't actually lead into a chimney. As a result, there was nowhere to go other than to squeeze into a corner with Tris propped up beside him. If Astolath and the others had been even slightly thorough in their attempts to find him, they would have spotted him as soon as they entered the room and it would already have been over for him.

As it was, his future was still far from certain as the smell of burning reached his nostrils and he realized that they must have started a fire somewhere downstairs. This left two possibilities: he could either try to sneak down and hope that they weren't outside waiting for him to do exactly that, or he could go upward and see how far up the spire he could climb. This might buy him enough time for someone to arrive and put out the fire, or it might just mean him burning to death a little later.

Watching the smoke start to pour up staircase, he guessed that the decision had already been made for him. Letting Tris gently to the floor, he muttered a goodbye and ran upstairs. Not stopping at the floor above where he'd found the spell book, he carried on into unknown territory.

The staircase came to an end in a wide square room with four huge opaque clock faces on each wall. Each clock face was set at the same time – two minutes to twelve – but there was no mechanism or machinery on view which might be powering them. Something was though. As he stood there wondering about this, the four of them advanced another minute in clunking mechanical unison.

With no time to marvel further, Priest looked for another means of escape and noticed that there was another staircase which wound around and up the inside of the spire which came to its apex a couple of hundred feet above him.

What could be up there?

He ran to the new staircase and darted up the first dozen or so steps before again being reminded of the present limitations of his body as he fought for oxygen and felt his legs turn into lead weights. As a result, the ascent wasn't as brisk as he had envisaged and it took him nearly ten minutes of hard slog – with frequent rest breaks – to get to the very top.

The steps terminated in a small platform with a metal door on the other side. After pausing once more to catch his breath, Priest grasped the handle of the door, pulled it open and stepped through.

Aiden Truss

## XXII
### Twists and Turns

Karl opened his eyes as if waking from sleep. Was it all a nightmare or had he just blacked out for a time? Regardless, he was wide awake now and once again unsure of exactly where he was.

Gazing about him, it seemed familiar. He was lying on a pink soft pile carpeted floor and looking up at a lopsided lampshade dangling from a light fitting on the ceiling. It had a pastel red, green and yellow 'ABC' design on it like something that might hang in a child's nursery. But, he was in a teenager's bedroom; this was confirmed by the presence of 'Forever Friends' posters covered in saccharin teddy bears and others depicting pouting young male pop stars and film stars. Pulling himself up, he noticed the bed with the Spice Girls duvet cover and the bedside table with a matching alarm 'Girl Power' alarm clock and lamp.

He was in the bedroom of an ex-girlfriend's daughter and, with a gulp, he realized that the nightmare was real. He'd been brought back to the place where he'd first taken advantage of his position as a supposedly responsible adult. Her name was Laura and, like the others, she'd led him on until he had to do something about it.

It had started one night when her mother had gone out. He'd put his head around her door and had offered to help her with her homework. She'd reluctantly agreed and he had sat down next to her on that very bed. He couldn't even remember now what the subject of the homework was as he'd feigned interest in it from the very start. Instead he'd started to tell her how pretty she was and that she shouldn't worry too much about schoolwork as she'd always be able to get work as a model.

He thought that he might have perhaps gone too far when he suggested that she change her clothes and model something for him. He explained that he had a 'friend' who was a fashion photographer and if he could take some photos on his mobile phone then he could get her an introduction. But she had gone for it hook, line and sinker and seemed to be flattered that he was taking an interest in her. She took an armful of clothes and disappeared into her mother's room to change.

Karl had tiptoed across the landing and had watched her through the crack in the door until he could contain himself no longer.

He forced himself upon her on the very same bed that he shared with her mother.

When the act was done, he'd told her again how beautiful she was and that she wasn't to tell her mother and that he'd speak to his friend about arranging that photo-shoot. Of course it never happened and instead he took to visiting Laura in her room at every opportunity. Her mother was oblivious to what was happening and only said something to her daughter after noticing that she had stopped going out and seemed to be withdrawing into herself. Laura never spoke to anyone about what was bothering her.

Some months later, her mother returned home to find Laura's body in the bath, covered with a liquid blanket of dark red. Only her pretty head and porcelain shoulders were visible above the still, dark murk. She'd opened the veins in both her arms and had left 'Viva Forever' playing in looped mode on her CD player in the doorway to serve as a melodic suicide note.

Karl had felt no guilt at what had happened. Was it his fault that she'd gone and topped herself? But he hadn't escaped all of the fallout. Laura's mother had no reason to accuse him of anything, but whatever was left of their relationship died that night with her daughter. A few weeks later, she'd put his belongings out on the street and had the lock on the door changed while he'd gone out for the day.

No amount of pleading through the letterbox would soften her attitude toward him and the last time he'd been here, he'd kicked at the front door in anger and walked away shouting abuse at the empty, darkened windows.

And now here he was again only this time he was the one that was frightened and uncertain.

He went to the door and tried the handle. It was locked.

The same went for the windows. Though he could see the street outside through them, no amount of banging and thumping seemed to make any noise that anyone might hear. He pushed the clock and the ornaments off the bedside table and picked it up to use it to smash the glass. His efforts were to no avail though and it merely bounced back at him as if it were made of rubber.

"OK, where are you?" he shouted in frustration.

"You mean me…?" a voice returned from behind him.

When he looked around, there was Rose, lying languidly on the bed and leaning up on one elbow.

She was still in her newly adopted form of a gothic goddess, but he recognized her immediately. What he didn't recognize was the fire and defiance in her eyes. In fact, he wasn't sure that he'd ever really looked her in the eye. Not from any sort of guilt, but that she had always avoided looking at him directly as if unwilling to acknowledge his presence.

"Whath going on Rowthe?" he lisped. "How did I get here?"

Rose sat up and swung her legs over the edge of the bed.

"You don't get an explanation Karl. You just get punished. It's only recently that I discovered that I wasn't the only one that you'd been abusing and now all I'll tell you is that on their behalf – as well as mine – I'm going to show you a bad time."

There was no triumph in her words, just a calm and matter-of-fact delivery that left him in no doubt of her steely purpose. But this in turn served to steel him too. Unsure of what was really going on, he was at the very least certain that he didn't want to end up with any more cuts and bruises. He stepped forward and took a swing at her with all of his declining might.

In the reflexive instant that most people might have raised a hand in defense, Rose instinctively erected a barrier around her that made Karl feel as if he had just punched a brick wall. He felt his knuckle bones crack and splinter and in almost slow-motion felt the shock travel through the bones in his hand where it ended at the carpals in his wrist and smashed them too. He gasped in agony and clasped his wrist. His hand was a mess and he could see bones jutting upward beneath the skin. In panic he pulled on his immobile and sickeningly misaligned fingers and felt a soft squelch and crack. This seemed to straighten the bones in the back of his hand, but the pain was unbelievable and he nearly blacked out again.

"You fuckin' bitch!" he shrieked pitifully. "I'm tho gonna fuckin' kill you!"

Rose merely laughed.

"How are you going to do that Karl? I'm the one with the power now. I'm the one who decides what happens to you next and how it happens. What does that feel like – to be afraid of someone stronger than you and who can decide on a whim to hurt you?"

Karl was beyond angry now. He felt a helpless rage that pulsed through his entire body and made ready to attack her again, regardless of the consequences. Rose sighed and shook her head when she read his intentions. Without a word, she concentrated and in her mind's eye saw him lifted from the ground, hanging in mid-air with both of his arms hanging uselessly by his side.

As she had imagined, so it happened.

Karl felt as if something had a hold of the top of his head, lifting him up until he was nearly touching the ceiling. Then the real fun began and he felt his arms being grasped and then slowly being twisted in their sockets. He heard a howling scream that cut through the air almost deafening him before realizing a moment later that it was coming from his own throat as both shoulders became slowly and deliberately dislocated. As the scream subsided, he heard the pop and crack of whatever held his arms in place before that were released to fall uselessly at his sides. He too was then released and fell to the floor with a thump.

"You bitch... you bitch... you fuckin' thtupid bitch..." he drooled on the carpet and tried to push himself up onto his knees by pushing his forehead against the carpet.

Seeing him in this prostrate position, Rose considered for a moment visiting on him something a bit more in line with his treatment of her. He was bowed before her and vulnerable to all sorts of punishment where he was. She weighed in her mind the arguments for and against what she might do to him. Could two wrongs make a right? Would she be any better than him if she were to abuse him further? And, how far should she take things – did she have the strength to leave him alive or was she going to put an end to his miserable existence?

This dialogue with her soul raged on inside her as she crossed the room to look out of the window. The street outside was bustling with everyday activity: children were coming out of a newsagent on the corner, sucking lollipops and laughing; a delivery van was being unloaded with a forklift by a man outside the electrical shop; two women were chatting animatedly outside the bakery; and an old lady was slowly walking along, seemingly being pulled by the small Yorkshire Terrier that she had tethered to her wrist.

It was all so ordinary and quotidian and yet she was in their midst. Was she the monster now instead of Karl?

This thought troubled her greatly. Her new, though limited, understanding of the cosmic order suggested that there was no great punishment or reward to come for her actions in either direction. But far from being liberating, she just felt crushed by the weight of her decisions. No one but she would be there to judge her – she who was her own harshest critic and accuser.

So where did this leave Karl if there was no divine justice? And, if she didn't punish him, then who would? No. This was down to her. She would be justice. She would right the wrongs of this pitiful creature and stop him from creating any more victims.

Turning back to the dribbling wretch in front of her, she dismissed her previous notions of giving him a grand monologue, a litany of his crimes and an exposition of how she had come to where she was. She would just end it here and now and put him from her mind.

"Don't worry Karl. It's over now."

Rose walked to the door, opened it and left.

***

It would be some months before anyone came into contact with Karl again. When they did, he was back on his sofa, remote control in hand and the giant screen TV set to Channel Four.

The council official and the police officer had to force entrance to the flat after repeated non-attendance at his job centre appointments. This had meant that his benefit payments had stopped and that his rent had not been paid. This was the only reason that anyone would want to talk to him so urgently.

Karl left the flat with them peacefully, a paramedic zipping him up in a black bag as they hoisted his body onto the back of an ambulance.

# XXIII
## Inspired

Astolath and his cronies sat down on some rubble and gazed up as the fire started to take hold of the church spire. At first they could see the yellow flickering of the nascent inferno casting its dancing shadows on the windows. But, as the light started to fade outside, the glow increased as the fire grew and spread. There was a pall of smoke now climbing into the air and a heat haze around the profile of the top of the building.

As they waited for signs of someone moving within, Eldredd appeared and sat down next to them.

"Did you take care of the bill?" Astolath sneered.

"I took care of the bill, my lord." Eldredd said with just the barest shred of grudging deference that he could summon. "I take that you found nothing and are now waiting for someone to emerge screaming from the flames?"

"That's about the size of it," nodded Astolath, "It had better not take too long though. Waiting greatly displeases me."

Edredd looked up, trying to discern any sort of movement at the windows, but could see none.

"And you're sure that this is the only exit from the building?"

"Moloch and Abraxas have checked and assure me that it is."

The two in question looked at each other. Could they be sure that they'd checked everything? Despite their doubts, they nodded in unison to their master.

"They'd both suffer immeasurably for their incompetence if it were not so," continued Astolath with another menacing grin in their direction.

Eldredd shrugged and kicked off his heels again with a sigh.

\*\*\*

High up above them, Priest had gone through the door at the top of the spire staircase and had emerged onto a small platform that led to a further set of small steps allowing access to an ornate dragon-shaped weathervane at the pinnacle. The base of the dragon was a gold obelisk covered in the same alien writing and topped with a pyramidion embellished with more engraved glyphs on each face. As he looked closer, he recognized them as the same ones that were on the cover of the book that he had taken from Tris' room. As the wind buffeted around him he hunkered down and pulled the book from his pocket. There was just enough light to see what he was doing as he flicked slowly through the pages looking for clues. Many of the chapters contained rough drawn illustrations and there was something about the dragon that prompted a recollection at something he had seen briefly while looking through the tome earlier.

After several minutes he found it. There in the very middle of the book, spread over two pages, was a picture showing the weathervane. The illustration showed a detailed reproduction of each symbol with what looked like some sort of explanation of their purpose beneath. Of more significance though, was the dotted line ending in an arrow that seemed to indicate that the vane could be turned somehow to point in the direction of each symbol.

Shutting the book and replacing it in his pocket, Priest looked up at the dragon and stood up. That was when he noticed that despite the ferocity of the wind, the vane was not in fact moving with it. Mounting the last few steps to the base, he grasped the metal rod which held the dragon, with both hands to see if he could twist it but could find no purchase.

Again he was buffeted by a strong wind and felt himself pushed sideways by its ferocity. In between gusts, he now smelled smoke and could feel the heat gently rising toward him. He looked out into the night at the lights of the city. The spire was not as tall as some of the modern buildings around it, but still provided a good view of the metropolis below. He wondered if he'd now have the opportunity to walk those streets and to discover their secrets, but his situation seemed desperate.

Another gust and this time he had to make a grab for something to hold onto. His hands found the sides of the obelisk and as they did so, he realized that they were hinged. Once he had steadied himself, he ran a nail along an opposite side and managed to pry it open. Inside the newly formed door was what looked like a lever. He tugged at it until it stood out at a right-angle to the pole and then he realized the purpose. Feeling for the edges of each side of the obelisk, he opened each door and pulled out the lever. When he had finished he had a means of rotating the dragon.

At the moment, the dragon was aligned with the diagonal cross-section of the pyramidion. With a firm push and a tug on the levers though, he was able to turn it to line up with the symbols on the faces. As he started to move it, he stopped to think where was he going to point it: north, south, west or east? Was he going to go with Anubis, Michael, Epona or Barnumbirr?

And, once he made the choice, what would that mean? Would it summon them to him, would he be summoned before them, or would something completely different happen? If only he could read what was written in the book!

With a push, he threw caution to the wind and slowly aligned the heavy weather vane toward the east and the symbol of Anubis. He was the first that Tris had summoned and so it made for some sort of logical choice that he'd plump for him first as well. With a groan, the vane finally turned at the way and clicked into place.

At first nothing happened. Priest let go of the levers and waited with a puzzled look on his face. Still nothing.

What was he going to do? He couldn't go back down and he couldn't stay where he was. He tried turning the vane to another point, back toward the north and the symbol for Epona.

Again, nothing.

He grimaced in frustration and backed down the steps onto the platform just below. As he did so, he heard a loud click and a groan as if somewhere some gears were turning. Looking up, he saw the doors on the obelisk close in unison and the dragon began to shimmer and glow brightly. A beam of light shot out to the north and a loud rumbling began which then became the more distinct sound of horses hooves followed by a great high-pitched neighing.

Out of the beam appeared Epona in all her naked, woad-stained and flame-haired glory, brandishing a spear and riding a white stallion which she gripped by the mane and clung to with her long legs wrapped around its sides.

"Come with me Priest," she beckoned and held out her hand.

Priest took it and they were gone.

***

A hundred feet below, Astolath and his small band looked up at the light show around the weather vane, saw a shape emerge and disappear almost as quickly as it had appeared.

In a nearby street, a young woman was returning home from work. As she rummaged in her handbag looking for her door key, saw thought she heard two terrified screams that were suddenly silenced. Walking to the end of the balcony outside her flat, she looked out into the street to see where it had come from but could see nothing unusual. Glancing across the road to the church, she fancied that she noticed a slight glow in one of the windows, but as she stared harder, it seemed to diminish and disappear until she wasn't sure if she'd seen anything at all.

With a shrug, she entered her front door and put the chain on behind her.

# XXIV
## Top of the Charts

Back at Lucifer's palace, there was an air of rare relaxation amongst its denizens.

The absence of both Lucifer and the new tenant, Astolath, meant that the various demons and creatures in residence had had the threat of imminent extinction removed from over their heads for the past few days. As a result, indolence reigned on a scale not seen in... well... ever.

At the gates, the guards were nowhere to be seen. In the kitchens, the cooks were asleep. In the armoury, the clanging and banging had ceased, and in the labyrinthine passages and hallways, normally bustling with frantic coming and goings, silence now held lease. In fact, there were only two people working in the entire edifice: a lookout on the highest tower named Barbas and, in his newly acquired office, our old friend Sinn.

Barbas was about as low down the hellish hierarchy as one could be and as a result, had no choice in the matter of his duty. Once some bright spark had realized that they could all have a holiday with no one around to boss them about, someone else piped up that they'd at least need one lookout in case Astolath returned unexpectedly. As a result, the officer class of demons drew lots to see who would get the job. After the third attempt to get some agreement on the matter, someone suggested simply finding the nearest available peon be sent up to the great tower under pain of slow disembowelment if he left his post at any time.

Barbas simply happened to be passing by on the way to the latrines when the door was flung open and before he could protest, he was grabbed by the throat and issued with his new orders. He'd been there now for three days under strict orders to keep both eyes on the horizon and that if he so much as blinked he'd be spitted over one of the kitchen fires. He'd taken the officers at their word and hadn't dared to close his eyes even once in all the time that he'd been there.

In more comfortable surroundings, Sinn sat eyeing an ornate chart of the very same demonic hierarchy that now crushed Barbas under its huge weight. He'd found it in the palace library and had been studying it intently for hours now.

At the very top sat Lucifer, the Lightbringer himself. Beneath him were inscribed the names of the Arch Demons: Asmodeus, Astolath, Lucifuge Rofocale and Belial. Next to this, the name of Astaroth had been crossed out – presumably when he'd been destroyed in the second civil war of Hell – and had been replaced with a series of four symbols instead of a name.

This is what was making Sinn scratch his head in thought. The Arch Demons traditionally held the balance of power in Hell and were appointed both by virtue of their age and power and because of their ability to hold Lucifer in check if he got out of hand. He was the supreme ruler, but millennia of squabbles had forced him into an agreement that there had to be some sort of equilibrium maintained. Lucifer wasn't strong enough to resist the Arch Demons, should they unite against him, but the Arch Demons were such an argumentative bunch, that they could never agree to attack Lucifer on a united front.

This was the situation until recently, when Astolath had managed to unite the other three in an unholy union against the Lightbringer. Astolath must have been sure of his odds of success or he would never have dared march on Lucifer. All had seemed to go as planned, but now that Sinn looked at the strange symbols, he wasn't so sure. Did this mean that there was a fifth Arch Demon that was unknown to the others, or that something else was meant to sit in that spot in the hierarchy?

As he pondered, there was a knock at the chamber door.

"Come in," he shouted, and in stepped Mulciber, grinning from ear to ear and muttering greetings.

"Sinn, old bean! How the devil are you?"

Sinn peered at him from behind the huge set of incisors that ran along the front of his gaping mouth. Realizing who his visitor was and unsure of his motives, he stopped what he was doing and quickly rolled up the chart.

"Mulciber! How nice to see you – do come in."

Mulciber crossed to the table and sat down opposite Sinn. He looked down at the rolled up parchment in front of him and then up at Sinn.

"Researching your family tree, eh?"

Sinn ignored the question and retorted with one of his own.

"So what can I do for you Mulciber?"

"Oh, this and that," Mulciber maintained his huge grin. "I've got news of one or two developments and was hoping that you might be able to enlighten me as to their meaning?"

"Oh?"

"Yes. They are mainly concerning my friend, Priest, and his visit to the human realm. You wouldn't know anything about that would you?"

Sinn eyed the other demon, weighing the ramifications and possibilities. *How much did Mulciber really know about what was going on?*

"I'd heard rumours that Priest had taken some sort of leave of absence, but nothing much beyond that. What do you know about this?" he asked cautiously.

Mulciber leaned forward, sitting one elbow on the table, and reached into his pocket. Producing the golden Ankh, he placed it slowly and deliberately in front of him and then sat back.

Sinn looked at the symbol intently and then back at Mulciber.

"Where did you acquire this?" he almost whispered.

"This? Oh, I was in the human realm myself quite recently and came across it there. It was in the hands of someone who is quite dead now. Properly and eternally dead I mean, as in not-coming-back-to-trouble-anyone-ever-again dead."

Sinn knew exactly to whom Mulciber was referring, but chose to keep playing his cards close to his chest until he knew exactly what was going on.

"That's very interesting, but why should it concern me?"

Mulciber had tired of the game already and decided to hurry things along. Standing up, he pocketed the Ankh and made to walk toward the door through which he had just entered.

"Never mind Sinn. Perhaps I've misunderstood. I'll take my little trinket and find someone who knows what to do with it."

Mid-stride, Sinn called him back.

"Very well Mulciber. Let us discuss this further. But first you must tell me how you came by it."

Mulciber shrugged and returned to his seat across from Sinn.

"I was looking for Priest in the human realm. He said that he needed to take some time away from things, as if he were suffering from some sort of existential crisis of some sort. I mean… really? He's spent so much time with the monkeys that he's started to appropriate their failings and weaknesses."

"Go on."

"Well, the last time we spoke he moped around the place for a while and intimated that he wasn't feeling too good about the way his life was going. I gave him a shoulder to cry on and listened to his bleating for a while. I do so like to seem a saint when most I play the devil. I told him that I'd been through the same experience and told him to go and find himself."

"And he believed you?"

"Why wouldn't he? We're old friends you see. I took him under my black wings centuries ago when I realised the potential in him. I didn't know what he really was, but I had my suspicions and these seem to be being confirmed more and more each day.

"Can I ask, is that the hierarchical list of demons that Lucifer keeps in his library?"

Sinn would have opened his eyes wide in surprise if it were physically possible. Instead he coughed slightly – something that was quite a noisily impressive sight when you recall that the top part of his body was just huge mouth.

"I have a similar list at home. It's in a copy of Alibek's Grand Grimoire that I obtained some centuries ago. Only my list is incomplete and I only have the names of four Arch Demons. Let me see…" he reached out for the list. "Does yours have all five?"

Sinn grabbed the scroll in both hands and suddenly pulled it away from Mulciber.

"I haven't finished with it yet. You may look at it when I've finished my research."

"Very well Sinn old man. But, I'd wager a few choice souls that yours has a gap in the list too. Am I correct?"

Sinn sighed in resignation. Perhaps Mulciber might be useful after all – at least until he had what he needed.

"It's not a gap exactly, but there is no name there either." He spread the scroll out before him again and rotated it so that Mulciber could see it. Mulciber in turn pointed mischievously to his name and that of Sinn in the third row of the tree of names in the chart.

"Oh look! There *you* are and there *I* am!"

Sinn failed to see anything amusing in this and instead just pointed to the four symbols at the end of the second line.

"No name, just strange symbols that make no sense to me."

Mulciber stroked his chin as he surreptitiously committed the shapes to memory.

"I've no idea either, but then again, they do look strangely familiar as well."

"You've seen them before now?"

Mulciber shrugged theatrically, "I said that they look familiar... if only I could place them..."

Sinn rolled up the chart again.

"You've seen the symbols. Now explain where you got the Ankh. It belonged to Thoth and hasn't been seen for millennia. Now you have it in your pocket and have an intense interest in the Arch Demons. I have shared and now you must."

But Mulciber now had all that he needed. He had indeed seen the symbols in the Arcanum library and he knew that Priest had been there. He also knew that Hermes Trismegistus had once been Thoth and that he had aided Priest in some way that had something to do with the symbols. His suspicions about Priest had been correct, but what was he missing?

"I'll tell you what Sinn old man," he said, rising from his chair again. "We'll agree to keep in touch and to share any further information that we stumble upon shall we?"

Sinn stood and bellowed at the other demon, "You're going nowhere until you tell me everything that you know! Stop or it'll be the worse for you. I'm respected in the new administration!"

Mulciber slowed but did not stop walking. He reached the door, opened it wide and then turned back to the fuming Sinn.

"Don't make threats Sinn. You've seen the chart and you know that we're the same level. You'd have a hard time getting the better of me and any battle would draw you a lot of unwanted attention wouldn't it?"

Sinn's mouth opened and closed in frustration but no recognisable sounds were emitted. In fact, he was so angry that he couldn't actually form any coherent words. Finally he overturned the table in frustration and hurled a ball of lightning energy in Mulciber's direction just as the other demon stepped through the door and pulled it shut behind him. The lightning hit the closed door and spread out, scorching the entire wall and leaving all of its hangings and adornments in a blackened and charred mess.

As he stood there seething, the door opened again swiftly and Mulciber's head appeared.

"Did you say something, old man?"

Mulciber pulled the door shut behind him and strolled casually down the hallway.

"No, I didn't think so..."

## XXV
## Great Balls of Fire!

Eldredd and Astolath returned to Al's Café to take stock of the situation, leaving the smoking bodies of Moloch and Abraxas on the waste ground behind the burning church. Astolath had given them more chances than most to please him, but in failing to find Priest they'd written their own death warrants.

As a result, Moloch had to watch his partner being turned inside out in front of him before having the same treatment himself. As a result, both demons were now wearing their snazzy black suits on the inside rather than the outside. Astolath had blasted them with a wave of searing heat just to make sure that they were finished off. In this regard, he had surprised Eldredd; he wasn't usually so merciful to his victims, instead preferring to let them suffer.

After dishing out his punishment, Astolath had thought first, not of his pursuit of the unchallenged sovereignty of Hell, but of an All-day Jumbo Breakfast before deciding what to do next. The 'Closed' sign still showed on the door, but he and Eldredd let themselves in anyway. Astolath sat down in the same place that he had sat earlier on that day and Eldredd took his place opposite.

"Where's that cook?" bellowed the Arch Demon.

In the excitement, Eldredd had quite forgotten what had happened to Al.

"I'll go and find him for you my lord."

Eldredd had seen Al throwing food onto the skillet on top of the cooker and so started to raid the fridge in search of bacon, eggs, mushrooms, sausages and anything else that he thought might be a part of an All-day Jumbo Breakfast. As it sat there in a great big heap he then had to figure out how to make it cook.

He turned knobs this way and that, he flicked switches and opened and closed doors looking for he knew not what. Determining that heat was required, he then took it upon himself to provide it. For the third time in twenty-four hours in that particular post code area of London, a demon summoned a fireball. Eldredd knew that he didn't want to incinerate everything and so used as much control as he had to summon a small, cricket ball sized flame at the tips of his fingers. As he did so, the flame introduced itself to the large amounts of gas that Eldredd had inadvertently released in attempting to heat the skillet. The result of their meeting was quick, violent and totally unexpected, as the whole room seemed to explode in an instant.

Next door, Astolath sat waiting expectantly when chairs, tables and cutlery suddenly flew past his head and the large window next to him shattered and blew out into the street. Outside, passers-by screamed and ran for cover behind parked cars while others watched dumbstruck as a large bald man in a suit and a stunning brunette in a short red dress stepped out of the smoking rubble, brushing themselves off casually as they did so.

"We will speak of this later," growled Astolath to his sheepish companion.

"Yes my lord," Eldredd almost whimpered, aware that it was only the fact that they had an audience that had saved him from painful oblivion.

The wailing of sirens in the distance made up their minds that they should vacate the scene as promptly as possible and so they headed back in the direction of their hotel.

When they arrived, Eldredd picked up their key from the receptionist and they quickly mounted the stairs in search of their room. Once inside with the door shut, Astolath glared at Eldredd.

"I've lost Priest and now I've lost my breakfast. Tell me something here and now to make me stay my hand from squeezing the life out of you where you stand!"

Eldredd stood rooted to the spot, painfully aware that his next words might very well be his last.

"My lord, we came seeking Priest in the hope that he would lead us to the Lightbringer. If Lucifer is indeed watching him, then it is logical to assume that he will also be trying to follow him. All we need to do is to keep a low profile until Lucifer appears and then we can either follow him or simply call for assistance and take him on the spot."

Astolath considered the options, slowly weighing things up in his mind, which as you know by now, wasn't built for deep and lengthy deliberation and cogitation.

Finally he broke his silence.

"Very well Eldredd, but this is your last chance. What do we do next?"

"Well my lord, now that we no longer have the assistance of Moloch and Abraxas, might I suggest that we summon more backup. This time, I think it best that you call upon your fellow Arch Demon allies. We need to ensure that we have all the necessary muscle that we need to contain the Lightbringer."

"Very well - see to it immediately."

"Yes my lord."

With that, Eldredd took his leave to return to Hell.

As he faded from view, Astolath sat down heavily on the double bed and looked around him. On the wall next to the bed was a sign saying, 'For room service, please dial 0'. The Arch Demon pondered the meaning before noticing the telephone with the big zero at the bottom of the dialling pad. He pressed the button and the hands free speaker leapt into life.

"Room service! How may we help you?"

Astolath grinned.

"Bring me three All-day Jumbo Breakfasts."

\*\*\*

Materializing back in his chamber at Lucifer's palace, Eldredd immediately set about changing back into his demonic form. He concentrated hard and his body shimmered and blurred before coalescing back into his jet black self. He peered into a large full-length mirror on the wall to confirm that he was indeed back to normal.

"That's better," he murmured to himself as he left the room to look for his counterpart, Sinn.

Striding through the hallways and corridors, Eldredd was struck by the lack of activity, oblivious as he was to the general 'go slow' policy that had been adopted about the palace.

Reaching the ground floor via the great staircase, he wondered to and fro until he actually managed to catch sight of someone. In one of the reception rooms, a serving imp was snoring beneath a table. After ineffectually prodding him with his toe, Eldredd finally gave the imp an almighty kick which had the desired effect of dragging him from his slumber.

"Where is Sinn?" he screeched in anger.

"He's in the library my lord. Please don't kick me again!"

Eldredd looked down at the sniveling form cowering before him and dismissed it with a wave of the hand. *What was Sinn doing in the library?*

The library was located at the other end of the palace and to reach it, Eldredd passed yet more indolent imps, dosing demons and shiftless succubi. The palace had obviously ground to a halt in the absence of Astolath and he determined that once he has spoken with Sinn he would start cracking the whip about the place and set things to rights.

On entering the library, he spotted Sinn leaning over a book. Once he caught sight of Eldredd, he sat up with a start and beckoned him over urgently.

"You took your time," he said by way of a greeting.

"I came back especially to thank you for meddling in my transition – my feet are still sore from those stupid shoes!"

If Sinn was grinning, Eldredd couldn't tell. He didn't appreciate the mocking sound coming from his companion's huge throat though.

Sinn turned back to his book.

"Let me guess, Priest got away and you've seen no sign of Lucifer?"

"How did you know?"

"Well, apart from the fact that we'd all know if Astolath had returned in triumph, I found out a thing or two while you were away. It seems that our old friend Priest is not all that he seems."

"In which way?"

Sinn pointed at the hierarchical chart on a nearby desk.

"Look at the second line down – the Arch Demons."

Eldredd scanned the document and fixed his eyes on the horizontal list of four names and one that was just made up of symbols.

"Yes and…?"

"It's not conclusive, but I think that the symbols are either some sort of representation of Priest or they are something to do with him."

But Priest's name is right here, on the same level as we are. He's no Arch Demon."

"Perhaps not yet…"

"What do you mean?"

"I had a visit from that oleaginous cretin, Mulciber. He was in possession of the Ankh of Thoth and had just returned from a visit to the human realm."

"Where did he get that from?"

"He wouldn't say, I think that he was trying to track down Priest himself. He also seemed to know something about the symbols but did a disappearing act before I could press him on the subject."

Eldredd began to pace the room in contemplation, mapping out permutations and configurations in his head and trying to piece the situation together. *If there were meant to be five Arch Demons, might Priest be aiming to take his place among them? Is that why he left Hell on his damned secret mission?*

"I think that Priest is planning on becoming the fifth Arch Demon. He may even have deliberately gone to ground in order to meet in secret with Lucifer in order to strike a bargain."

"It's possible I suppose," agreed Sinn, "But he never really showed any ambition in that direction before. He even berated you and me when we suggested that he join us. He said that he wasn't interested in politics."

"Well that's exactly what he would say if he wanted to put us off the scent of what he was really about. It's more important now that I get back to Astolath and warn him of what we may be facing. If there's no balance of power, then our war is doomed and there'll be no mercy for any of us."

Eldredd stopped pacing.

"I'm going to summon the others to return with me. We must stop the Lightbringer from forming an alliance with Priest."

With that he stalked purposefully from the room, leaving Sinn to his books.

"Fantastic!" moaned Sinn. "Bloody stuck here again!"

# XXVI
## Epona

Strangely spent from her efforts, Rose found somewhere quiet and familiar to rest up and to gather her thoughts.

When she'd been on the streets, she'd often visit the park next to the cemetery a short walk from her old house. She wasn't interested in the graves so much as the near complete quiet there – a quirk of the landscape as it sat in a depression, something that might once have been a small valley. The trees surrounding the park meant that in some places you might imagine that there was no city outside its boundary fence and that you might be back in time somewhere before the world started to become covered in concrete.

Now, she sat on an old wooden bench, surrounded by the traditionally funerary Birch, Cedar and Willow trees which seemed to swing mournfully in the breeze around her. Her favourite spot overlooked a small pond which was devoid of birds, but rippled with Pond-skaters, Water boatmen and Mayflies amongst myriad other tiny creatures that made it a home or a hunting ground.

In the summer months when the weather was warmer, she would often sleep here on the bench knowing that she wouldn't be bothered and had even carved her name into it with the edge of the silver Claddagh ring that she wore on her right hand. If anyone else ever came here, she had never seen them. Perhaps the cemetery was no longer accepting new occupants and everyone that had a relative there was now gone too. Certainly those graves that she had examined seemed to be quite old, with the most recent seemingly Victorian.

Rose considered what the last couple of days had brought to her: her apparent death and resurrection, a meeting with an otherworldly being who was apparently a demon and who had given her his powers, the death of her mother at her hands and finally, a reckoning with the man who had single-handedly ruined her life for her. And now, she had the power of the universe in her hands and couldn't think of a single thing to do with it. She was used to thinking about matters from one day to the next, such as where she might sleep, where the next meal or the next wash might come from. She'd never really wanted anything extravagant, just peaceful normality: a job, a flat, a car, and in time, perhaps even a boyfriend that would love her properly. Her mind raced with possibilities, but beyond finding Priest again, none appealed to her. She felt all at sea and in need of guidance, but above all she just wanted someone to talk to that understood her. She closed her eyes and reached out to find him.

The visions came all at once, out of chronological order and in a stream of raw flashes of experience: She saw the library and a dead body dressed in strange clothes; next came a sudden flash and the appearance of a strange woman in the air astride a white horse; then a huge bald man in a suit and sunglasses with an uncomfortable-looking brunette in a red dress; finally she saw four glowing symbols on the front of an old book. Her inner eye then lost focus, and her vision faded.

Trying to piece things together, she realised that Priest was still in the human realm, but also that he was somewhere else. This confused her. It didn't make sense, almost as if he had become some sort of ghost flitting between dimensions as she felt him fading in and out of contact with her.

Where on Earth was he?

***

Some miles away, in the same geographical proximity and more or less in the same dimension, Priest was the guest of Epona.

Like many others of her kind, she'd not had a particularly good couple of millennia. The sacred feminine field was dominated by the worship of one female: a young Jewish girl who'd failed to meet the virginal criteria for her marriage and who had cooked up the biggest excuse in the history of the world for her sexual exploits. Recent times had also seen a prostitute contemporary of hers experiencing a rise in popularity as well and between them, they had the entire milieu sown up in terms of followers.

Oh, the Wiccans and the new agers had brought about a small resurgence in worship of some sort of indistinct triple goddess, but their numbers were mainly limited to teenage girls into 'dark fantasy' literature or old women with a penchant for henna and a nostalgia for the nineteen-sixties.

Epona had lived on in the fringes of memory in her role as a psychopomp. For those deities assigned this role in addition to their other areas of patronage, it was like having a nice pension that paid out on retirement. There were always four gods or goddesses whose job it was to oversee the transition between realms, the main one of course being that from life to death. The need for her to fulfil her role had kept her from oblivion and maintained much of her power.

Hermes Trismegistus alone had known how to summon the four of them via ritual, but when Priest had stumbled across his notebook with the instructions for using the summoning obelisk and had used it - albeit clumsily - she had responded and had come to his rescue.

Epona lived in lots of different places, moving on a whim or where her duties called her. Like the other Celtic deities, she liked in-between places: the sea shore, a riverbank, the edge of a forest - those liminal places between worlds and between times.

For the time being she had settled in that most between of places, Battersea Power Station on the Thames. Once an art deco monolith of energy and industry, it too had been protected by a preservation spell. Over the decades since its construction and decline, it had been bought and resold on countless occasions, but no one could ever decide on what to do with it. For a while it was going to be an amusement park, then a football stadium and even a shopping mall with a hotel, but all plans had failed to come to fruition. Every deal struck on the place had fallen apart at the eleventh hour and nobody could ever offer an explanation as to why.

Being an in-between site, Epona had managed to do it up a bit without attracting any attention. The main body of the building now stabled her favourite horses and she'd converted one of the huge chimneys into her living quarters overlooking the rest of the city. It was alongside her that Priest now sat, calmly sipping a cup of herbal tea and flicking through a copy of Country Living magazine that he had found the top of a bookshelf.

Despite the panoramic view of South London, the interior of Epona's home looked like a cottage in the Home Counties. The blue curtains in the windows were tied back with ostentatious gold ropes and the walls were painted a pleasing terracotta colour. The furniture was also contemporary, but with a touch of chintz – big flowery cushions and drapes everywhere. Homely is how it would have been described by anyone other than Priest. To him, it was as exotic as a chamber in his own palace might have been to a human visitor. He did however discover – although it was unknown to him at the time – that like his pursuers, Astolath and Eldredd, he had a liking for tea, albeit of the fruity variety, rather than the English builder's tea that they had sampled.

Epona slipped back into the room and sat down opposite him. She'd put on some clothes: a pair of blue jeans and a white blouse and she'd tied her long red hair back into a ponytail but still looked ravishingly beautiful.

Priest put down his cup and saucer.

"So what now, Epona?"

She smiled at him but shook her head at the same time.

"Uh, uh. You've got one month – minus three days now – to fulfil the terms of your agreement. Did Hermes Trismegistus not explain everything to you after the ritual?"

Priest shifted uncomfortably in his seat.

"Well, we talked a little while I was recovering, but someone killed him after I left. When I went back to see him, I found his body. I managed to find his book, which is how I managed to summon you, but there are a lot of gaps which I need to fill in."

Epona sat quiet for a moment, absorbing the news of Tris' death.

"So, there is now one fewer of the old gods…"

"You knew about that?"

"Of course! Hermes Trismegistus used to be known as Thoth and was worshipped by the Egyptians. He once performed the role that Anubis now holds, but chose to give it up."

"Everyone seems to know about this except for me. Tris was labouring under the misapprehension that it was his big secret. I've known him for centuries and he only told me yesterday."

Epona smiled at this.

"Hermes Trismegistus' secret was only known to a few of us. If anyone else knows of it, then they came upon it by foul means."

"You think that his killer might have found out before he died?"

"It's possible, but then you've only just told me of his death. I know nothing of the circumstances."

Priest took this opportunity to explain to her the whole story of what had happened, including his fascination for Rose, his pursuit by Astolath, and the fire at the Arcanum. Epona listened with unblinking attention and was quiet for some time after he'd finished imparting all of the facts.

"Then your time among men is now not just a matter of your own journey of discovery. For some reason, you are wanted by others who are willing to kill and destroy to find you."

"Yes," shrugged Priest. "That's about the size of it. I've divested myself of everything that I need to protect me just as the worst of the Arch Demons decides to get better acquainted with me. Though I can't see why; I've only met him once and then he barely said two words to me. He had bigger fish to fry no doubt."

"So, your priority now must be to get your powers back."

"Well, obviously I'd like to get them back eventually, but as far as Astolath is concerned, I'm really not interested in any squabbles that he might have. Hell can go to... well... Hell as far as I'm concerned."

Epona winced at his shocking lack of concern over anything that might not affect him directly, before remembering that despite his current situation, he was still a demon and subject to all the selfish and (usually) evil whims that this entailed.

"Well, demon, as far as I can see you may have no choice in the matter. But, as our only way forward seems to be to get you to fulfil your quest as quickly as possible then perhaps we ought to begin."

"But that's just it. It was never made clear exactly what I have to do – it was all a bit vague. Tris said something about shackles and spheres and about guiding men back to the right path or something but the old man met a grisly end before he could fill in the blanks."

Epona tried to be understanding. She had made a promise to Trismegistus as a part of the ritual that she would help to protect Priest, but she didn't foresee having to do it alone.

"I have snatched you from the clutches of your pursuers, but can do no more for the moment. Have you slept recently?"

At the idea of sleep, Priest's face opened into a huge yawn. This was yet another thing to which he needed to become accustomed. He'd slept for a while when he'd been with Rose, but hadn't closed his eyes since escaping from the Arcanum spire the night before.

"No, I must confess to feeling a bit fatigued. Is it always like this?"

Epona shrugged, "I wouldn't know, I've never been human either. They do seem to spend a fair amount of their existence unconscious though. Sleep for now and we'll decide what to do with you afterwards."

She then paused as if listening intently for something.

"What's the matter?"

"There's someone trying to find you."

"Astolath?" Priest sat bolt upright and spilled some of his tea on his lap.

"No, I don't sense any harm being meant toward you, but she wants to make contact with you urgently."

"She? It must be Rose. Can you take me to her?"

"Sleep and I'll find her for you."

\*\*\*

Rose knew immediately that something had changed.

She stood and walked to the edge of the pond, watching the tiny ripples spreading out across the water as the bugs played upon it and then everything became suddenly calm. The pond became still like a liquid mirror and all activity disappeared.

As she pondered this change, she felt a hand on her shoulder. She spun around to suddenly face Epona, who stood smiling at her.

"I didn't mean to startle you child."

"Who are you? What do you want?"

Epona retreated to the bench and sat down.

"My name is Epona and I want you. Priest is with me but is unable to rouse himself at present. I said that I'd fetch you and bring you to him."

"Where is he?"

"He's somewhere safe Rose, don't worry."

Rose was about to ask how she could be sure of her visitor, but then her new senses kicked in and she realised that she was being told the truth. She could literally divine the divine and knew immediately that Epona was no ordinary person. She shone with a golden aura that seemed to confirm her good intentions. Epona knew that she was being studied and weighed up and waited patiently for Rose to come to her own conclusion.

"OK, how do we get there?"

Epona stood, broke into a beatific smile and extended her hand to Rose.

"Come with me."

## XXVII
## The Gathering at the Gape

Marshalling the support of the other Arch Demons was not as straight forward as Eldredd had imagined. The fact that Asmodeus, Lucifuge Rofocale and Belial had entered into a pact with Astolath did not mean that they were willing to jump when he told them to jump, much less at the bidding of a lesser demon like Eldredd. And, to make matters more difficult, after the march on Lucifer's castle, they had each returned to their own domain and so he had to visit each in turn to explain the situation and to request their attendance in the human realm.

Eldredd had sent out messengers to politely request the attendance of the three Arch Demons somewhere on neutral ground. He hoped that this would mean that they wouldn't feel that they were being summoned at Astolath's behest – which of course they were. He'd selected the Gape, otherwise known as the Mouth of Hell, as a meeting place. It was far enough from Lucifer's palace to reassure them that they were not being lured into anything and, as it sat at the very entrance to Hell, it was non-aligned territory where none of them could claim dominion.

The Gape was a huge gateway which marked the entrance to Hell. It was fashioned to resemble the face of a huge dragon with its open maw allowing entrance to all that fell from grace. The gates were always open (unlike heaven, no one was ever denied access to Hell), and were formed from razor-sharp tooth-like spikes. From outside the gates, the comparatively undramatic landscape was disguised by a simple illusion maintained by the impish wardens. This depicted dancing demons and screaming humans being tortured and carried off by a winged demon. To anyone looking in from the outside, they saw the inferno.

Once you were inside though, the illusion was revealed for what it was: smoke and mirrors, a bonfire and a large banner reproducing Luca Signorelli's depiction of the Last Judgement from Orvieto Cathedral. The denizens of Hell had little time for pitch forks and all of that nonsense, but had agreed to keep up appearances in order to deter visitors. Lucifer had decided that Signorelli's work was a particularly apt representation of Hell in the old days and had offered the artist a commission himself. The devout Italian, however, had balked at the idea of a personal visit but had offered to reproduce his great fresco on the understanding that he never hear from Lucifer again.

Over the ages there had been many who had laid claim to being truly evil and on speaking terms with the devil. Almost all of them had been revealed as pseudo-Satanists as soon as they had caught sight of the Gape. Suddenly the idea of an eternity in the company of Hell's minions didn't seem so appealing. For most, this revelation was far too late, but for those who had sailed close to the wind and had come within touching distance of the place; this tableau was convincing enough to deter them.

The Gape was approach by a long bridge spanning the river Acheron, which looked like it was full of molten lava, lapping at the imposing black, crenelated walls on either side. It was here on this bridge that Eldredd had convinced the Arch Demons to gather.

Asmodeus, 'The Prince of Lechery', arrived first, limping slowly with the aid of two sticks toward the centre of the span. He was quite handsome as far as demons went, with a pleasant face and small golden horns protruding above a mop of dark, slightly curling hair. On top of this sat a golden crown topped with a trident device but other than this, he was quite naked with an unsettlingly large penis which swung like a pendulum as he moved. His limp was explained by his right leg which, unlike the left, was skinny and wrinkled and ended in a claw rather than a foot, as if it had been transplanted from a giant chicken.

"Well Eldred, I'm here. Where are the others and where is your master?"

Eldredd bowed low before Asmodeus.

"I am sure that they will be here soon my lord. As for my master, he cannot attend, but I have authority to speak on his behalf." He didn't have any authority at all, but if everything went to plan, Astolath wouldn't care about this slight overstep.

Asmodeus walked to the side of the bridge and peered over the edge. He had things to do and, like anyone with an over-inflated sense of his own importance, didn't like to be kept waiting, especially by climbers like Lucifuge Rofocale and Belial.

"You can have five more minutes of my time and then I'm leaving," he said curtly without turning back to Eldredd.

Eldredd bowed again.

"Thank you, my lord."

As he spoke, two other figures appeared at the end of the bridge.

There was no mistaking Lucifuge Rofocale, with his three horns, long serpentine tale and cloven feet. Unlike Asmodeus, he had a little more decorum about displaying his genitalia (or just a smaller penis), and wore a skirt about his midriff covered in scale-like plates of armour. About his shoulders he wore a similarly crafted set of armour which partially covered what would have been a 'Mr. Universe' winning physique had he ever deemed to enter the competition.

His companion, Belial, looked from a distance more like a centaur than a conventional demon, having as he did four equine-like legs instead of two. He too had an impressive set of horns atop his skeletal features and instead of eyes, two small flames burned in his deep ocular cavities. Aside from looking very impressive, it also had the unsettling effect of making you never quite sure whether he was looking at you or not. As he walked, his hooves sparked against the stone of the bridge, adding to the awe-inspiring effect of his appearance.

Even Eldredd trembled slightly at his appearance - that was until Belial opened his mouth in acknowledgement of him and Asmodeus.

"Well, we're here now. Where's Astolath?" The voice that emerged sounded something like Mickey Mouse. It was a high squeaky and shrill falsetto totally at odds with his demonic appearance. For a second, Eldredd said nothing, waiting for this Crown Prince of Hell to perhaps clear his throat with a cough and to speak with his true voice. But the ridiculous noise continued with the next sentence. "I asked you a question Eldredd. Belial, Asmodeus and I are here, now tell us why!"

Eldredd did a double-take and had to summon up every ounce of restraint not to break into a roar of laughter at what he was hearing. Through a tight-mouthed grimace of concentration he attempted to explain why they had been called together.

"Thank you for coming, my lords," he bowed again, both to make a show of respect and to buy a few valuable seconds of self-control and composure.

"I've asked you to come at the behest of my Lord Astolath, who is currently in the human realm attempting to find the whereabouts of Lucifer, who has fled Hell. We believe that he is attempting to find Priest, who also left Hell recently for reasons that we can't quite ascertain."

Lucifuge Rofocale seemed to wake up at this point to ask a question of his own. Eldredd noted that his voice was much more suited to his appearance; a deep mellifluous basso more in keeping with an Arch Demon and he was grateful for a break from having to listen to the stupid sound that Belial kept making.

"Why has Astolath decided to pursue Lucifer? He gave up the crown and walked away."

Eldredd cupped one hand inside the other in a teacher-like gesture as he attempted to explain what he thought was happening without sounding too condescending to creatures that were above him in the hierarchy but who he also regarded as morons unworthy of their positions.

"We, that is, Lord Astolath and I, think that Priest may in fact be the fifth Arch Demon and the one to tip the balance of power back in the favour of Lucifer. This is conjecture at present, but circumstances seem to point toward it being the case. I don't need to spell out to you what this would mean for the future of Hell if Lucifer sought retribution…"

The Arch Demons looked at each other as the import of Eldredd's words hit home.

Asmodeus broke the silence again.

"What do you propose that we do about this?"

"Well… that's where we might have a bit of good fortune. Priest has decided for some reason to forego his powers temporarily. I won't bore you with the whole story, but it's some sort of experiment that he's embarking on. Now, we don't even know if he is aware of his importance, but if we can get hold of him before he recovers his powers then we can remove him from the scene before any damage is done. Between us we can then do away with Lucifer for good."

This news went down well with the other demons who then allowed themselves to grin and clap each other on the backs in anticipation. Each one hated the others, each one wanted the crown for himself and each one saw an immediate opportunity to get rid of all of the others at some stage and that included Astolath. Eldredd understood that this was why they were so pleased. Indeed, he'd already thought things through himself and decided that should a favourable chance for his own advancement present itself then he wouldn't be backward in coming forward to meet that opportunity.

This train of thought was derailed violently by another ludicrous interjection from Belial.

"I think that I can speak for all of us when I say that we are with you Eldredd… and of course, with our valued ally Lord Astolath."

Eldredd was again forced to stifle a laugh.

"Good… ahem… then we must leave at once for the human realm where my Lord is waiting for us."

Eldredd saw the look of shared doubt pass between them. They obviously thought that there was the possibility that this was just as likely to be some sort of trap as much as it was to offer them some advantage. Of course this is what they would think – they were demons after all and lived in a world of constant duplicitousness and spite in which they had risen to near the very top.

"What assurances do we have that all is as you say it is, Eldredd?" challenged Lucifuge Rofocale, crossing his arms across his broad chest and jutting out his chin defiantly.

"You have no assurances at all. You stay here and await the return of my lord Astolath in fury that you did not come to his aid, or you come along and see to the demise of the Lightbringer. This is the choice before you. I cannot compel, I simply point out the options."

With this, he bowed for the final time and went to walk back into the Gape. As he did so he muttered to himself silently.

"Come on you imbeciles, come on. You must come with me or I'm the one who's going to be spit roasted!"

"Wait, Eldredd. Wait for us!"

Before turning back, Eldredd allowed himself a huge grin of triumph.

"As you wish my lords…"

# XXVIII
## Access Denied

Far from returning home, Mulciber had merely removed himself from the scene and had decided to stay as close to the action as possible without being seen. At present he was ambling along the Victoria Embankment alongside the Thames along with the usual crowds of office workers and tourists that made their way along this artery that took in so many of London's attractions. From here you could see the Houses of Parliament and the London Eye, and were within walking distance of Trafalgar Square and Piccadilly in one direction and The Strand and Covent Garden in another.

The high tide was just a few feet under the low wall that lined that stretch of river. Stopping to peer into the swirling depths of the murky water below, he leaned against the edge to think.

Reaching into his jacket pocket he retrieved the Ankh and scrutinised it, turning it over and over in his hand, trying to divine its secrets. But he felt nothing from it and wasn't even sure that it had any use anymore. He'd seen its lack of potency when Trismegistus had tried to use it against him but he couldn't be sure that it didn't have some other purpose of which he wasn't yet aware. He was tempted to toss it into the river and to walk away but couldn't quite bring himself to do it.

The other thing that was bothering him was the notion that Priest might not have believed his story about finding the old man. Priest was still of use to him as a 'friend' and it would just complicate things if the two were at odds. He should seek him out in the capacity of an apologetic and concerned companion who wanted to ensure that he was OK after his experience. Then he would be able to tease out what was going on.

Continuing his walk, he followed the course of the Embankment before coming to a large statue of a rampant dragon marking the boundary of the old City of London and so knew that he was heading back in the right direction. In the distance was the dome of St Paul's Cathedral and beyond that, he could see the tip of the spire of the Arcanum church building. What little he could see from where he was didn't look right. The top was blackened and the weather vane was tilted at a strange angle.

His contemplative stroll now gave way to an anxious jog and then a full-blown sprint down the twisting and turning warren of side streets until he reached the Arcanum. Looking up at the building, he could see the blackened steeple, broken windows and now ragged spire. Leaping the fence he ran into the building and was confronted with the scale of the destruction. Everything was blackened and broken and the air was still full of smoke and motes of ash and powdered concrete.

The marble tiled floor was cracked and split in places, making it uneven to walk on as he moved down the aisle toward the staircase he stopped in his tracks. What had been the helical staircase spiralling up to the floors above was now melted and twisted completely out of shape. It was obvious that it was impassable and so Mulciber had no choice but to shift into his real form and use his wings to reach the library.

He braced himself once again and made the shuddery transition. Once complete, he stretched out his huge blue wings and bounded into the air before heading out through the shattered round stained glass window and up the outside of the steeple. Catching the sill of the first floor window, he bounded in through its ruined frame.

The library was in the same state as the church below: everything was blackened and charred. From what he could see, none of the books had survived and the great table in the centre was now just a rectangle of ashes on the floor. Kicking through the debris he found nothing that resembled a body and so flung himself headfirst back out through the windows and up into a window above. It was the same story there, everything destroyed and nothing to indicate that Priest had ever been there. The staircase wasn't in such a tortured state here though and he made his way up and into the clock tower.

The clock faces were another smoky ruin and the hands had melted straight down to the six o'clock position where they had fused together into a flowing mess. Looking up, he followed the path of the staircase to the top of the spire and leapt toward the platform at the very top. Pushing the door open, he emerged at the base of the weather vane and saw the obelisk at the bottom with the strange glyphs on each face. He climbed up to examine it further, tracing each symbol with a taloned index finger and committing them to memory. The dragon weather vane above him was bent at almost a right angle to its base and now gave no indication that it had been used to point in any particular direction. As such, Mulciber disregarded it completely.

Although he didn't know exactly what he was looking for, his intuition told him that the symbols held the key to locating Priest. There was nothing else he could do, but return to speak to Sinn and see if he could shed any light on the subject. If he couldn't, then a spell of research in Lucifer's library might yield something useful. Returning to Sinn felt like admitting failure but he couldn't see any other course of action. Besides, there might have been further developments since he had last been there.

Mulciber leapt from the spire high into the air and disappeared at high velocity toward the horizon in a small sonic boom that startled the pigeons roosting in the tops of the nearby tower blocks.

\*\*\*

Lucifer's palace meantime was a hive of bustle and activity. Before leaving to meet with the Arch Demons, Eldredd had put the wind up its inhabitants with his best 'wait-'til-your-father-gets-home' speech. Of course he was referring to Astolath and addressing the hellish creatures that dwelt in the palace, and not a mother threatening her children, but the effect was much the same. Suddenly everyone had something to do – in fact they were falling over and bumping into each other in their attempts to look busy.

Helnocker was particularly grateful for Eldredd's intervention. After Astolath's departure his authority had seemed to evaporate. Despite his attempts to whip up some discipline, his heart wasn't really in it. He'd become a time-server, only he wasn't waiting for retirement but his inevitable messy death at the hands of his lord and master.

He'd spent years in the service of a lunatic and now couldn't take any more. As a result he had reached a career crisis from which he could see no end. When Eldredd had shaken the rafters with his dire threats, his subordinates seemed to suddenly remember who he was and had started to show some respect. But he knew that it was all still just a matter of time before the axe (or the sword, or the halberd, or the blunt instrument of some kind), fell on his neck.

***

Arriving back at the palace, Mulciber resumed his smartly-dressed persona with a flick of the wrist and walked up to the main gates which this time were shut for some reason. This time he was actually challenged by the two enormous ogre-like guards there and asked whether he had an appointment with 'Minister Sinn' after he had asked for admittance.

*Minister Sinn? Who did that puffed up freak think he was?*

Mulciber shrieked, howled, cajoled and threatened the two guards as loudly and as intimidatingly as he could but it was to no avail and the palace was closed to him. So, Sinn had shown his claws?

He could have turned the two guards into sticky paste in an instant, but that still left the rest of the garrison and hell knew who else that Sinn had in there with him to deal with. Luckily for Mulciber, his common sense got the better of him. Had he decided to bludgeon his way in, he would have sooner or later come across Eldredd in the company of Asmodeus, Lucifuge Rofocale and Belial all preparing to leave for the human realm. Against the combined might of the Arch Demons who would have stood no chance.

With his options limited, the best course of action, he decided, was to try to find Priest again. If he could charm his way back into his confidence then he could find the answers that he needed and perhaps get one over on Sinn and his friends.

Aiden Truss

# XXIX
## A Nice Cup of Tea

Priest wandered drowsily into Epona's living room. His long hair had come out of its ring and hung about his face like a lion's mane. He didn't remember undressing for bed, but found himself barefoot and wearing a pair of old fashioned green paisley pyjamas. With a wide yawn and a stretch he looked about for his clothes.

"Why did you undress me, Epona?"

Epona smiled indulgently at the strange sight that he presented.

"It's what humans do at bedtime. Some even sleep naked, but I didn't want you to feel bashful when you woke up. I borrowed the pyjamas from a friend."

"Thank you – that's most considerate of you."

"I've had your clothes laundered and pressed. They'll be ready soon. Would you like some tea?"

Priest nodded and walked to the window.

"What time is it?"

"It's just after ten o'clock in human terms of reference. If you're to spend much time in their realm then you'll have to get yourself a watch."

"To be honest, I don't actually know why I asked. Time has never meant anything to me up until now."

"Could it be that you're truly becoming mortal? Humans are utterly obsessed with the concept of time. They're always wasting it and then complaining that they never have enough of it."

Priest saw the good-humoured dig for what it was and returned an exaggeratedly hurt frown at the goddess.

In the background a whistle started quietly and then quickly grew in shrill volume.

"Ah, that'll be the kettle for the tea," Epona headed for the doorway to what he assumed was the kitchen, before turning back to him. "Oh, and if you'd like your tea in the kitchen, you have a visitor as well."

Priest started and then followed her with a puzzled look on his face.

In what appeared to be a cozy country cottage kitchen, Rose moved back and forth setting out cups on saucers before filling a china teapot with hot water. She turned back to see the dishevelled Priest in the doorway looking awkward in his new jammies. His appearance nearly made her drop the tea tray with laughter.

"You've got to be kidding!" she snorted.

She managed to reach the table and set the tray down before she almost lost control of her arms and legs in the paroxysms of mirth that were now racking her body. She laughed noisily and gaily as if she hadn't a care in the cosmos before grabbing her sides and complaining about her hurting ribs.

Calming down, Rose went to him and gave him a crushing hug and a kiss on the cheek.

Priest was confused by her reaction to him but was also pleased to see her again.

"I hope that your ribs are alright now?"

"Yes, fine. It's funny isn't it," she sat down at the table. "My heart doesn't beat but my sides still feel like splitting if I laugh. How can that be?" For a second she became serious again adding, "I'm not complaining though. I haven't laughed like that in what feels like a hundred years…"

"I'm glad that I can be the source of so much pleasure to you – especially in light of what we may soon have to face."

"Trust you to put a downer on things."

"I'm sorry, but as Epona has already pointed out to me, I'm finding time to be a new obsession of mine."

As he said this, Priest turned to Epona, only to find that she was no longer in the room.

"Epona?" he called out to the other room.

"I think that she's made a diplomatic retreat so that we can talk."

Priest shrugged, not completely understanding, but happy nonetheless to sit and drink tea with Rose for a brief time.

"So, how have you been enjoying my powers?"

Rose paused, looking down at the table and fidgeting with her saucer.

"I wouldn't say that I'd been enjoying them exactly. It's been scary and liberating all at the same time. Strangely enough though, I've not been tempted to go back to see all those strange places throughout the cosmos that you showed me before. It's been the things here on Earth that I've needed to take care of."

"Such as?"

"My mother and my step-father. I've been to see them both and managed to find closure in my relationships."

"That's good."

"No it's bloody well not!" Rose's mood suddenly turned sullen. "They're both gone now and no longer a worry."

"I'm confused Rose…"

"Neither of them was good for me. My mother hadn't been a mother for years and my step-father is the reason that you found me where you found me. I owed them nothing but what I gave to them in the end."

"Which was…?"

"Which was, the ending that you took away from me. They're both dead and its down to me and I feel no guilt and no remorse about it. I thought that I would but I don't. I found myself enjoying the feeling of control and even toyed with Karl – my step-father – before allowing it to end."

Rose calmed herself before continuing.

"But ever since, I've felt all at sea. I can go anywhere but want to go nowhere. I can seemingly do anything but want to do nothing. I don't know where to go next, at least not on my own."

"What do you mean?"

"I need someone with me. I need you with me. I've spent so long on my own that I don't want to go where no one has gone before without someone to share my experiences."

Priest sighed before draining his cup and returning it to the table.

"I'm sorry Rose, I truly am. And believe me, until recently I didn't know what sorry was. I might have had more time to be your cicerone of the great beyond - or at the very least your Virgil of the underworld, but it's not to be I'm afraid.

"Even the idea that I might show remorse is totally alien and shocking to me. For the longest time I did what I wanted whenever I wanted with no one to stop me. I may even be unique among my kind that I grew tired of this and decided to look for something else. I think that you're learning already what it took me millennia to realise: that life can be pretty meaningless whether you were born of a woman or you were hell-spawned like me."

"But how do you find meaning? I mean, if you can't do it with all of your experience and power, then how can I?"

Rose's question was met with a shrug from Priest.

"I was trying to find the answer to that by embarking on my little sojourn to your world. I've not had the time to find anything out yet though as it's been hard to leave the politics from home behind me.

"I've never been a joiner, you see. When all the others want to clan together to wage this war or that, or when so and so has gotten too big for his boots and a coup is required, I just can't be bothered to get involved and I never have."

Rose smiled at this.

"You're just like me aren't you – a square peg continually trying to fit into a round hole. And even if you find a square hole, invariably you're the wrong size to fit comfortably."

Priest raised an eyebrow and protested playfully at this.

"I've tortured many people in my time, but none have ever been subjected to the agony through which you've just put that metaphor."

"And I thought I was being most profound," giggled Rose. "Come to think of it, it did sound a bit wanky, didn't it?"

Priest tilted his head and raised an eyebrow in an 'if-you-say-so' sort of gesture and before folding his arms across his chest and letting out a long sigh.

"It's the worst timing possible though isn't it? I fear that I've put us both in danger."

Rose straightened in her chair.

"We need to swap back don't we?"

"Well yes we do, but it's not that straightforward. I've given my word to fulfil some sort of good deed for mankind within one calendar month or it's all over. I'll be mortal and lose my powers forever."

"What will that mean for me?"

"I just don't know. My powers brought you over and my power still maintains you. If it's all gone for good then I assume that I'll have to eke out a living as a human and that you'll just stop existing in your current form. As to where you go after that, that's not my call."

"Thanks a lot. That's so reassuring!"

"I'm just stating facts Rose. Don't blame me. You'd be dead in a doorway if I'd not found you."

This fact sobered Rose and she saw that it was pointless being angry at Priest. He was right. She'd no doubt be lying in a pauper's grave in some council cemetery by now if not for him. But despite everything that had happened and despite all that she'd seen, she was still having trouble taking everything in. It was a scary adventure where she didn't know what was going to be thrown at her next.

She'd gone from dossing in a shop doorway to taking tea with a demon in the high-rise kitchen of a Celtic goddess fallen on hard times. There was no 'Idiot's Guide to Afterlife Etiquette' that she might have stumbled across to offer guidance on what was now happening. All the god-type books that she'd ever read in her life were about preparing you to get to heaven and to steer clear of hell. None of them thought to provide guidelines on what you had to do once you got there.

"So where do we go from here then?" she asked.

"That's the big question. I still need to work out exactly what Tris was asking me to do. Once I figure that out, I'll need your help to get things done. Whatever it is, I'm sure that my powers will be useful in some way. I'll just have to direct as to how to best use them."

"So when do we go?"

"Why now of course – we haven't any time to lose," Priest stood up as if ready to leave at that instant.

"Aren't you forgetting something… or are you planning on walking the streets in your PJs?"

"Oh, I forgot about that. Where did that goddess get to with my clothes?"

Right on cue, Epona appeared in the doorway with his black suit hanging over her arm, his shiny polished boots in one hand and freshly ironed black shirt and starched white dog collar in the other.

"I'll leave these on the bed for you, shall I?"

## XXX
## A Passing Shower

Astolath was just on the point of losing it completely. He'd been wandering this strange city aimlessly for hours now. Like most demons, he'd been a visitor to London in the past, but now he didn't recognise anything.

For a start, when he'd last been there it was a tiny place. It was mainly fields and marshes criss-crossed by rivers and their tributaries. The city itself was a walled island in this landscape of green and brown, but the city gates and walls that he had known were now gone and so he had trouble getting his bearings.

Sticking close to the river he tried to orientate himself from east to west but a promising start failed when he took a turn and found that the old church at the top of Ludgate Hill had been replaced with a big white building with a dome on the top. The ancient cross at Cheapside was also nowhere to be seen and there now seemed to be dozens of bridges crossing the Thames instead of just the one.

As a result, he'd ended up in a Georgian Square in the West End (although he didn't know that), where for the last ten minutes he'd been staring at a bright red post box in contemplation of finally taking his frustration and impatience out on Eldredd in the most horrific way imaginable, which at that moment involved using said post box as an improvised Iron Maiden (he would have to wing it with the spikes somehow).

His frustration was compounded by the knowledge that he had all the power in the world but could use none of it for fear of drawing attention to himself. Lucifer would know the instant he appeared and the element of surprise would be lost.

He crossed into the garden at the centre of the square and parked his huge bulk on a seat in a small shelter just as it started to rain. Not just a shower or a downpour, but a deluge complete with thunder, lightning and hailstones which bounced off nearby parked cars and set off several alarms. As this happened, the other occupants of the garden began to head for cover, first at a brisk walk and then at a sprint to avoid the possibility of a concussion as well as a drenching.

Something in the air other than precipitation warned Astolath that someone or something was inbound and he was even starting to find himself slightly impressed at the biblical quality of the spectacle. But it was all very much like an 'end of the pier' magic show when it finally happened. During a lull in the storm there was bang followed by a brief popping sound, a puff of green smoke and a whiff of brimstone. And then, there he was, Eldredd, the object of his ire. If his appearance had changed, then his arrogant gait gave him away.

This time he was flanked by three other figures that Astolath struggled to recognise at first sight, but as the smoke cleared Eldredd stepped forward in an attempt to get the formalities out of the way.

"My lord, may I present the lords Asmodeus, Lucifuge Rofocale and Belial. They are here to aid us in our mission."

As he introduced them, each gave a cursory nod of the head in acknowledgement before Belial stepped forward, pushing Eldredd to one side. Eldredd had thus far made the latest transition unscathed and appeared, like his fellow travellers, in black, formal suits and sunglasses. They were human in appearance and all clean cut and square-jawed. In fact they looked like the latest recruits for the Men in Black or perhaps clones of Agent Smith from The Matrix – both references for comparison that would have escaped them unless they had steeped themselves in science fiction movies. Which, of course, they hadn't, as their time was spent constantly contriving Machiavellian manoeuvrings in hell.

Astolath acknowledged their arrival with a slight look of surprise mixed with contempt and then promptly followed by a scowl of displeasure. What did that idiot Eldredd think he was doing? If he was going to find Lucifer then he wanted the pleasure all to himself. Hell was one thing – there he needed their cooperation - but here in the human realm he was going to take the Lightbringer by surprise himself and end his reign once and for all.

But before he could say anything to the new arrivals, one of them decided to act as spokes-demon for the others.

"We are not here voluntarily, Astolath," Belial began in his screeching caterwaul of a voice. "The terms of our alliance said nothing about having to do your dirty work for you."

This did not sound like a greeting to Astolath and he was also having trouble discerning the necessary quantity of respect and fear in the broadside he had just received. Just as he was about to redefine the word 'apoplectic', Eldredd stepped in again to play the politician.

"Lord Astolath, your fellow arch demons have come to offer their aid in your indisputably brilliant stratagem to hunt down the Lightbringer. I'm sure that you would want to show your appreciation for their support in this matter."

Astolath fixed him with a look so savage that it would have impaled a mere mortal. What in the name of Beelzebub's big bulging bollocks was Eldredd doing? He couldn't yet make out what was his game was. If he'd lured them here to be assassinated then that was one thing, but to share the credit in taking down the Morning Star was going too far.

In his most impressive act of restraint yet, Astolath decided to play along to see where this was leading.

"Quite right, Eldredd. It's good that you are here my demonic brothers. We can share in the glory of our impending victory."

The new arrivals looked at each other in wonderment before turning back to Astolath. He had never spoken like this before and they were sure between them that if Astolath in fact possessed a dictionary, then the page with 'Magnanimous' was definitely missing from it (as was a significant part of the 'M' section also containing: Merry, Magisterial, Mannerly, Merciful, Munificent and Marmalade amongst others).

Almost reassuringly though, Astolath then continued in the manner in which he had become best known. Rising from his seat he approached Belial and stood towering over him menacingly.

"But," he continued, "If I hear that preposterous voice of yours again, I'll renege on our agreement and not only will I slay you on the spot but I'll continue to wage war on your corpse for some time after you have ceased to occupy it!"

He stepped back and turned his back on Belial who was bristling with an indignation that was only just tempered with enough common sense not to push his rival too far without being absolutely certain of support from Lucifuge Rofocale and Asmodeus. That they had arrived as a trio came with no guarantees that they would all march one way when it came to possible conflict.

Astolath continued, "If you must communicate with me, pray do it through Eldredd here. He seems to have a higher level of tolerance than I do."

Again, Eldredd was swift in his attempt to salvage the situation.

"My lords, if we can agree that for now we have the best chance of apprehending Lucifer if we locate Priest, then we can move forward with our mission."

Leading them away from Astolath he continued to pour treacle in their ears with regard to the possible future that they were going to see under the new regime. He mentioned casually the possibility of a quadrumvirate at the top of Hell's hierarchy and tried to appeal in general to their megalomaniacal appetites. Again, none of these things had been discussed with Astolath but if he'd left things to him, then they'd well and truly be on their own.

After a few minutes, Eldredd returned to Astolath, leaving the other three demons engaged in conversation in the middle of the green.

"They are with us my lord but you may need to honour – or at least seem to honour – some promises later on."

"You are playing with hellfire Eldredd…"

"Yes my lord, but I'm very adept at that." When no reaction came from Astolath he went on, "We now have the other Arch Demon's onside. As well as them staying their hand at moving against you in your absence, we now have their particular skills at our disposal."

As he said this, Lucifuge Rofocale wandered over to them.

"The others are in agreement – for the moment. I'll locate this Priest and return once I've located him. It will not take much time."

With that, he walked off toward the garden gate and disappeared into the city beyond.

"And in the meantime Eldredd, what happens?"

"Not much more waiting now my lord. We are nearly upon our quarry and Asmodeus has somewhere that we can go to await the return of Lucifuge Rofocale."

***

As the men in black moved away, the rain seemed to follow them. As they followed the path around the floral display at the centre of the garden then downpour stopped and the sun reappeared in its place.

On the main square and watching through the wrought iron railings just outside the garden, stood Mulciber. And, after a prudent amount of time had passed to give them a little distance, he followed discretely.

This was going to be easier than he thought.

# XXXI
## Chapter Thirty One

The elder priest and his younger assistant stood at the bedside of the young boy. What was normally a bright and cheerful room was dim, with just enough light to read by, and on and around the bed was arrayed a collection of Christian paraphernalia: various impressively large-looking bibles; a chrism of holy oil; a small pot of salt; a gently smoking censer; and an impressively ornamental aspergillum sitting in an equally showy silver aspersorium.

They'd been at his side for some time now, praying and invoking a litany of saints and reading from various scriptural texts and were about to embark on the full Roman Catholic ritual of exorcism with all of its theatricality. Both men donned identical purple stoles with embroidered golden crosses on the neck and began the rite in earnest. The older man led and the younger priest supplied the responses as well as periodically making the sign of the cross with his thumb on the forehead of the boy.

"I adjure you, ancient serpent, by the judge of the living and the dead, by your creator, by the creator of the whole universe, by Him who has the power to consign you to Hell, to depart forthwith in fear, along with your savage minions, from this servant of God, David, who seeks refuge in the fold of the Church.

"I adjure you again, not by my weakness but by the might of the Holy Spirit, to depart from this servant of God, David, whom almighty God has made in his image. Yield, therefore, yield not to my own person but to the minister of Christ. For it is the power of Christ that compels you and He who brought you low by His cross. Tremble before that mighty arm that broke asunder the dark prison walls and led souls forth to light. May the trembling that afflicts this human frame, the fear that afflicts this image of God, descend on you. Make no resistance nor delay in departing from this child, for it has pleased Christ to dwell in him.

"Do not think of despising my command because you know me to be a great sinner. It is God himself who commands you; the majestic Christ who commands you. God the Father commands you; God the Son commands you; God the Holy Spirit commands you. The mystery of the cross commands you. The faith of the holy apostles Peter and Paul and of all the saints commands you. The blood of the martyrs commands you. The continence of the confessors commands you. The devout prayers of all holy men and women command you. The saving mysteries of our Christian faith command you. Depart, then, transgressor. Depart seducer, full of lies and cunning, foe of virtue, persecutor of the innocent..."

It was then that, to the shock and trepidation of the two priests, the young boy sat bolt upright in his bed.

Fixing the older man with a malicious grin, the boy addressed him directly, not with an adolescent voice, but with that of a much older man, with a deep rumbling voice cloaked in a slightly Germanic-sounding accent.

"What do you want, old man?"

In thirty years of being the official Catholic exorcist for the Archdiocese of Southwark, the priest had never actually had this happen. He'd seen the movies of course and had even been on a residential course at the Vatican itself in order to qualify as an exorcist (he had a certificate and everything), but he'd never seen anything like this in real life.

He tried to continue with the ritual.

"Give place, abominable creature, give way, you monster, give way to Christ, in whom you found none of your works. For He has already stripped you of your powers and laid waste your kingdom, bound you prisoner and plundered your weapons…"

"…He has cast you forth into the outer darkness, where everlasting ruin awaits you and your abettors. To what purpose do you insolently resist?"

It was the boy who had interrupted and who seemed to be reciting the ritual back to him verbatim.

"Am I correct priest? Is that what you were going to say next?"

With a fear that gripped his innards, the priest realized that he was not just on shaky ground, but that the Earth was very likely about to disappear from under him completely. The younger priest looked at him for reassurance that wasn't there.

"What's happening, Father Michael?"

The boy crossed his legs under him, folded his arms and mimicked the trembling voice of the young priest.

"Yes, what's happening, Father Michael?"

Father Michael fumbled for the crucifix at his neck and held it up in front of him in the hope that if would give the appearance of more strength and confidence than he had. He'd seen Max Von Sydow do the same thing and had admired his self-assurance.

"What is your name vile creature?" he asked in the most authoritative voice he could muster.

The boy spoke again in the deep voice.

"Oh yes, you want my name and then you are supposed to have some sort of power over me aren't you? Quod nomen mihi est and all that? Very well, my name is Asmodeus, King of Demons, and arming yourself with that knowledge will gain you nothing."

The old priest's jaw dropped so suddenly that he was in danger of having two broken feet. Reeling from the notion that he might be dealing not only with a real demon, but also that he might be confronting one of the Top Ten, Hall of Fame, Grand Slam and Premier League evil entities of all time.

Asmodeus was in all the text books, grimoires and occult tomes and by all accounts he was a thoroughly nasty piece of work. But, as Father Michael had never seen anything like a real demon, he had assumed that the creature with whom he was now apparently conversing was just a myth.

"How do I know that you are who you say you are?"

The boy continued to fix him with a stare but also went through the motions of checking his pyjama pockets for something.

"Let me see... where is my Union of Demons membership card?" Failing to produce anything he continued with a shrug of his shoulders, "Oops, I must have let my subscription lapse – silly me."

The sarcasm wasn't reassuring to the old priest at all. He was absolutely stumped as to what to do next. He should continue with the ritual and ignore his tormentor (according to page twelve of the 'How to be an Exorcist' course notes and PowerPoint slide show), but his mouth was dry and his legs were in danger of moving quickly for the door under their own volition.

Basically, he was shit-yer-pants terrified but the younger priest cut in above the panicking chatter in Father Michael's head.

"Father Michael, what do we do now?"

The old priest turned for the door.

"I-I just need to get something from downstairs. I w-won't be a moment."

The younger man then watched as Father Michael went through the door and closed it behind him.

In the quiet of the room, he could hear the old man descend the stairs and mutter something urgently to the parents in the room below. He then heard the front door shut, a car door slam and then an engine starting, followed by a loud roar and the screeching of tires trying to find traction on the road surface.

Then he was alone with a real demon.

The boy was looking straight at him now with the same nasty grin on his face.

"Well Father John, what shall we talk about?"

"T-talk ab-b-out?" he blabbered, pleased that at least he hadn't fallen into the cliché of asking how the demon knew his name.

"Yes, I have a little time to kill. Your dead mother sends her regards by the way."

"My mother's not dead."

"Yes, but I'm expected to say something like that am I not?"

Sinister chuckling and then silence.

"That was a very pregnant pause - it was overdue - it may even need to be induced…" the demonic voice provoked, "I could perhaps rotate this child's head through seven hundred and twenty degrees, dislocate his arms from their sockets and make him vomit pea soup?"

The boy's head started to turn slowly away from the young priest.

"No, don't harm him… please!"

Concern made him courageous and Father John took a step forward.

The boy turned back to him suddenly.

"You have more courage than the old man but you're just as misguided. Do you think that your ritual could do anything against someone like me? You're deluded."

"But you can't be allowed to infect this poor innocent child; you must be banished and returned to Hell from whence you came."

The boy laughed a sickening, mocking cackle.

"From whence I came…? I just came from a few streets away – would you like me to go back to Bedford Square?"

"I don't understand."

"Of course you don't – why should you, you're only a feeble-minded monkey. But you and your kind persist in continuing the illusion that you can keep evil at bay with your silly books and your misguided dogma. What even makes you think that it is worth my time trying to possess a child – and if I did, do you really think that shouting obscenities, speaking in tongues and levitating adolescents achieves anything to further the ambitions of hell?"

Father John was really puzzled now. He'd been petrified but now felt more curiosity than fear. He was actually in dialogue with a demon and his mind raced with the questions that he could ask.

"So why do you possess people."

"We don't."

"But Father Michael said…"

"Father Michael is a fraud and a coward and is right now contemplating a messy suicide brought on by a sudden crisis of faith. In fact, I'm sure that we'll be meeting on a more formal basis in the very near future, not because your pathetic god dictates it, but because as far as I'm concerned, all those who squander their brief lives deserve an eternity of painful reflection."

"But you and your kind have fallen from God's grace."

"God's grace? What does that even mean? Do you people ever listen to yourselves?" the voice sounded incredulous and the child tilted its head to one side, as if trying to comprehend something completely nonsensical.

"I'll give you an example of your faulty logic: you believe that your Christ died to save your whole tribe of monkeys from original sin. This original sin was supposedly committed by two people who couldn't possibly have existed outside of a primitive metaphor. Ergo, your Christ died for nothing."

Father John had heard this line of argument before and had never really managed to get a handle on it. He would have had trouble arguing a five year-old out of this reasoning, let alone an Arch Demon. But he wasn't going to show any weakness if he could help it.

"I believe that Christ is our lord and saviour!"

"You may believe what you wish, but believing so doesn't make it so priest. You peddle lies and then have the unmitigated gall to tell your flock to fear the devil. Hell is full of priests who got there on the back of their sterling service to the Lord of Lies. They reside with the false prophets, the pederasts, the lying politicians and the strange creatures known as 'Reality Television Show Commissioners' in a special circle of the inferno for those whom hell cannot decide upon a punishment commensurate with the gravity of their sins."

The priest blinked as he tried to process the incongruity of false prophets and TV execs butting up against each other in hell, but Asmodeus obviously knew what he was thinking.

"Yes priest. We know of your culture and your obsession with the facile, the banal and the superficial. It's why Hell has so little interest in you anymore. What's the point of trawling the Earth for souls when so many of you are without one? Believe me, there is nothing intrinsically interesting about humanity. There may have been once, but that time is passed."

"Then why are you here inside this innocent child?"

"Technically, I'm not. I'm just manipulating his physical form as a diversion. When your clumsy attempts at exorcism began, I was nearby and sought a brief diversion. It was either sit in on your little ritual or jump on the 'Big Red Bus Tour' with the other tourists. In fact, I'm right behind you with two others of my kind."

Father John froze in terror, torn between wanting to look around and wanting to crawl under the bed until the nasty monster went away.

In the end he had no choice as he felt his feet leave the floor and his body begin to turn. He fought to close his eyes but the lids remained wide open, filling with tears. His body shook fearfully and he mouthed a prayer through dribbling lips. It was meant to be the twenty third psalm but sounded like something completely alien as he both forgot most of the words and how to pronounce the ones that he could recall in his sheer over powering dread of what he might be about to see in the room with him.

It was worse than he thought.

Standing next to a poster of the wrestler, John Cena, were three of the most hideous creatures he'd ever seen. They were alien and yet familiar to him. Demonic to a tee, they were like the images he'd seen in so many books and paintings and yet here they were standing before him and glaring at him with their glowing golden eyed gape. In their stillness, he could almost have been looking at a medieval triptych, but for the visage of Cena visible just behind Belial and Eldredd. He was waving his hands in front of his face under the words, 'You Can't See Me!' As a result, it looked like the line up for a diabolic tag-team match was lined up before him.

It's strange what the mind will conjure up in the midst of great trauma and fear. Not so surprising was what his bowels conjured up as they emptied into his underwear and down the leg of his trousers.

The one he assumed to be Asmodeus raised his head and took a step toward him, inspecting him like one might inspect an exhibit in a museum. When he spoke, the voice confirmed his identity.

"This has been mildly diverting, priest, but now we must depart."

The demon's breath was rank – a mixture of sour milk, backed up drains and wet dog. Father John still couldn't bring himself to answer other than to whimper pathetically and to begin to cry like a baby.

"Mmmh," mmh'd the demon. "It's always the same. Their tiny monkey minds depart them under duress. No one will believe the story that he now has to tell."

Belial grunted, still smarting from his dressing down by Astolath, but Eldredd piped up.

"It just underlines my puzzlement at Priest's fascination for them: they're just so breakable."

## XXXII
## Fight or Flight?

The trio left Epona's home by means of yet another helical staircase which wound its way around the inside of the giant chimney. Emerging at the bottom, they crossed the meadow at the bottom until they reached the banks of the river.

Looking back, they couldn't see the power station, only the exterior of a thatched country cottage. This pastoral image swam slightly as they looked at it, with the huge power station fading gently in and out of view. It was like looking at a TV image with the ghosting of another channel in the background.

Priest acknowledged to himself the ingenuity of Epona's magic. It was similar in effect to that which had been placed on the Arcanum library, but on a much larger scale. The Arcanum would have fitted inside the power station several times over.

Reaching the river, Epona explained where they were.

"Your pursuers are not far from here Priest, but we are hidden from them for the moment. This is the Thames as it was centuries ago and we are walking in that time outside of the normal flow of years. Unless they know *when* as well as where to look, you'll be safe. But, you must leave this place in order to complete your journey."

Priest nodded, resigned to the realization of the trials ahead (or the impending death ahead at the hands of the angry Arch Demon in pursuit). At this stage, Priest was quite unaware that the numbers of those hunting him had increased by three. Had he known, there might have been a little more urgency to his departure.

Epona continued.

"Head out of the city by following the Tamesis (she used its ancient name) to its source in the West. I will follow you there when I have made arrangements here. From there we can plan our next move."

"How do we get there," enquired Rose. "Do we walk?"

As if in answer to this, a small barge appeared as if from nowhere, with a tall hooded figure at the prow. It looked like Charon, the ferryman of Hades, but of course, this was the wrong river. The barge came alongside them and stopped but the strange boatman said nothing.

"This is Brutus. He will make sure that you arrive safely at your destination," explained Epona.

Priest and Rose climbed into the barge and sat down on the wooden seats that lined its length. Before another word could be said, Brutus pulled back on his oar and started to scull his way out into the fast moving current. As they moved along, the river, the scenery around them leapt in and out of view as the power station had done. They were looking at trees and hills and animals in pastures, but as they did so, they could also see the vehicles and people and steel and glass buildings of the modern city.

As they journeyed on, they could see the shadows and ghosts of bridges spanning the river and reaching over them and every so often another boat would flicker into view and pass right though the space they occupied. For Priest, the notion of interstitial travel was nothing new, but for Rose the experience was truly magical. She continually pointed at people and places as they passed, jumping up and down and screaming at the top of her voice when it seemed that they were about to collide with other boats and ships. After ten minutes of what he deemed to be childish behavior, Priest finally snapped.

"Will you sit down and shut up, Rose? You'll have us over!"

"Sor-ree Mr Serious!" teased Rose. "Don't you think that this is absolutely mad – being in two places at once?"

"You get used to it," he returned with a shrug, as if it were something that people did every day, like riding the bus or commuting on a train.

"So you've done this lots of times before then?"

"Let's just say that time is not as linear for us as it is for you. My sanctuary is situated in between times and places for instance." He explained this as if it made everything clear and put an end to any further discussion on the matter.

Rose decided that he was obviously preoccupied with something and decided to try to calm down and just enjoy the ride for what it was. As they passed out of central London, the river narrowed and became gentler. The scenery around them still faded in and out of view but the differences were not so pronounced between past and present as the view on either side took on a more rural aspect.

As the mysterious Brutus pulled his oar back and forth, Rose began to relax slightly, letting the motion of the boat lull her to the verge of sleep. She couldn't quite relax fully though, without knowing a little more about their pilot.

She nudged Priest in the back to attract his attention.

"What do you want?"

"So who is he?"

"Who is who?"

Rose was trying to keep her voice just above a whisper.

"Brutus – the big mysterious bloke with the oar!' she rasped.

"Oh him – I'm not entirely sure. There is a legend of a Brutus who supposedly founded the city of London. He was the grandson of Aeneas, the last survivor of the sack of Troy. Whether it's true or not, I couldn't say…"

Rose looked back at Brutus, trying to make out the face beneath the cowl. Every so often she'd catch a glimpse of a man's face and not the skeletal figure that she had imagined. But that was all she saw. The cowl that he was wearing seemed to cling to him to protect his face from exposure. She fancied that he looked at her once or twice, but she couldn't be sure.

She turned back again to face the front of the boat. Priest was still seemingly deep in contemplation, letting his arm hang over the side of the boat and dangling his fingers in the water.

Suddenly he stood up and turned around to face Brutus.

"Take us back."

The boatman stopped rowing but said nothing, as if considering the request, before leaning into the oar and continuing on his way.

"Didn't you hear me? I said take us back!"

"What's wrong Priest?" Rose made to get up, but with all three of them standing, the boat got a little unsteady and started to rock precariously.

"I don't want to run from this, I want to confront things and bring it all to a conclusion. Isn't that the right thing to do?"

"Yes, if you're on the run from the tax man, but not if half of Hell is after you."

Priest nodded his understanding of the situation. He was fully aware of the facts but had decided that if he didn't have his powers then he wasn't going to hide from a fight. Besides, he had Rose with him and could guide her to use her power to protect them.

Ignoring Rose, he addressed the boatman yet again.

"Brutus, this is your last warning. Stop or it'll be the worse for you."

Rose shouted at him this time, "What are you saying? You don't have your essence anymore!"

When Brutus again failed to take any notice of him, Priest spread his legs to straddle the sides of the boat.

"I don't need my essence Rose. Just sit down."

With that, he started to rock from side to side, forcing the boat to sway violently. Rose held on with both hands and screamed for him to stop.

Brutus only lasted a few shoves before finding himself in the water. Despite being a boatman, he didn't like getting wet and his cowl now clung to him and made it difficult for him to swing to safety. He foundered, gargling and spitting out the brown Thames water before disappearing beneath the surface. Rose watched where he had vanished, waiting to see if he would resurface, but there was nothing there now to suggest that anyone had fallen in at all.

Priest stilled the boat and then stepped over Rose to grab the oar himself and without a backward glance he started to turn the boat back in the direction from which they had come.

"You've killed him!"

"I haven't killed him. He's a river god – he'll find his way home."

"But he was trying to help you."

"Hey, I asked him nicely and he ignored me – twice! I don't like being ignored."

"So where are we going now?"

"Back into the city - they'll be searching for us there. And I'll need you to perform a little magic to make sure that once we are there we are in the correct time period."

"Oh yes, no problem, I'll do that. I do it all the time of course!"

"I don't like sarcasm either," Priest complained. "Besides, I'll tell you what you need to do; you just need to follow my instructions and we'll be fine."

"Ok, what do you need me to do?"

"I'll keep on rowing but you need to reach out to your surroundings. It will take a little concentration but you must fill your mind with the city as it is, as you know it and not as it was."

"Do I need to close my eyes or something?"

"Do whatever you need to concentrate. Just fill your mind with the city, see its monuments and hear its sounds. Ignore the old and fixate on the new."

231

"How will I know if it's working?"

"You will know, now just concentrate."

Rose looked forward of the boat where she could just make out Putney Bridge. It looked like most other London bridges, but she could tell where she was from the sight of the nearly identical church towers at either end. She'd been there once on a school outing and had climbed to the top of one, but couldn't remember which. There was a local legend that the churches had been built by two sisters – nuns who couldn't decide what to call the new church that they were planning and who instead had decided to build two. They were obviously not little sisters of the poor if that was the case.

As the bridge faded in and out of view, she tried to hold it in her mind. After a few moments, she thought that she could hear the traffic moving back and forth over it before it disappeared again.

"Keep trying," railed Priest. "You nearly had it then!"

Rose did as she was told and stared hard, straining to see what she had seen before. Slowly but surely the railings of the embankment alongside Bishop's Park came into view to their left. Then a big sign for the 'Star and Garter', a local pub, appeared on their right.

"It's working!" she shouted.

"Yes, keep going. Keep it in your mind!"

And then they were back.

The countryside around them had been replaced with the familiar scenery of South West London. The traffic roared in the distance, joggers ran through the park and high overhead, an airplane buffeted the clouds with the din of its engines. The air smelled thick too – as if she were trying to breathe in liquid. The transition between time zones had served to highlight the polluted air of the modern city. Rose noted with sad irony that if she hadn't been dead, she'd do something more to get involved in environmental concerns. The air in London would defy the Trades Descriptions Act if they tried to sell it.

This realization was felt alongside a strange elation as it dawned on her that she had just moved them physically through time, even though she still wasn't sure quite how she'd done it.

Priest broke in on her thoughts as if he'd been listening.

"It just took someone to see things as they really were to break the effect of the magic. We were existing between times, almost in two places at once, but it took someone with sufficient power to break through the illusion. If you know what to look for then it's easy. Luckily our pursuers didn't know where or when to look for us. We should have the jump on them now."

"I see... sort of. I'm sure it will all make sense later when I've had time to take it all in."

"No time for all that, just go with it and do as I tell you."

"Yes sir! Don't forget that I'm the one with the power though."

"And a fat lot of good it will do you if you try to take on our foes without my guidance. This is serious Rose – more serious than you know."

"But I still don't know why they're after you."

"Nor do I exactly, but I'm not about to try to enter into dialogue with Astolath. He's what you'd call a 'kill first and ask questions later' kind of demon. I'm not sure exactly what I've done to incur his wrath but I'm sure that will become clear in due course."

"So we head back into town and just wait for them to find us?"

"Sort of... I don't know how much they know about you – if at all. I'll draw them out into the open and you can spring the trap."

"Me? Taking on demons?"

"Exactly!"

"I'm guessing that it's not going to be as straightforward as it sounds."

233

"Well, that's another trouble with humans: you never see the possibilities, only the risks. It's what holds you back and keeps you as a third-rate species."

"Charming!" Rose bridled. "So what's to keep me from just walking away and letting you get on with it all yourself?"

"You could indeed do that, but I wouldn't advise it. I will recover my powers and I will chastise you for an eternity if you cross me."

Priest was finding the physical exertion of sculling more draining than he had imagined. It even made it difficult keeping up with the conversation, "Don't mistake my interest in you for some sort of altruism or philanthropy Rose. You have much to gain from an association with me, but I don't serve anyone but myself. If you become a liability then you cease to be of use or interest. I'm sorry, but that's how it is."

"Yes, you're a cold-hearted demon aren't you?" Rose was on the verge of tears. "I keep forgetting that fact."

"I am what I am Rose," he panted. "Now this is more difficult than I imagined and I'd appreciate not having to converse for the time being."

It struck Rose yet again how alone she was. Priest had reminded her how he was the only connection that she now had with anyone and he had other priorities on his mind. *So where did this leave her once he had achieved his aims? Would he tire of her and consign her to oblivion or was there a worse fate in store for her?*

On balance, she decided that perhaps it was best to be useful and to keep in his good books. As selfish as he was, he was her only means of getting the answers that she needed. She'd gone from a human with no purpose or aim in life to a… well… something else with no purpose or aim in the cosmos but seeing to the needs of Priest.

As she ruminated on this, she brushed the wetness from her eyes with the back of her hands. When the glassiness cleared, she fell into shadow as they passed beneath yet another bridge.

Emerging on the other side of the span, she looked up to try to identify where she was but her eye was caught suddenly by the sight of someone looking straight at her over the railing between the crenellations on the side.

It was a man in a black suit who then smiled at her and proceeded to climb the railing and to sit hanging his legs over the edge of the bridge. Then, without a sound, he leapt into the air and arced toward them before landing lightly on the end of the boat in front of her.

He then turned to face them both.

"Greetings Priest. Astolath sends his regards."

"Who are you?" Priest barked at him, trying to disguise the feeling of panic.

"My name is Lucifuge Rofocale. We've not yet had the pleasure of acquaintance, but perhaps you've heard of me?"

"Yes, I know of you. I know that you're an Arch Demon and that you have struck some sort of a bargain with Astolath. Other than that, I know your reputation."

"Good, then you'll have an idea of why I'm here. Come with me or I'll hurt your companion."

The threat was delivered almost matter-of-factly, and without any malice or drama. He might have been stating that he was about to offer her an ice cream or take her out to lunch. For Rose, this didn't make the menace any less unsettling. If anything, the casual threat of violence was even more concerning. This was obviously someone who would think nothing about doing harm to her and then afterward, think even less about what he had just done.

For his part, Priest gave nothing away. He dropped the oar, raised his chin and stepped carefully toward his opponent. That Rose was now between the two of them didn't make her feel any better.

"What does Astolath want from me?" Priest asked with as much confidence as he could muster.

"I'm not here to discuss the matter. Come with me and he can explain things himself – if he can restrain himself from pulping you for long enough." There was a dark humour in the voice.

As he spoke, he put his hands around Priest's arms, as if he were about to pick him up bodily and throw him out of the boat. Instead, he started to rise on invisible wings, taking Priest up with him.

"Now Rose!" shouted Priest.

Rose had been staring with scared fascination at what was happening and only now realized that she should have been doing something to aid him. Unsteadily, she stood and raised her hands in what she hoped was a magical gesture and thought of fire.

Her hands began to tingle as if she had pins and needles in them. Then they started to warm and then her fingers started to glow. Flames flickered into life around the tips before combining and growing into a fiery ball. She released it with her mind, partly in fear that she might burn herself, and partly in the knowledge that it was meant to hit Lucifuge Rofocale. She let go and watched it shoot toward its intended target.

There was a small explosion and a splash.

Priest was in the water, frantically doing a doggy paddle back toward the boat and Lucifuge Rofocale was still in mid-air, covered in flames and screaming in agony. As he writhed, pieces of his clothing fell off and splashed into the river. Then, it seemed like the very flesh was dripping off as well.

Could it have all been that easy? Had she destroyed a demon?

Such thoughts died at birth as she realized that he was in fact just shedding his disguise and reverting to his true form. He discarded his flesh as easily as he might have cast off his suit and soon the reality was there before them in all of its horrifically horny glory.

Lucifuge Rofocale bellowed with rage, every muscle in his body taut with frustration. He hung there in the air above the water, seemingly summoning up a magic projectile of his own. His hands danced in front of him, as if his fingers were playing a concerto on an invisible piano and then the water around the boat started to bubble and heave as if it was boiling around them.

"We need to move Rose – he's summoning some help!" yelled Priest.

Rose concentrated again, visualizing the boat rising out of the river and they started to rise slowly. As water dripped from the bottom of the boat, it hissed as it returned to the Thames. The water was indeed rising in temperature and steam started to form like a mist about them. This was accompanied by the surfacing and popping of eels and fish that had been cooked to bursting by the extreme temperature.

Meanwhile, all along the bridge and on the embankment on either side of them, crowds were gathering. Bewilderment gave way to cheering and applause as word soon got round that there was a movie being filmed on the Thames. Passers-by stopped to take out their mobile phones to record the action and within minutes the web was alive with chatter about which movie it might be and who was starring in it. Video sharing sites were also already streaming the epic battle to the world.

The early speculation was that Priest might be Brad Pitt in a wig, perhaps reprising his Interview with a Vampire role. Rose, it seemed, looked like Angelina Jolie or perhaps Megan Fox and the flaming demon was wearing such convincing makeup that he could have been anyone from Matt Damon to Robert Downey Jr. Early betting was on a hitherto secret 'Brangelina' team up, perhaps in a Marvel Comics adaptation.

The boat continued to rise until it was almost alongside the bridge at which point Rose and Priest leapt off and into the waiting crowd who started to cheer loudly, seemingly all hands aloft to capture the moment of phone cameras which continued to supply a steady stream of digitized images for consumption by the voracious social web sites.

Despite the elapsing of only a few minutes in which the river born drama had begun, conspiracy theorists and religious nuts had already started to come out to have their say. Depending on your particular bent, it was either all CGI enhanced footage, meant to look like it was happening in real time, or it truly was an end-of-the-world confrontation between a holy man and a demon (with the Whore of Babylon caught in the middle of the two). These ideas had only minutes to find their way out into the blogosphere before the protagonists provided even more to talk about.

The river became suddenly calm again, before suddenly erupting violently and showering the onlookers with scalding water. This should have given everyone a big clue that they should start panicking, but the spectacle overrode any thoughts of self-preservation.

The reason for the eruption became quickly apparent as a huge creature rose from the water to tower above them.

Now people are used to sea monsters. They've seen them in the cinema, they've read of them in books and they've even defeated them in video games, but none of these things was proper preparation for the thing that confronted them now.

Yes it was green and had scales, yes it had teeth and yes it had claws. It also stood the requisite height above the surrounding buildings to qualify as a proper sea monster. It was serpentine and reptilian and looked like it was covered in some sort of slimy substance. However, what made this one stand out in particular was that it was right there in front of them and not being projected onto a cinema screen. It was immense and stank and it was noisy and it was right now beginning to pull people from the bridge into its gaping mouth.

Once hitting the pavement, Priest had broken into a frantic run, urging Rose to follow him. They'd managed to escape the frantic mob which was now mesmerized by the creature that was busy dining on some of their number. Amazingly, many still had phones and gadgets still held aloft to capture the final moments of their fellow gapers.

"He's summoned the Leviathan!" Priest called behind him as he pumped his arms and legs furiously.

"Where are you going?" Rose shouted after him, struggling to keep up.

"Away from the Leviathan," replied Priest without turning back this time.

Rose could feel the road shaking beneath her now. Risking a glance backward, she saw the creature brushing parts of the crowd aside, treading on some and casually snacking on others as he began a slow and lumbering pursuit of them up Putney High Street.

As it moved, the creature swept its huge tail from side to side. As a result, the first major building casualty of the Leviathan was the church that sat on the Putney side. The slimy appendage the size of a tube train raked across the road, smashing the doors down and undermining the square tower which collapsed raining dust and bricks all over the road.

The Odeon cinema which sat at the bottom of a high-rise office building nearby was next. In one stroke, it took out the lobby packed with filmgoers, leaving glass, blood and extortionate popcorn and overpriced cola everywhere. Survivors of the incident would later ruminate on the irony of literally having popped out to see a blockbuster.

The Leviathan lurched on, smashing cars, shops and restaurants as it went and continuing to inflict a variety of nasty deaths upon anyone not fast enough to get out of its lumbering way. All the time, it had its eyes fixed on Priest who was still desperately running away from it with Rose in tow.

"Rose, concentrate on bringing some of the buildings down behind us to slow it down!"

"But that will kill more people!"

"So? Just do it!"

Rose didn't comply straight away. The thought of being the cause of so much death was abhorrent to her and she didn't understand how Priest could suggest it so casually, as if he was just asking her to shut a door behind them.

"I can't just kill people!"

Priest stopped in his tracks and grabbed her by the shoulders, barking into her face.

"It's either that or let it kill us. I care nothing for these people and they are the very same that left you to rot on the streets. Just do it!"

Rose looked back to see the Leviathan bearing down on them. She didn't want anyone to suffer but by the same token, she didn't want to end up in the digestive system of that creature. Also, Priest was right. No one had ever cared for her, so why should she care for them…?

In the end, she reached a compromise with her conscience and told herself that burying the monster beneath a few office blocks would be far better than to let it continue its trail of destruction unchecked. She might even be saving more lives.

With a deep sigh, she turned around and visualized the buildings collapsing on either side of the High Street. As she did so, cracks started to appear in the facades, windows imploded and brickwork and roof tiles started to rain down. Just as the Leviathan drew level with the buildings, she pushed with her mind and let them fall onto it.

The creature shrieked with pain before collapsing under the weight of two firms of solicitors, a copy bureau, a pizza restaurant, an employment agency and the offices of a large local firm of accountants. Noting the casualties, Rose felt a little better about her actions. She had nothing against pizzas, but solicitors, employment consultants and accountants weren't going to be missed surely?

When the dust settled, the screams of those trapped in the rubble formed a noisy chorus with the bellowing of the creature. It was buried up to what she assumed was its waist, with one huge arm trapped by its side and the other flailing desperately, trying to grab for something to pull itself out. But, as it grabbed at other buildings, it only managed to bury itself further in debris.

Priest slapped Rose on the back in triumph.

"Well done, you've stopped it!"

"Yes, but for how long?"

"Long enough for us to administer a coup de grace I hope."

As he said this, a piece of the tarmac exploded in the road behind them. Lucifuge Rofocale was standing on the roof of another building above them and firing bolts of lightning at them from his fingertips.

Priest employed his favourite English language curse.

"Cunting hell! I'd forgotten about him!"

"What do we do now?" shouted Rose.

"Throw something back at him!"

"Like what?"

"Another fireball!"

"Oh… yes, ok."

Rose raised her hands and thought fiery thoughts again. This time though, Lucifuge Rofocale wasn't taken by surprise and batted the fireball away contemptuously where it exploded on the roof of a double-decker bus which had been emptied of its terrified passengers.

"Don't waste your energy woman, you are no match for me," he shouted down at her. "Go now and leave Priest to me and you'll come to no harm. I have no interest in you, whoever you are."

As he spoke, he stepped off the roof and fell, landing on his feet with a loud thud that left cracks in the pavement. Approaching the two of them menacingly he flexed his muscular arms, opening and closing his hands as if preparing for a fight.

Priest stood behind Rose and whispered into her ear.

"Just delay him long enough for me to get away will you?"

Rose nodded and stepped toward the demon.

"I will not let you take him!" she shouted, raising her hands again to summon another fireball.

Lucifuge Rofocale was on her in an instant, one hand around her throat and the other twisting an arm behind her back with so much force that the pain took her breath away.

"No you don't. I don't give second chances. Now, get out of my way."

Picking her up off the floor he threw her easily to one side where she felt her head pass through a pane of glass, a display stand full of DVDs and a shelf full of magazines. WH Smith's had thus far escaped any major damage, but now the front window was a mess. Rose laid still, half stunned and half pinned down by the pile of periodicals, journals and newspaper titles that had cascaded down on to her.

Lifting her head she saw that several copies of Hello Magazine had fanned out across her midriff. One the front page, an orange-coloured woman with collagen-inflated lips and huge breasts barely concealed by her tiny t-shirt was pouting at the camera while wrapping her arms around a skinny guy with unkempt hair. He was wearing sunglasses and had a cigarette hanging out of his mouth in that tired old clichéd rock star pose. They'd obviously just stepped out of a night club and been caught by the paparazzi. She didn't recognize either of them, but even through her pain and bewilderment, she decided that she hated them.

Through the shattered remains of the front window she saw the demon approach Priest and grab him by the shoulders before taking to the air like Superman. She tried to move again, but gave up when a pain in her back got too much. She then focused on moving the detritus about her with her mind and that proved more successful. Slowly but surely, everything lifted from her and she was finally able to move. Once free, she stepped out of the shop and allowed everything to crash back down with a bang and a spray of dust and glass shards.

She looked up; scanning what she could see of the sky but Priest was nowhere to be seen. Further down the High Street, the Leviathan had managed to free itself from the rubble but was now heading away from her; presumably back to the river from where it came. The air was filled with sirens and the distant flapping sound of helicopters, presumable from the police and the press. She could still hear screams and shouts from all directions as people stumbled from various vehicles and buildings, trying to make sense of what had just been visited upon them.

Rose hugged herself and shook her head, unsure of what to do next. She walked away from the damage, sat down to think and once again found herself huddled in a shop doorway.

# XXXIII
## Lucy in the Cave with Minions

Enjoying the spectacle, Mulciber stood on a nearby rooftop. As he watched Lucifuge Rofocale and Priest rise into the darkening sky, he had to make a choice: either to follow them or go to Rose and ingratiate himself with her in order to harness her powers for his own ends.

After a brief deliberation he decided that he might have time to do both. Swooping down to ground level, he found Rose brushing herself down and shaking dust out of her hair.

"If you hurry, we may still be able to help him."

She looked up at the dapper demon standing with his hand extended toward her.

"Who are you?"

Mulciber frowned and beckoned with a motion of his head, "Can I explain en route, there really isn't any time to lose."

Taking the proffered hand, Rose stood up.

"Follow me if you can," challenged Mulciber and rose quickly into the air.

Rose followed him with her eyes and then began to rise toward him. Her initial fear of the height to which she was ascending soon gave way to nervous elation as she realized that she wasn't going to fall. It was as if something had hold of the top of her head with a woolly grip. It hoisted her higher and higher until Mulciber came into sight again and she willed herself toward him.

Below them, she could see the destruction of the High Street, the flashing of blue lights and the movement of people climbing in and out of the rubble. A helicopter flew straight by her, but the pilot didn't appear to notice her, so concerned was he with what was happening below.

Rose came alongside Mulciber.

"What now?"

Mulciber pointed toward the city and the two figures moving away from them in the distance.

"We follow!" And with that, he accelerated away from her.

Of all the strangeness that had overtaken her recently, Rose thought that one of the strangest was this guy flying about in his tailored suit. As terrifying as the demon that she had just fought was, he kind of seemed at home in the air, with his fantastic appearance. This one on the other hand looked like he should have been more at home in a gentlemen's club.

They flew over the river and the park and then on over the labyrinthine streets of the London sprawl. She recognized parts of Fulham and Chelsea, then Victoria, the West End and The Strand snaking back into the Square Mile. Twenty-first century buildings nestled cheek by jowl alongside the Victorian and the Georgian, with references to Gothic revival and neo-classical in between. London was as much a melting pot in its architecture as it was in its ethnicity and culture. And now of course, trans-dimensional beings had just been added to that heady mixture.

Just what it was that was attracting Hell's high flyers to the city was a puzzle. Sure it was a great tourist destination, but she doubted very much that they were all after a ride on the London Eye or a trip to Madame Tussauds. Yes, they were after Priest, but what had brought *him* there originally?

Perhaps it was just its coldness and its reputation as a huge temple to Mammon. She remembered reading a book once that had even suggested that the M25, London's orbital motorway, formed a huge occult symbol when you traced its outline. This made even more sense when one considered that it had been officially opened by that old witch Margaret Thatcher. All of this floated through her mind as she floated over the metropolis.

Ahead of her, she saw Mulciber stop and hover, looking all about him. In her reverie, she'd lost track of Priest and the other demon. Had he lost them too?

Mulciber suddenly looked at her, beckoned with one hand and plunged downward. They were somewhere in the East End, but she didn't recognize exactly where they were. He'd dropped down into a quiet back street lined with uniformly grim-looking terraced houses on both sides and backing onto a stretch of what looked like a canal.

As she drifted slowly to the ground, Mulciber signaled to her with a motion of his head to follow him. They darted down a covered alleyway between two of the houses and emerged on a litter-strewn towpath alongside the stagnant and still green water of the canal, complete with the mandatory shopping trolley half buried in the mud on one bank. The stench coming off the murk and slime was almost overpowering. It smelled like a watery graveyard for the local urban wildlife, and looked like it too, liberally dotted as it was with torn open foxes, bloated cat corpses and schools of dead fish.

Mulciber stopped and took a deep breath of the pungent miasma and even seemed to savour the deep lungful that he'd taken.

"Is it permissible now to ask who you are and why we are here?" enquired Rose with as much casualness as she could muster in the circumstances.

"My name is Mulciber and I'm an old friend of Priest's. In fact, I'm probably his oldest friend." Mulciber made an old-fashioned bowing gesture as if he were doffing a hat. "As to where we are, I'm not quite sure. I merely followed Lucifuge Rofocale and we wound up here in this delightful little slough of despond."

"Lucifuge Rofocale – he was the other demon?"

"Yes that was him. He's one of the Arch Demons of Hell. Did he not introduce himself?"

"No, we've not had the formal pleasure yet."

"Don't worry. Now that you're in his bad books, your paths will cross again. In fact, if you want to see Priest again, you're certain to meet him very shortly."

Rose didn't like the sound of this.

"Can't you get him back without me – I don't really know what I'm doing."

"Oh no my dear, you are absolutely crucial to recovering our friend. On my own I'm no match for Lucifuge Rofocale, but with your aid, I think I can tip the balance in our favour. Just do as I say and we'll get him back."

"It feels that I spend all my time at the moment being told what to do by demons!"

"Now now my dear. This is no time for a tantrum."

This made Rose want to explode.

"Don't you fucking patronize me you bastard! I don't care who you are and I don't care for your attitude. Do you think that I'm just some helpless female?"

Mulciber looked at her with something approaching admiration. Yes, he could see why Priest was attracted to her: she had spirit and courage. Certainly no human had spoken to him in such a manner before. Once he revealed his true self to her, he was sure that she'd be more compliant though. She had Priest's powers but not his experience. It would be no contest if she really decided to attempt to throw her magical weight around.

"Rose, I'm sorry if you take me wrong – I have the utmost respect for you. It's just that we are very near our quarry and I'd rather not announce our presence too loudly if it's all the same to you."

This did little or nothing to assuage Rose's anger. If anything, it made her even more livid. Mulciber seemed to have something of smarmy and oleaginous bureaucrat or the politician about him, where every word was condescending and vaguely insulting. Even his attempt at an apology was infuriating.

But, she decided that retrieving Priest was more important than having things out with Mulciber there and then and she decided to keep her anger as bottled up as possible – at least until later when she decided that she might test some of her other powers out on the swanky bastard.

"I apologise, Mulciber," she said, exhaling a deep sigh. "What would you like me to do?"

Mulciber nodded with satisfaction, assuming that she'd seen the error of her ways.

"Follow me and keep your wits about you."

With seemingly no effort, Mulciber bounded across to the other bank of the stagnant canal and walked toward a low graffiti-covered iron bridge that carried a road across the water. Rose followed him with a single bound and the two of them passed under and into a circle of flickering light from a broken street lamp. Just inside the circle was the outline of a door. It looked like it provided access to some sort of maintenance tunnel under the road and was secured with a hefty padlock under a large 'KEEP OUT' sign spattered with various shades of spray-paint.

"I believe that we'll find him inside here," said Mulciber.

With that, he grabbed the padlock and ripped it casually from the door before tossing it into the canal where it landed with a soft *plop*.

As the door opened, the already fetid air around them became even more noisome. It was as if something huge and decaying had exhaled its malodorous breath into their faces and despite Mulciber's seeming indifference, Rose gagged and was ready to disgorge herself all over the pavement.

"I'm OK," she said, composing herself and answering the questioning look from her accomplice.

Mulciber nodded and proceeded into the gloom inside.

Rose blinked hard, trying to force her eyes to become accustomed to the lack of light but she could barely see her hand in front of her face.

"I can't see a thing," she complained.

"Try using your eyes my dear!" retorted Mulciber in his irritating manner.

"I am using my eyes!" Rose hissed. "They aren't working!"

Mulciber stopped suddenly and she bumped into his back. She then felt him turn to face her.

"Use your powers, you stupid girl. You can see far beyond the limited spectrum of your human senses. Just reach out as you've done with all of your other new skills."

Rose took a deep breath – as much to concentrate as to still the voice inside her that was prompting her to reach out to Mulciber and attempt to scratch his eyes out of his head.

As she centred herself, she began to see that they were in a long sloping passageway, rather than the claustrophobic box that she had assumed that they had entered. It stretched out for about a hundred yards ahead of them, tunnelled out of what looked like solid rock, before terminating in yet another doorway. As she brushed her finger-tips along its surface, it felt lined and scratched, as if had been dug out by huge claws rather than any machinery.

They moved their way toward the second door and as they approached, she saw that the door was much older than the first. It looked like it was made of solid oak but had a small barred porthole in it two thirds of the way up.

Mulciber peered inside and nodded to himself.

"This is definitely the right place. Take a look."

Rose joined him at the door and stood on the tips of her toes to look through to the room beyond.

It was huge – a cavern rather than a room and from what she could see, it looked like a nineteen-sixties horror movie set - something out of a Roger Corman interpretation of Edgar Allan Poe. There was no floor as such; it looked like a series of metal walkways held together with chains, through which could be seen what looked like a lake of glowing molten lava several meters below. The craggy walls were lined at intervals with sconces holding flickering torches and in the centre of the cave was what looked like a rectangular black stone altar with a supine figure upon it. Through the red glow and the heat haze, she immediately recognized Priest and without thinking went to call out to him.

As she took in a deep breath to shout out his name, she felt Mulciber's hand close tightly over her mouth and drag her backward a few paces.

"Keep quiet!" he hissed at her. "It's him, but he's not alone – our other friend is with him. Look for yourself."

He gently released her from his grip and at her nod, signaling her understanding, allowed her to walk back up to the barred window. She could still see Priest but where was Lucifuge Rofocale?

Her eyes scanned back and forth, sweeping the scene in front of her, trying to detect signs of movement.

"I can't see anyone else," she whispered, turning back briefly, but when she looked back again through the bars her heart nearly stopped.

Starring back at her were the flaming eyes of Lucifuge Rofocale.

Rose screamed as the demon roared – their combined voices amplifying and echoing off the walls around them. She jumped backward in fright just as the door crashed outward revealing the Arch Demon in all of his fury. There was nothing for it – Mulciber was right behind her and so she couldn't run away. The only thing she could do was to rush forward and try to do as much damage as she could in the hope that he'd join in as soon as he could get alongside her. She summoned up every ounce of strength and courage and rushed headlong at Lucifuge Rofocale.

It was like hitting a brick wall.

As she rammed her head into his chest, she could feel the shockwave trace its painful way down the back of her neck, before descending her spine and ending up somewhere down in her heels. Instead of knocking him down, she ended up on her backside, stunned and trying to work out what day of the week it was.

Fortunately though, this meant that she was no longer in Mulciber's way and he let loose a wave of energy from his fists that rammed the bigger demon back through the doorway and into the cave beyond. As Lucifuge Rofocale thudded onto his back on the hard rock floor and screamed at them in his considerable rage, Mulciber ran in after him and leapt onto his foe. As he closed the gap between them, his appearance changed into that of his real self and as they collided again, the two enemies literally locked horns, rolling around and wrestling on the floor as each tried to get an advantage over the other.

Rose picked herself up and followed Mulciber with the intention of giving her own blast of something to wear Lucifuge Rofocale down, but couldn't get a clear shot without running the risk of hitting Mulciber.

The cave into which she emerged was even larger than it had seemed through the window in the door and was covered in the same scratch marks as the tunnel. For the first time though, she noticed a massive throne-like chair at one end, surrounded by a group of seven or eight small creatures which she took immediately for imps. They were all naked and hideously ugly, with deformed faces and limbs with pointed ears and noses that all seemed to be dripping with something slimy. They stood watching impassively as the two demons continued their struggle in the dust, like a collection of grotesque courtiers waiting to see if their ruler would prevail.

While Mulciber and Lucifuge Rofocale were occupied with each other, Rose ran to the black altar to rouse the unconscious Priest. As she did so, she fully expected the imps to fall upon her, but they continued to stand motionless where they were, completely fixated with the fight.

She grabbed Priest by the shoulders and shook him. There was no response; he didn't even seem to be breathing. She leaned further over him and slapped his cheeks gently, calling his name as she did so.

"Priest! Priest it's me, it's Rose. Wake up!"

Again there was no reaction.

She went to the other end of the altar and swung his legs as far to the side as she could, before running back to the head end and trying to push him into a position where she could maneuver Priest into a semi-standing position. That way, if he remained unconscious, she might at least be able to drag him on her shoulders or hoist him toward the doorway. In the end though, it all proved surprisingly easy. Priest either weighed about the same amount as a small child or she had grown massively in strength. As she pulled him toward her, she managed to pick him up in her arms easily and made toward the door.

Mulciber wasn't doing so well against Lucifuge Rofocale. Although they were almost evenly matched in size, it was clear that he was outmatched both in terms of physical strength and magic power. Lucifuge Rofocale threw his opponent around, landing blows in between tosses and following these up with bursts of energy that made the air crackle and spark. It was all that Mulciber could do to fight off each attack just to stay alive.

When he finally started to run out of resistance, Lucifuge Rofocale slowed his assault, seeming to take pleasure in the opportunity to tease his adversary.

"Is this what you really came for, Mulciber?" he spat through clenched teeth.

"You know what I came for Lucy old man!"

"Do not call me that! I've told you before never to call me that!" screamed the Arch Demon.

Mulciber smiled a huge smile before spitting a mixture of blood and sputum onto the floor between them.

"Don't be so touchy, old man, you used to like that particular sobriquet."

Rose looked on at the conversation and realized that Lucifuge Rofocale was actually blushing. His face had turned from a demonic greenish grey to a demonic reddish grey. She couldn't believe her eyes at the sudden change of pace and atmosphere. One minute the two of them were engaged in a small war of attrition and the next, Mulciber was proving that although sticks and stones could indeed break bones, names could really do a lot of damage too.

Lucifuge Rofocale looked from Mulciber to Rose, back to his imp minions and then returned his gaze to Mulciber again.

"That was a long time ago."

Mulciber decided to press home his temporary advantage.

"Embarrassed are we?"

"I am one of the Arch Demons of Hell. Your words cannot hurt me!"

"No, but they've stung you a little haven't they…"

Rose noted that the stronger demon seemed lost for words for the moment, as if weighing up his options. What was Mulciber playing at, and what did he know that so unsettled Lucy? She couldn't help grinning as she applied the name to the monstrosity standing before her. Quietly, she lay Priest against the tunnel wall beyond the door and then returned to see how the confrontation would resolve itself.

Mulciber had pushed himself backward from Lucifuge Rofocale and had moved to one side so that the other demon was now standing in between him and Rose. Almost indiscernibly, he raised an eyebrow at her, hoping that she would be receptive to some sort of cue to attack the Arch Demon. For her part, Rose hoped that the raised eyebrow she had just seen meant that Mulciber was working up some sort of plan to get them out of their situation. Perhaps if she could incapacitate Lucy from behind, they could buy themselves enough time to escape?

Mulciber continued speaking.

"Don't Astolath and the others know about your nickname, or, more to the point, how you came by it?"

This turned the other demon's shame to anger.

"No, and they never will know about it as you'll be too dead to tell them!"

"How do you know that I haven't told others?" said Mulciber, gesturing his head slightly toward Rose.

Lucifuge Rofocale turned around to look at her and for a second she feared that he was about to fly at her. The second though, was all that Mulciber needed to turn his disadvantage into an advantage that would be very painful for his adversary.

He quickly brought one leg back under himself and used it to propel himself forward. As he did so, he tilted his head so that his spiraled horn stood foremost and rammed into the demon from behind. He'd gone for something to produce a grievous wound, something to slow the other down a bit, but as luck would have it, he managed to place the tip of the horn right at the entrance to Lucifuge Rofocale's fundament. It slid in nicely and as Mulciber felt it enter, he turned his head and twisted himself so that the curly horn corkscrewed its way further into the orifice.

Lucifuge Rofocale stood bolt upright and made possibly the most disturbing sound ever uttered in this particular dimension. Without forming any discernible words, he managed to articulate his pain through this eardrum shattering wail. It described the slow journey of the horn through his rectum and into the large intestine, where it passed through his sigmoid and descending colon, up into the transverse colon, pinched his duodenum and then finished up embedded in his stomach.

It took Mulciber a little time to realise exactly what he had done. The top of his head was now wedged tight up against Lucifuge Rofocale's hairy buttocks. Once he made sense of his situation there was nothing for it but to press home his unexpected advantage. Pressing against the back of the other demon's thighs, he proceeded to try to pull his horn free. This time, he didn't try to twist it, he just tugged with all of his might, eliciting an even more unpleasant but equally articulate noise that described the horn's downward journey back out the way it had come but with the added description of having it pull out everything with it upon its egress.

Moments later, Mulciber was left kneeling on the floor, covered in blood, bile and bowels but both looking and feeling distinctly pleased with himself. Lucifuge Rofocale lay twitching and groaning next to him.

"Is he going to die?" asked Rose timidly, still too chary to move any closer.

"Oh I do hope so – don't you?" replied Mulciber. "Imagine how angry he's going to be with us if not."

Rose looked around the chamber and back toward the throne. The impish minions had all disappeared but she couldn't see how they'd made their escape. They hadn't gone past her in the doorway and she couldn't see any other obvious means of exit.

"What do you think this place is?"

"Lucy here prefers to stay underground when he visits the human realm. Where the other Lucy – Lucifer - is the Lightbringer, our boy here is named after 'he who flees from the light'. He is – or was – the top of the pile of a particular strain of the demon orders who feel most at home in the darkness – hence the subterranean lair. It's all such a cliché I know, but there you are."

As he finished, Lucifuge Rofocale appeared to breathe his last.

Seeing his motionless form, Rose suddenly remembered that she had left Priest propped up in the corridor and ran out to retrieve him. As she got there, he was stirring and moaning, shaking his head and muttering something unintelligible.

Rose knelt next to him.

"Priest, are you alright?"

Priests' eyes suddenly opened and looked about him as if he had just woken from a nightmare.

"Rose? Where are you?"

Realising that the passageway was in near complete darkness, she sought to reassure him.

"Don't worry Priest. Here let me help you up."

She pulled him gently to his feet and put an arm around his shoulders, guiding him toward the doorway. Back inside, he blinked as the torches seared his eyes and so Rose led him to the throne and sat him down.

Once he'd become accustomed to the light level, he looked around him. He remembered being stunned and then there was a gap. Then he remembered being carried and thrown on his back and lots of little creatures flitting about him and jabbing and pulling at him before running away. Peering out of his memory was the face of Lucifuge Rofocale and then more darkness. Climbing unsteadily to his feet, he approached the stone altar and ran his fingers across its cold surface. How long had he lain there?

Rose came to him and put a hand on his shoulder.

"Are you feeling OK now?" she asked tenderly.

"I think I'm alright. I just feel a bit groggy," he replied, rubbing the back of his head and then examining some blood on his fingers. "Ah, that will explain it – a concussion probably. Someone must have hit me on the head."

Mulciber joined them at the table.

"Good to see you up and about, old man!" he exclaimed jovially.

Priest just looked at him. He hadn't seen him for quite some time in his natural form. He'd certainly never seen him in his natural form and covered with gore and excrement before.

"What have you been up to Mulciber?"

Mulciber said nothing and instead looked back at the mound of already decomposing matter in the corner that was formerly the Arch Demon Lucifuge Rofocale.

"You killed him?" said Priest incredulously.

"How very astute of you to notice. It was an unintentional but not unwelcome outcome to our confrontation."

Rose chimed in, "He would have killed us all Priest - it had to be done."

Priest walked to the remains and prodded them with the toe of his boot.

"He was an Arch Demon, Mulciber. There will literally be Hell to pay for this!"

"You are very welcome my friend," bridled Mulciber, scraping some of the filth from his neck before sniffing at it and then putting it into his mouth.

Rose thought she was going to be sick and doubled up as her stomach retched in a long dry heave, but she had nothing inside her to bring up. Mulciber laughed at her reaction and continued to groom himself, his long black tongue darting out over his fingers to lap up the blood and muck that covered them.

This time, it was Priest who had to be reassuring.

"Don't mind him Rose, it's part of the process. He has killed a higher level demon and now must devour as much of him as possible, finishing with the heart. Once finished, he will become imbued with the power of Lucifuge Rofocale. The thing is that demonic remains don't wait around long before decomposing."

"Absolutely correct old man," agreed Mulciber. "Do both excuse me while I tuck in will you?"

With that, he crouched over the remains and started to devour them noisily, tearing and gnawing at flesh, snapping bones to get at the marrow and popping out little delicacies like the eyeballs and sweetmeats to enjoy separately. It was a truly disgusting sight and made Rose once more want to heave the gorge.

Priest had seen this before and so was a bit more phlegmatic about the whole business. He also understood the full implications of the act as well: if he was allowed to continue, Mulciber would now become one of the four Arch Demons. Where this left the already parlous state of politics in Hell was anybody's guess. He decided to get his old friend to fill in some of the gaps in his understanding of what had happened.

"So, old friend, how did you know where to find me?"

Mulciber paused his eating without turning around.

"I followed you here from the river. I saw Lucy here summoning the Leviathan and the mess that it made and then I found Rose and brought her to rescue you."

Priest took this all in, trying to make sense of everything.

"But how did you know to be there in the first place? You were at the Arcanum when Tris was killed too. Have you been following me?"

Mulciber dropped a slither of muscle that he had been chewing on and turned to face his friend.

"Of course I was. You said that you were going through some sort of crisis and I wanted to make sure that you came to no harm." Mulciber smiled a great blood-stained smile at his friend as if to reassure him of his good intentions.

Priest wasn't reassured at all by this answer; too many things just didn't add up to him. Of course he had every reason to trust Mulciber. He'd known him for centuries and the older demon had always taken him under his wing. But then again, this in itself was odd when he thought about it. Demons formed relationships with each other, but usually out of some sort of mutual gain or benefit and not out of altruism or real affection. Now Mulciber was on the verge of ascendance to the next level in the hierarchy, he wondered how this might affect their 'friendship'.

Rose had recovered and had come to his side to join in the discussion. She leaned against the altar, but still couldn't bring herself to look at Mulciber as she spoke.

"I can't speak of anything before we fought the monster and the demon in Putney, but it's true – he did find me and bring me here to rescue you."

"Don't think that I'm not eternally grateful to both of you, but I'm just trying to understand why half of Hell has suddenly tried to pursue me wherever I go... it makes no sense. I have no power at the moment; I can't do anything to upset anyone. All I want to do now is to restore my essence and take myself off somewhere away from everyone else."

Rose was hurt by this outburst. Where did this leave her? She'd done as she was told at every step of the way, like some pawn in a demonic game of chess and now that she'd seemed to serve her purpose, was she just to be cast off and forgotten?

"Well, you're very welcome to all the help I've given you Priest. I'll just take myself off and keep out of your way shall I? I'll leave your friend Mulciber to aid you in retrieving your precious powers. Just give me a little bit of warning before you finally strip them from me, just in case I'm in the middle of something important, like doing a bit of shopping for Satan or something!"

The outburst took both demons by surprise, but Mulciber was the first to reply.

"Now Rose, don't be like that. Priest meant nothing by what he said. He's just struggling to come to terms with what has happened recently."

"Oh, and it's just Priest that's had his life turned upside down in the last few days is it?" replied Rose.

"Now I'm the one being talked about as if I'm not here!" complained Priest.

There was only one thing for it, and it risked his friendship with Mulciber, increased the danger to him and Rose and possibly put him in some sort of breach of his agreement with the four psychopomps. He looked at Rose making to leave and at Mulciber temporarily paused in his consumption of the remains of Lucifuge Rofocale and made up his mind. Before anyone could react, he rushed to the corpse, forced his hand up into the body cavity and felt for the heart. Once he had it in his hand, he pulled hard, separating it from the arteries that had secured it and ripped it out.

Mulciber screamed at him, "No, don't!" But it was too late.

Priest brought the dark organ up to his mouth and bit into it. His human constitution wasn't used to such things and he had to fight the urge to gag as the stinking muscle filled his mouth with bitter, metallic tasting liquid that had already started to grow cold. Fortunately, for such a large creature, Lucifuge Rofocale had a very small heart and it was gone in four deeply unpleasant mouthfuls, but this still left Priest green in the face with nausea. Each piece that he swallowed burned him on the way down his throat and felt like it caught fire as it hit his stomach. As the last piece descended, he fell to his knees in agony at the burning sensation and he took his turn to scream out.

"Ahhh, it's killing me, it's killing me!" he roared, falling onto his side and clutching his belly.

Mulciber crawled backward on his hands, "No, this can't be happening – that was mine. You've ruined everything!"

Rose tried to go to the aid of the agonized Priest, but as she approached, he suddenly rose up from the floor and spread his arms wide. The room was hot anyway, but the heat now coming off Priest was unbearable. As she watched, his clothes started to smoke and smolder. She could see the buttons melting and dripping off his jacket and the leather crackle on his boots. Then it seemed that his entire being reached its flashpoint and everything erupted into flames.

Both Rose and Mulciber looked on at the fire engulfing Priest, the former sneering in anger and mouthing unheard words and the latter with her hand up to her mouth as if stifling the urge to burst into tears.

Finally, the conflagration burned itself out and Priest fell to the floor covered in what looked like black tar. It had set hard but as he hit the ground, it cracked and fell from him in great lumps. He pulled the rest from his body and emerged like a butterfly from a chrysalis.

Only this wasn't the Priest that either of them recognized.

# XXXIV
## Peripeteia

Astolath had been left waiting again and, as usual, he wasn't happy about it. Lucifuge Rofocale had promised to track Priest down but had not returned. And, on top of that, he'd just been informed by Eldredd that, prior to disappearing, he'd fought a pitched battle on the Thames in front of a huge audience and then he'd summoned the Leviathan which had laid waste to a half-mile stretch of the city. As a result, their chances of a clandestine end to their foray into the Earth realm were practically non-existent. The exorcism had been an amusing diversion, but now he was on the edge of losing both his advantage and his temper.

The Arch Demon was sitting with Belial and Asmodeus in the upstairs bar of a pub called The Rising Sun when Eldredd returned with the news. They'd repaired there after enquiring of a local as to where they could find a quiet hostelry and were told in no uncertain terms to "Try the Rising Sun, it's a shit-hole and there'll be no one in there at this time of the day."

At the first rude word from the unwelcoming landlord, Astolath had impaled the discourteous man on his own beer pump handles. He was still slumped there, groaning and leaking bodily fluids all over the bar and into the drip trays behind. They'd locked the doors after them and settled in to wait upstairs for news, rather than listen to the noise that he was making. That they could have silenced him by putting him out of his misery had of course been considered and dismissed.

On the huge flat screen TV on the wall opposite their table, they were watching the news. A reporter was standing behind a police cordon which was sealing off what was left of Putney High Street. Eldredd stood listening with the others to the young blonde who was talking animatedly to concerned voices in the studio: *"...has left locals feeling scared and bewildered by these events. What looked like some sort of publicity stunt or even a movie shoot has turned out to be something completely different. We don't know who the people are that were involved, but the police are obviously anxious to interview them and anyone who knows who they might be.*

*In terms of getting back to normal in South West London, this has left the bridge closed to both pedestrian and road traffic for the foreseeable future and has caused what looks like millions of pounds worth of damage to property. On top of that, there were obviously many casualties..."*

As she spoke, images of the Leviathan and of the fight between Rose and Lucifuge Rofocale flashed up in the background, captured mainly from mobile phones. The last piece of footage showed the demon in full flight, with Priest in his arms.

"He's got to be somewhere in the vicinity," Eldredd explained. "It's just that I'm not exactly sure where my lord."

Eldredd realized that by saying this he may well have just signed his own death warrant but he pressed on regardless. He was beyond the pale now, he'd gone too far, he'd crossed the Rubicon in a pair of neon waders while holding loft a sign saying 'There's no going back!' and he was past caring. Events had now gotten so far out of his hands that he threw all caution to the wind with his next statement.

"Might I suggest that instead of sitting there, you three remaining Arch Demons use some of that power that you've amassed and do something for yourselves for a change?"

Eldredd thought for one split second that he would just stand his ground and take whatever was coming to him, but in that second, self-preservation got the upper hand and he decided to flee. It was too late for any discretion; the genie was out of the bottle. With this in mind, he made a dive through the nearest window and took to the air before his fall could take him as far as the pavement. As he raced skyward, he shed his disguise in contempt, to reveal his natural shiny jet black form.

For the second day in a row, Londoners were faced with the sight of strange flying creatures darting about above their city. They were used to strange occurrences and to constant inconveniences from terrorists, protest marches and sporting events and so not many were panicked by these sightings. Other than the internet continuing to be awash with unexplained footage and crazy theories about the appearances, the only group who had mobilized in any numbers were those belonging to the various evangelical and related Christian sects who had taken to the streets in large numbers to proclaim that the end was nigh (yet again!). They'd been sure about this in the past, but now they were doubly sure about their predictions. The advent of the demons was a sure sign of the imminent arrival of the Second Coming.

Without the counsel of Eldredd, Astolath had no ameliorating voice to calm him and to make him think about his actions. Without thought, he leapt through the hole left by Eldredd's hasty departure, followed closely by Asmodeus and Belial. Like Eldredd, they abandoned their 'Men in Black' outfits on the wing and accelerated upward in pursuit of the fleeing recalcitrant underling.

***

There was nowhere in Hell safe for Eldredd now and he had to think fast about his increasingly limited options. If he could reach Priest himself, he might be able to persuade him that he had known nothing of Astolath's plans. Perhaps whoever was hiding him might hide him as well? It was a long shot, but he didn't see what other choice he had. At the same time, if Lucifuge Rofocale had been successful, he might be able to ingratiate himself again with the Arch Demons by returning to them with the news of a successful capture. Who knows what sins might be forgiven in such circumstances? But, where to look?

Orienting himself by the Thames, he headed up river, surveying the bridges for signs of damage. He could see from a distance that there were flying machines hovering over one of them, along with a huge pall of smoke drifting up from buildings nearby. This must have been where it happened. Eldredd didn't dare getting any closer in case Astolath, Belial and Asmodeus got the same idea and tried to trace him there. Then it struck him that he might be able to get a lead on where Lucifuge Rofocale had gone.

He knew that the other demon was an underworld dweller by nature – 'he who flees from the light'. If he had fled below ground, then Eldredd might be able to locate him be employing a handy spell with which he was familiar. But how to get underground quickly?

Another flash of inspiration hit him as he recalled the underground railway beneath London. If he could get access to that then he might be able to work his magic. Swooping lower, he doubled back on himself, hugging the river and looking out for one of the signs that indicated an entrance to the tunnels below. Approaching Charing Cross he spotted what he was looking for, a circle with a bar through it saying 'Embankment'. There was no time for disguises. He'd not seen anyone following him, but he couldn't be sure that he was safe.

With this in mind, he landed in a small park next to the entrance and blithely walked into the atrium. As he did so, he received very few second glances, most people assuming that he was promoting a shiny new gadget or perhaps a peripatetic art installation. Londoners are hard to impress at the best of times and rarely make a fuss over such things.

Eldredd crossed the small enclosed area to a row of ticket barriers. Not understanding their purpose and not being in possession of a travel card, the barriers wouldn't budge as he approached, instead eliciting an annoying electronic beep along with a sign which lit up next to him saying 'Seek Assistance'. Behind him, several commuters huffed and grunted at being inconvenienced by his failure to enter smoothly, and backtracked to other barriers to enter the station.

A moment later, a London Underground official was at his side.

"What's up mate – ticket not going through?"

"Ticket?" Eldredd shook his head, not understanding what he was being asked.

"Ticket? Oyster card? Travel card? How were you trying to travel?"

"By going under the ground of course."

This was as much as the official was going to take.

"Alright smart arse – no ticket eh?" Pulling Eldredd by his arm to one side, he officiously pronounced judgment for all to hear. "You either pay a ten pound penalty fine or I call the Old Bill. 'S'up to you mate?"

Eldredd looked at the man and then around at the small crowd of onlookers, some of whom had already started to take photos on their phones.

"I don't have time for this you dolt. Get out of my way!"

With that, he put his hand on the man's chest and flung him backward into a stand full of tourist leaflets. That was when the screaming shouted.

"He's hit him!"

"Somebody call the police!"

"Did you get a photo of him?"

Eldredd turned back to the barrier nearest him, forced the two rubber flaps open and walked through toward the stars. In front of him was another sign indicating a choice between the East and West bound platforms. Picking one at random, he leapt down seven or eight steps at a time, rounded a corner and found himself on the station platform.

His arrival caused a few heads to look up from newspapers, but most people just ignored him. That was, until he leapt down onto the track and started to dig at the stones in-between the rails. It was then that the screaming began again.

"There's a man on the track!"

"Is it a terrorist?"

"I don't know - he looks weird!"

"Did you get a photo of him?"

Eldredd ignored the chatter and the crowds beginning to line the platform to see what he was doing. It didn't matter anymore if anyone saw him. They wouldn't understand and they could do nothing to stop him.

Reaching under the stones, he felt for the hard floor of the tunnel and spread his fingers wide, pressing his palm down hard against the concrete surface. As he did so, he closed his eyes and reached out for his quarry. Pulses of energy left his fingertips, firing in all directions, racing through the stones, through the tunnel walls and even through the steel rails, fanning out in search of a contact from someone from the demon realm. It took only seconds to receive a reply, a chthonic echo that indicated in which direction he needed to go.

The pulse indicated that he should head toward the east and so he got to his feet with every intention of flying through the tunnel in that direction. It was then that he felt the floor trembling and could see the rails on either side of him vibrating. In the distance he could see two lights shining down the tunnel, heralding the approach of a train. The screaming began again and people shouted at him to get off the tracks. On this particular train line, the east and west direction tracks were side by side and so he simply jumped to the next line before the breeze behind him indicated that a train was approaching from that side as well.

At this point, the noise of screaming and shouting from the crowds lining the platforms was almost as loud as the approaching trains. Eldredd realized that he could either jump onto one of the platforms – but that would risk him being mobbed – or he could simply hop onto one of the trains. He waited until the train behind him got to within about fifty feet and he prepared to jump onto the roof and ride it as far as he could. The problem was that the driver saw him on the track well before this and had already started to apply her brakes to pull into the station. The train ground to a screeching halt a few yards from where he was and stopped dead. For what seemed like a very long time, the demon and the driver just stared at each other through the glass screen of the driver's compartment. Eldredd cursed his bad luck at having to make his own way, but took off all the same, running down the track and into the darkness of the tunnel.

\*\*\*

Priest stepped from the charred husk and threw his arms wide and then stood on tiptoe, stretching his arched back and yawned as if he had just woken from sleep. Finally, he stood there spread-eagled, like Da Vinci's image of the Vitruvian Man, naked as a baby, refulgent and completely white but for his golden eyes. As he stood there, colour started to spread out across his marble skin and he started to darken. Next, his hair started to grow back, cascading down his shoulders and back. He was being reborn right in front of the watching Rose and Mulciber.

Still on his knees among the filth and the blood, Mulciber was the first to speak.

"You've denied me the right to take my rightful place among the hierarchy old man. It's too bad that we couldn't stay friends." As he spoke, he climbed to his feet and snorted threateningly and raked his feet, like a bull about to charge.

Priest said nothing.

"What are you doing Mulciber," asked Rose.

"I'm going to end this travesty once and for all my dear," replied the hopping mad demon. "I was never one for prophecies, but now that Priest here has just fulfilled one – albeit not in the way that I suspected he would – I may as well bring things to a conclusion."

"What do you mean?"

"Are you asking for some sort of dramatic exposition, like a theatrical villain?" mocked Mulciber. "Well, you'll not get one. Priest here is about to end me and then he can explain it all to you if he chooses."

This was the cue for Mulciber to leap, horns first, at the naked Priest. For his part, Priest merely raised a hand which stopped his attacker in his tracks. Mulciber struggled but found that he couldn't make any movements forward or backward – he was held in place by virtue of the lightest touch of Priest's finger on his forehead. Priest brought Mulciber's face upward until their eyes met. He smiled briefly and then gently grasped the older demon by his horns.

Rose watched in horrified fascination as Priest proceeded to pull the horns apart. He tugged them in opposite directions as Mulciber screamed in the throes of the most horrendous agony. Instead of coming away from his head, the bases of both his horns were pushing inward, cracking and crushing his skull. Priest obviously now had the strength to make a quickness of it, but continued to push slowly in opposite directions. Mulciber's eye's which had been fixed on him throughout the torment now looked in opposing directions as well as his cranium was rent in two under the enormous pressure. At length, a terrible crunching sound heralded Mulciber's demise and Priest let him fall onto the floor where he was.

Finished with his revenge, he turned to Rose, who stood petrified still looking at the body on the floor.

"Would you like an explanation, Rose, or shall we just carry on?"

Rose couldn't bring herself to speak for a minute. The Priest that she'd known for the last few days had been without any power and had shown a vulnerability that had fooled her. He'd seemed so human in his outlook and innocence that she'd almost forgotten that she'd inadvertently befriended a demon. Priest's outrageously demonic behaviour had just disabused her of this way of thinking. *If he could blithely rip his oldest friend apart, what might he do to her if she upset him in some way?*

"You don't owe me any explanations Priest," she began tentatively. "If you want to tell me then you will."

"So be it, let's go."

Rose suddenly had a reason to intervene.

"Don't you think that you ought to put some clothes on first?"

Priest looked down at himself almost self-consciously.

"I see what you mean," he answered brusquely and proceeded to close his eyes tight in concentration. As he did, his outline shimmered and dimmed before his usual black suit appeared, complete with dog collar and shiny black boots. "Is that better?"

"Much!" Rose almost smiled but was still feeling a bit on edge from witnessing what had just transpired. For his part though, Priest just stepped away from the pile of bloody detritus at his feet and seemed more concerned that he might dirty his boots than anything else.

"Now," he began. "The decision is whether to wait here, assuming that our friend Lucifuge Rofocale meant to hold me here until his companions arrived, or whether to take the initiative and to go in search of them?"

\*\*\*

Eldredd had run for what felt like miles, stopping every so often to dart out of the way of a train and then to repeat the necessity of putting his palm to the tunnel floor in order to re-orientate himself in the right direction. After a while he found

271

that the tunnel gave way to daylight though the track continued to run unbroken beneath bridges and roadways. He continued to cause consternation at several more stations along the way as he bounded on past commuters and day trippers on the platforms. Each appearance elicited shouting and commotion followed by frantic announcements on loudspeakers.

Not that such knowledge would have bothered him one iota, but Eldredd's traversal of the rails had caused an almost complete shutdown of the tube system as staff and police monitored CCTV feeds to find out why a costumed man was running through the tunnels and to find out where he was heading. All trains had now been stopped where they were, many crammed full of people who were resigned to the odd delay but who by now were almost as one thinking that this time, London Underground really was taking the piss. Those who had not seen a demon racing along the tracks assumed that the delay was down to one of two usual reasons: signal failure or suicide.

In fact, commuters were so blasé about people throwing themselves under trains on the system that there was never any hint of sympathy when it happened. Instead, the usual complaint to be heard was, "Why couldn't he/she have done it at the weekend instead of during the rush hour?" This was as opposed to what one would think would be the human reaction of, "Oh dear, think of his/her poor family. He/she must have been desperately unhappy, poor soul!" But no, two thousand years of war, conflagration, famine, disease, civil unrest and smart phones had bled the last remnants of sympathy or empathy out of Londoners. As such, it was probably surprising that more demons hadn't decided to move to the metropolis and make their homes there.

Eldredd stopped once more between stations and felt the echo return much stronger this time. He was near to his destination but the returning pulse indicated that following the train track was of no more use to him. The signal branched off through a brick wall which didn't appear to have any means of entrance. This meant either flying up to try to pick out a likely spot from the air, or a spot of tunneling of his own. In the end, the decision came down to practicalities. Aloft he would be easier to spot by Astolath et al. and so he decided to go through the wall. If he was lucky, he would emerge somewhere in another tunnel closer to his destination. If not, he'd have several courses of rugged Victorian brickwork followed by rock, concrete, steel and who knows what to work his way through.

In the event, Eldredd was fortunate. Smashing through the wall with his fists, he emerged on the other side and into a service tunnel that seemed to run for miles in either direction. This was punctuated every so often by doors and hatches that seemed to lead off at right-angles from the tunnel. Perhaps this would bring him closer?

Once more touching the floor to get his bearings, he followed the corridor to his left and then, after a hundred yards or so, opened the second door that he came to and followed the corridor to which this led. He could see and feel that the long passageway was on a slight downward incline and by the time he reached the door at the far end, he must have gone down another thirty or forty feet.

The door had one of those 'Push Bar to Open' signs and so Eldredd did as it suggested. The smell hit him immediately as it swung open. He emerged under a small bridge over a stream of what looked like some sort of foul smelling green soup. Directly opposite him on the opposite bank was yet another door, this one covered in messy painted writing over a 'KEEP OUT' sign. Dropping down to one knee, a final probe confirmed that he was nearly at his destination. Eldredd rocked backward on his heels before propelling himself across the green liquid to land softly on the other side.

Entering, he found himself in the same tunnel that Priest and Rose had traversed earlier on. In fact, he also found himself face to face with the two of them as they made to leave the lair of Lucifuge Rofocale.

For a few seconds they all just stared at each other in surprise, before Eldredd broke the silence with an opening gambit.

"Priest! Just the demon I was looking for. Thank Beelzebub that you're still alive!" He put on his best smile and threw his arms wide as if he were about to embrace Priest.

For his part, Priest eyed Eldredd suspiciously and pulled Rose back so that he was between her and the unexpected arrival. Eldredd noted the protection that he gave her and continued with his outpouring of relief.

"I thought that Lucifuge Rofocale had taken you."

"And you came to make sure of it?" Priest replied dryly.

"No, of course not. I came to warn you of his intentions – you know of course that Astolath is after you don't you?"

"No more games Eldredd, I haven't time for this. In fact I'm off to find Astolath now in order to bring this whole silly thing to a head." As he finished, Priest made to brush the other demon to one side and leave the passageway, but Eldredd grabbed his wrist as he did so.

"I wouldn't be in such a hurry to dismiss my help Priest, especially in your current condition."

The two of them were eye to eye now.

"Just what condition would that be, Eldredd?"

As he asked, Priest's eyes glowed brightly and a gentle ripple ran through his visage as if he were about to alter his appearance. Eldredd got the hint straight away and let go of his wrist as if it were a hot poker.

"You've recovered your powers then?" he asked, looking at Rose to see if he could discern any difference in her as well.

Priest smiled and continued to walk on past. As he stepped through the door he peered back at Eldredd.

"Just keep walking until you reach the end of the passageway. All will be revealed there."

He let the door swing shut behind them and left Eldredd in the gloom.

Emerging into the shadow of the bridge and then into the full daylight, Priest turned to Rose and half-smiled.

"You can ask your questions now if you wish. It's the least I can do before asking of you what I'm about to ask."

Rose didn't like the sound of this, but liked being kept in the dark even less.

"Very well then – as you're offering…" she said archly. "Do you want to explain absolutely everything that happened back there?"

"Do you mind if we walk and talk?" he returned. "Once Eldredd sees what happened back there, he's going to be back with questions of his own and I'd like to get moving." And so they fell into step along the grimy towpath and began to walk back toward the city.

While they couldn't exactly have passed as young lovers – not with him dressed in ecclesiastical garb – they did at least seem for a while like two good friends on a leisurely stroll. At least that's the way they seemed to the fraternity of the canal: the two young boys in hooded tops who tried to mug them and were now floating face down in the green canal; the elderly bag lady who tried to panhandle them before shrieking madly when they told her to go away and who was now in pieces and stuffed inside several of her own carrier bags; and lastly, the stray bulldog who had been startled by their passing and which had attempted to extract his own pound of flesh from Priest and was now impaled on a fencepost outside a house that backed onto the slimy water.

The body count was mounting and it wasn't just Priest who was to blame. Rose had grown her own tally to three (hers was the old bag lady!). While her mother's assisted demise was what she saw as an act of kindness and the lonely death of her former step-father a deserved retribution, she realized that she hadn't been as repulsed by the whole notion of killing as she thought she would be. Even when on the streets, she had fought to maintain some sort of morality and dignity however lowly. Now that she realized that it was all just one big game of dice, that there was a god up there but who was as interested in her as the sole of a boot might be in the passing of an ant, she didn't feel the crushing compulsion to act with any reserve or restraint. She was powerful now and kept company with the powerful. There was something beyond and death no longer held any fear for her. Even if she were now destined for Hell, she might even have an ally or two to look after her on the inside.

She'd not grown callous, just indifferent. She realized now that humans weren't special, not the chosen ones created in the image of a benevolent deity. She wasn't special, her mother hadn't been special and Karl certainly hadn't been. What kept society on the straight and narrow was even further beyond her now that she knew what she knew. It wasn't even really possible to blame the demons for their behaviour. Yes, they were a capricious and argumentative lot whose peccadillos seemed to spill over into the Earth realm periodically, but then they didn't regard humans as equals. The monkeys (as the demons often called the humans), were a diversion for some, but mostly they held no more fascination for them than humans do for house flies or earthworms.

In between rude interruptions and the resultant slayings, Priest relayed to Rose his reasons for killing his friend Mulciber. Although ignorant of Mulciber's true motives, he simply couldn't let the older demon eat the heart and ascend the hierarchy. This was not because he feared him becoming an Arch Demon, but because it was Priest's only sure way of gain back enough power to protect himself. It had been a purely selfish act and had he been human, or had he remained in semi-human form, might have had cause to regret his actions later if not sooner.

There had also been Mulciber's words that made Priest certain that he was being played like a pawn in some sort of game. Mulciber had mentioned some sort of prophecy being fulfilled, as if there was an end game that Priest had inadvertently stumbled into. Priest knew of no prophecy but he was no stooge. Self-preservation was the first order and he'd leapt headfirst into that obligation. By the time he'd felt the transformation, he knew that he was now an Arch Demon himself and had inherited much of Lucifuge Rofocale's knowledge as well as his powers. This meant that the whole of the conspiracy was now opened up to him.

He knew that Astolath was following him in order to ambush Lucifer – who no one on any plane of existence had seen since the coup d'état in Hell – and he also knew now that he was going to be used to maintain some semblance of a balance of power there now. By extension, this meant that if the Lightbringer wasn't originally looking for him, then he certainly would be now.

There it was in a nutshell. Priest had chosen the worst possible time to go on his experimental sabbatical and to hand off his powers. And, of small comfort to Rose was the fact that he had someone else's essence inside him and had no idea what this meant for either him or her in terms of returning things to normal. But he did know that now he was notionally in the highest echelons of the hierarchy, he had no intention of staying there. The power plays, jockeying and vying for position held no interest for him still. Unfortunately he also realized this was no longer a matter of his own choice.

There was also the small matter of a bargain with a group of deities that was also to be sorted out. If his essence was to be forfeit after thirty days, then it would be both gone forever for him and mean the end of Rose. This wasn't a part of the exposition that she was particularly anxious to hear him expand upon.

Rose listened with both fear and fascination to what he had to say. It clarified the situation somewhat, but provided no reassurance. In fact, the whole thing started to irritate her again.

"So, did we learn our stupid behaviour from you or did you learn it from us?" she asked pointedly.

"What do you mean?"

"Well, all the politicking and power-grabbing. It's bad enough down here, but to know that it goes on in other dimensions as well is a bit depressing to say the least. I thought that we were the only ones who got life so out of whack."

"Well, we've been around a lot longer than you have, so I suppose that we were the forerunners. But no, it's pretty much the same all over. It's just nature isn't it – everything fights for ascendency and control. The only difference is that we higher beings have the wherewithal to cogitate on the issue and to ponder our decisions."

Rose stopped walking at this point.

"How can someone supernatural speak so casually of nature? You know nothing of nature."

Priest laughed, "Ah, there's a solipsistic point of view if ever I heard one. You assume still that everything evolves about the human realm. Do you know how many realms there are?"

Rose was stumped by this one.

"No… how many?"

"Thousands," Priest replied with obvious glee. "Perhaps even millions, I don't know. I've only visited a small number of them. But I can tell you this much – each one has a small backwater somewhere in it that thinks that everything was designed purely to cater for its needs. The Earth realm is no different."

"So what is the point of everything?"

"You mean the answer to life, the universe and everything?" Priest paused for a moment. "There isn't one Rose. You people have a truism don't you – 'life's what you make it'. Be happy with that and find your own meaning."

"Like you did?"

"No, I failed in that and I'm still looking. Perhaps the meaning of my life is to end up as a corpse somewhere in London… I don't know. I don't think that I want to let that happen though. I'm going to pay Astolath a visit and have all of this out with him. But I could use your help Rose. In return, I'll try my best to make sure that this all works out OK for you – in whatever way you choose." Priest extended his hand. "Do we have a deal?"

Rose smiled and gripped his hand.

"Good. Now remember that you're not helpless. You still have my powers and it'll be almost as hard for them to kill you as it will be for you to kill them."

"That's so reassuring!"

"I thought it might be. Now, this has been an interesting walk and everything, but it's about time that we made our date with destiny."

So saying, Priest and Rose took silently to the air.

# XXXV
## At the Crossroads

The flat roof of the high-rise Centre Point building on New Oxford Street had three new additions to the usual population of roosting pigeons that afternoon. Astolath, Belial and Asmodeus stood peering in different directions from the brutalist glass and concrete edifice, scanning the skies for anything resembling a flying demon. But, other than helicopters, planes and yet more pigeons, they'd seen nothing to pique their interest for the hour or so that they'd been there.

In boredom and annoyance, Asmodeus sat down on what looked like an air conditioning unit to take the weight off his hooves for five minutes. Glancing down beside him he was surprised to see a sleeping bag and various bottles and cans covered in a layer of feathers. Just off to one side of this was a cardboard sign with 'Property of Old Bailey' scrawled on it in thick pen. Absent-mindedly, Asmodeus prodded the litter with the point of a hoof and briefly wondered who Old Bailey was and why he'd choose to live in such a high-up place.

His train of idle thought was derailed by the sound of Astolath barking and pointing to the East of them at two growing shapes in the distance. Asmodeus and Belial immediately ran to his side and peered in the direction that he was indicating.

"It must be Lucifuge Rofocale and... and... a woman?" squawked Belial excitedly, forgetting Astolath's prohibition on him speaking. Luckily for him, Astolath seemed to have forgotten this in the rush to identify whoever was inbound at that moment.

As the moments ticked by, the shapes started to resolve themselves into something recognisable but by that time, Priest had the jump on them and announced his arrival with a well-timed bolt of something big and fiery that exploded on the roof and shook several of the large 'CENTRE POINT' letters from the side of the building. The letters crashed onto the building site at the base of the tower and the screaming and mobile phone photography started once more. The three Arch Demons on the roof were thrown from their feet, but all recovered in time to take to the air in order to confront their attacker.

Priest stayed close to Rose and gave her instructions as to what to do next.

"Here they come Rose. They won't know who you are, so hopefully they'll leave you alone. As they get closer, peel off and try to get behind them."

Rose nodded in understanding and took off at a right angle to Priest. As he had suspected, the three demons were only interested in him and flew straight for him in an attempt to grab him. As he suspected, they wanted to take him alive rather than kill him immediately, or else the air would have been burning and thundering already. Astolath held back a little and let his two partners close in.

"Don't make this any more difficult than it needs to be, Priest!" boomed Asmodeus.

"Fair enough. Why don't you just turn around and leave, Asmodeus. Seems easy enough to me!"

"Your insolence does you no favours, Priest," squealed Belial.

Priest did a double-take when he heard the strange noise that the Arch Demon forced from his mouth.

"Belial, I presume? Do you have a sore throat or something?"

Belial bristled at this and instantly forgot any notion of taking Priest a prisoner. It was one thing having Astolath ridicule him – he'd pay later – but to have a lesser demon do it was intolerable. He accelerated toward his foe with the intention of impaling him on his horns.

Priest had anticipated this and hovered waiting for him like a toreador at the approach of a charging bull. At the very last instant he spun to one side with a flourish and Belial sped past him into the distance. This left Asmodeus isolated with Priest in front and Rose coming in from the side. At a nod from Priest, Rose hit Asmodeus with everything she could summon and at a gesture, the air between them heated and expanded violently, exploding around the demon and causing him to founder and flail wildly with his arms as if flapping them might keep him up in the air.

This was Priest's chance to do some real damage. He flew into Asmodeus himself and accelerated as fast as he could. In a deadly embrace the two of them rocketed on a downward trajectory before smashing into the gaudy orange, green and yellow Mechano construction that constituted the nearby Central St. Giles building. The impact took the both of them through the glass side, into the atrium and then into a faux-Italian restaurant on the ground floor where they landed among the well-heeled diners in a heap of furniture, serving trays, spaghetti and cursing waiters.

Shock and surprise among the diners turned quickly to fear and then outright terror as the two interlopers didn't even stop to dust themselves off before resuming their brawl. Quickly herding themselves toward the nearest exist in the most disorderly of fashions – many of them finding egress via the broken windows – a fragrant stampede of suits and posh frocks found its way quickly out into the street. Of course, this left more room for the two demons to fight but it was still too confined a space to use the more spectacular weapons in their respective arsenals and so they had to resort to good old fashioned pier six brawl complete with fisticuffs, slobberknocking, donnybrooking, chair throwing, bitch slapping and a generally rampant session of arses being well and truly kicked. It was something straight out of a comic book with neither initially gaining the upper hand, both trading the most outrageous of blows that had some of the male diners (and one or two of females), turning back to watch the action.

The tides started to turn when Priest got Asmodeus in a headlock and managed to ram him bodily into the large coffee machine on what was left of the service counter. The larger demon's horns pierced the side of the device and wedged there. As he tried to struggle free, steam and boiling hot water erupted from the holes that he'd made. This quickly scalded his head and neck, eliciting screams of agony. Priest wasted no time in capitalizing on his opponent's compromised position and pile on the pain by smashing a jar of chillies over his head to add to the burn.

This was too much for Asmodeus and in fact gave him the strength out of desperation to pull himself free of the machine. Trying to blink away the stinging chilli powder he rounded on Priest and come for him in an even greater fury. Tables were ripped from their fixings, walls crumbled, doors were knocked from their hinges and porcelain smashed from its mountings as he pursued Priest into the gents toilets under the weight of a flurry of wildly angry and mostly indiscriminately aimed blows.

Like an expert pugilist, Priest let his enemy come on, tiring himself out and wasting his energy. Finally, he sidestepped a particularly powerful but badly aimed attempt at a punch and tripped Asmodeus into one of the cubicles where he sat down heavily on a toilet seat, shattering the bowl as he did so.

With his opponent temporarily run out of steam, Priest looked about to find something to use as a weapon. Options being limited, he stepped over to the condom machine and tore it from the wall, showering the room in brick dust and shards of white tiling. Returning to the cubicle, he smiled at Asmodeus who looked back at him with resignation and defeat. Turning the machine in his hands, Priest lined up a sharp corner to lead with and rammed it into the face of the compliant Arch Demon with all of his might. Not sure of exactly what it might take to prove fatal, he then repeated the act several times, each impact meeting with less and less resistance until it felt like he was pounding something of the consistency of cheesecake – soft and gooey, with crunchy stuff underneath.

He dropped the machine and surveyed his handy work but it was no sugary dessert that met his eyes. It was a demon's body with a large flat splat erupting up the wall where the head once was. Even then, he couldn't be sure that Asmodeus was dead. In the mixture of water, blood and urine pooling on the floor and spreading out beneath the cubical was one eye that had escaped from being mashed. It must have popped out during one of the initial impacts but now stared up at him accusingly as if it was still watching him. Priest reached down for it and mouthed an apology into the staring cornea. He then almost tenderly placed in back on the floor before stamping down on it as hard as he could.

The next problem was what to do with the remains. He'd eaten one heart recently, dare he consume another? Even he wasn't sure what this would mean for him, but there was always the risk that one of the others might find him and do it instead. There was nothing for it but to bite the bullet and see what happened. Fortunately, Asmodeus was already hanging open and it didn't take much to free the quickly blackening organ. Priest held it aloft and stared at it as if he were inspecting a precious jewel in the light.

"Oh well, here goes!"

He took a bite and then another…

*** 

Meanwhile, back over the West End, Rose was breaking all sorts of records: Fastest female airspeed, fastest female over one hundred, two hundred and fifteen hundred meters and then an unofficial shot-put attempt whereby she tore the glowing sphere from the top of the London Coliseum and hurled it all the way over as far as the Duke of York statue near The Mall, on top of which Belial had been perching. She'd missed him, but was still very pleased with her effort and her amazing new strength.

Beneath them, chaos was spreading through the city. In their usual evocation of the 'Blitz Spirit' during a crisis, a great many Londoners had decided to carry on as usual, even as debris and bodies rained from the haven around them. Others though – mainly the younger ones - had taken to running around like headless chickens, either panicking or trying to break windows and loot stores as if one more broken window just wouldn't matter.

In all directions, sirens wailed as police, ambulance and fire brigade attempted to coordinate a response to something that they'd never planned for in all of their worst doomsday scenarios. Terrorist attacks and dirty bombs they could cope with; demons going ten rounds at high speeds above their heads had left them looking much like the aforementioned decapitated fowl.

Rose took time to look down upon this and reflect briefly upon what it all meant to her. She was fighting against some of the nastiest creatures in any time or reality but she suddenly realized with a shocking reminder that none of what she was doing was for any of the dupes down below eking out their feverishly empty lives. *So what if some of them were caught in the cross-fire? What did she care for them when none of them had ever cared for her?*

And their terror made her giddy with excitement. As she passed low over them or fought among them, she could see the fear and wonder in their eyes as they cowed in awe of events that they had no part in and no control over. All around her, time stood still for these insignificant beings as they sought desperately to make sense of what was happening. They'd been so conditioned to seeing everything remediated through the spotlight of internet, television and advertising that as something truly stupendous unraveled before them they immediately struggled to see it framed within one of those familiar terms of reference. That so many of them were struck dumb and yet still taking in the scene through their mobile camera lenses was proof of this. In the moment it was just all too much to take. But at their leisure, at home and in front of a screen, they could play it all back and attempt to make sense of it through their online social networks. Here they would find their answers. Here they would pull the wool over each other's eyes so that they could return to the cozy and doped up sleep of unreason. It might be going a bit too far to say that she sympathized with the demons but at least now she understood them a bit better.

Right now though, she had one demon on her tail and another – the biggest one – who seemed to have disappeared and could turn up at any moment to catch her off-guard. She assumed that Priest had managed to take care of the third, but she hadn't seen anything of either of them for some time now.

Her thoughts were rudely interrupted by a fork of lightning which hit the rooftop on which she was standing. Around her more windows shattered, cracks appeared in the brickwork and concrete around her and sparks arced, crackled and danced in between TV aerials and satellite dishes. Rose herself was thrown backward and off her feet and landed with a crash against a wall of almost vertical roof tiles which shook and broke around her. Looking up, she saw the source of the lightning as Belial swooped down from out of a cloud, howling with vicious laughter.

Thankful that she was still alive - though not sure how - Rose struggled to stand upright on legs that had turned to jelly. This probably saved her life though, as she stumbled forward and fell to one side, another bolt impacted against the tiles which exploded behind her. The building was on fire now and this gave her the impetus to keep moving so that she was sheltered behind the low wall at the front on the roof. This meant that she was away from the flames and out of sight of Belial for the moment.

As the feeling returned to her limbs, she risked a glance over the wall but other than distant helicopters it seemed empty of supernatural beings. The light was fading fast now but the darkening clouds lit up periodically as if there were a storm over the city. These flashes were joined in some places by searchlights and green and red laser lights where the authorities had obviously decided to act at last against the aerial threat.

Rose looked around and thought for a moment how she had never seen the city look so vibrant and beautiful. It was London as it was meant to be, a place of excitement and danger, coldness and illusion, magic and mythology. Somehow it seemed exactly right that it should have demons in its skies and imps in its subterranea. It fitted that there should be ancient and occult non-places rubbing shoulders with the high-rise modern city and that there should be a hidden lake of lava bubbling beneath the District Line.

Her reverie was once again harshly shattered, but this time not by a bolt of lightning. It felt this time like the whole world shook and not just the building where she was hiding. Peering down into the street, she could see people being thrown from their feet, cars and buses screeching and skidding to a halt and a black cab disappearing sideways into a newly opened fissure in the road. She watched as the driver and his passenger frantically waved for help before they vanished from view.

Priest then appeared, walking down the road toward her. He was naked again and this time was covered in a glowing golden aura which danced and shimmered around him as he moved. Leaping from the roof, Rose slowly descended to land next to him.

"What's happened to you?"

Priest shrugged, "Must be something I ate."

"You killed another one?"

"I killed another one," he replied casually.

"So are you going to get dressed again?"

"It's hardly worth it my dear – my appetite is not yet sated."

As he said this, Belial dropped to the road behind them and laid down a challenge to them both in his most menacing squeak.

"How convenient to have both of you here at the same time. It will make my work much easier to take you both out with one blow!"

As he said this, the street emptied quickly as people rushed to avoid being caught in the cross-fire. But Priest just sighed and gently moved Rose to one side before raising a hand, palm forward, toward Belial.

There was drama, no noise and no flash of light, just a sudden red splash as Belial seemed to be standing there defiantly one second and the next he was falling all around them in big drops of red rain and slithers of lightly cooked flesh.

Rose looked again at Priest.

"What about his heart?"

"Oh, I didn't want it. I've taken the powers and attributes of each that I've killed so far. What if I'd have ended up with that ridiculous voice?"

As the rain ceased, Rose stood there laughing like a mad child at the insanity of it all. In fact, she felt her mind on the edge of a precipice, it looking over and willing itself to jump. Priest's next words brought her back from the brink.

"We still have Astolath to contend with and I have no idea where he is at present."

"Oh, for a moment there I forgot about him and thought it was all over."

"Far from it," Priest smiled grimly. "In fact, we've had it easy so far. Astolath is in a different league entirely to those we've yet faced."

As he spoke, nascent horns began to spring from his forehead along with small green wings that sprouted from his shoulder blades.

"You're changing Priest!"

Priest reached up for the swelling nubs that had appeared on his head and shrugged.

"I feared as much. It's as I said, I'm taking on some of the attributes of those who have contributed to my diet recently – I've no control over it at all."

"Well at least your bottom half has remained the same. Talking of which... can't you at least put some trousers on?"

"Very well," Priest shrugged briefly and black trousers appeared on his legs. "Is that better?" He gestured at his legs. "Really, you humans should get over your bashfulness at your own anatomy."

"It's nothing to do with being shy," she hesitated. "It's just that I've not had any luck in the past with men who were all too ready to show me what was in their trousers."

"Oh yes... I'd quite forgotten." Priest at least made a valiant effort to look abashed at his insensitivity. "From henceforth, it stays out of sight!"

Rose felt that discomfort at being too close to the edge again. She was here in this apocalyptic scenario with a full-scale demon war erupting around her and she was complaining that one of their number might be a bit more modest with his outlandish anatomy – the horns and the wings were fine, even the carnage and collateral damage were understandable, but no showing Mr. Winky okay!

*What the Hell was she thinking?*

As if reading her thoughts (perhaps he was...), Priest smiled and changed the subject tactfully.

"Let's head back to where we first encountered Astolath et al. Perhaps he's still there."

Rose agreed that this was the best course of action and hand in hand they both took to the air again.

\*\*\*

Astolath was indeed waiting for them back at the Centre Point building. This Priest was a relatively minor player – though he had a bit of a reputation for being a schemer and one of the more intelligent of Hell's host – but he was levels below them in the hierarchy and shouldn't have taken too much trouble to dispense with. That neither Asmodeus nor Belial had returned, though, was troubling.

Night was now here and he still had nothing to show for his efforts. And it had started off so promisingly with that amusing diversion that Asmodeus had provided with exorcism and the monkey priest. For a while there he'd even forgotten about all the hassle of having to maintain his position at the top of the greasy pole that led to the top of the Hellish hierarchy. But now it looked as if he would finally have to get his hands dirty. After all, they were out in the open now, laying waste to swathes of one of the most highly populated cities on Earth and there was no way that The Lightbringer didn't know where they were by now. Besides, he'd already challenged Lucifer to combat on his own doorstep and he'd walked away like the coward that he was. What had he, Astolath, to fear from him? He was surely a spent force and truly now the most fallen of fallen angels.

Looking down, he saw a sudden stampede of people running down Oxford Street toward where he was. Many stopped every so often to look behind them and point to the sky above. Just coming into sight was an unfamiliar demon and Priest's woman. They were flying low over the street but were they holding hands or was the demon holding her captive? Perhaps he was something to do with another one of

Eldredd's plans that he hadn't seen fit to share with him. He'd still punish him thoroughly when he got hold of him, but perhaps he'd be a bit more lenient if this worked out in his favour after all.

Stepping off the edge of the roof, he plummeted toward the ground before coming to a gentle stop. He stepped onto the pavement as if he were just stepping down from a train carriage. Seeing him in all his demonic glory, the crowd changed direction and darted down toward Tottenham Court Road, leaving the crossroads clear for them.

From the distance someone was shouting at him something about putting his hands up and lying face down on the road. Looking down Charing Cross Road, he could see a police cordon manned by dozens of armed officers in riot gear. Behind them were several police vehicles – vans and patrol cars – from which even more officers were alighting. A lone figure at the front was shouting into a megaphone and making demands of him.

Casually, Astolath stepped over to a wooden hoarding that ran around some building works at the base of the high-rise from which he'd just descended. His intention was to rip the wooden wall from its moorings and to throw it across the end of the road to show his contempt for their puny threats. Once the hoarding was down though, he saw the collection of plant machinery sitting there waiting for the next day's crew to begin work again. Of most interest to him immediately was the huge road roller that sat at the end of a stretch of fresh tarmac. Picking it up as if it were no heavier than a box of toys, he hoisted it above his head and tossed it toward the road block.

Amazingly, as it flew toward them, the front row of police officers all raised their riot shields as if this might be enough to save them from the several tons of machinery that was fast approaching.

It wasn't enough.

On a day of carnage, Charing Cross Road bore the brunt of some of the worst as the road roller took out the entire cordon and then careered into the vehicles behind and then, seemingly unstoppable, carried on, crossing Shaftesbury Avenue and on toward Trafalgar Square. It was finally stopped as it smashed through several book shops, undermining the structure of the terraced building on that side of the street and causing the entire thing to fall down. The road roller ended up buried along with hundreds of its victims.

Satisfied with his work, Astolath now turned back toward his new visitors who were standing in the middle of the crossroads and waiting for him patiently.

Priest opened the conversation.

"Greetings Lord Astolath. I trust that your visit to London has been a pleasant one?"

Astolath grunted his appreciation of the humorous remark.

"It has had its ups and downs," he smirked. "Now tell me demon, who are you?"

"Do you not recognize me? I'm a little dash of Lucifuge Rofocale, a smidgeon of Asmodeus, and a few drops here and there of Belial." Priest grinned broadly. "Oh and the rest of me is most definitely the one that you know as Priest."

"What is this? What do you mean?"

"Simply that your accomplices are now no more and I am here in their stead. I think that this also moves me up in the rankings slightly so I'm now your new fellow Arch Demon!"

Astolath actually looked dumb-struck for a few seconds. His mind turned over trying to compute the ramifications for the hierarchy now that the balance of power seemingly all lay in the hands of this interloper.

"And who is the woman?" he asked, stalling for time to take everything in.

"This? Oh, this is Rose. Rose, Astolath. Astolath, Rose." Priest grinned through his insolent introduction.

Rose, for her part, decided to play along.

"Pleased to meet you Astolath – I've heard so much about you."

"Ah, the female monkey that we've been hearing so much about," replied Astolath. "How are you enjoying your last few minutes of existence?"

"If it sees the end of you, then it will have all been worthwhile," countered Rose defiantly.

She'd obviously never met Astolath before – she was pretty sure that she would have remembered if she had – but she found herself well and truly hating him for all that he'd put Priest through. She thought this even though she knew that Priest didn't particularly care for her beyond the fact that she was of use to him at the moment.

Astolath ignored the jibe and turned back to Priest.

"It is time to put an end to this."

"I agree."

"It's a shame though. With your new position, you and I could have been allies and ruled Hell together. I was never after you, I was after the Lightbringer."

Priest seemed to consider this for a moment.

"I'm still not clear as to why you or Lucifer might have any interest in me, but I'm not interested either way. I don't want souls, I don't want power and I don't want your friendship. I just want my freedom from all this nonsense that concerns all of you so much. If I'm now an Arch Demon then as the humans say, that's just tough shit. I resign, I walk away from it all and you can have my key to the executive washroom."

Astolath struggled to follow the idioms but got the gist of what Priest was saying and it made no sense to him at all. Who wouldn't want unlimited power, to hold sway over others and to have them tremble at your every word? This was madness!

"I can't allow you to walk away Priest. Whether you like it or not, the hierarchy is in disorder now thanks to you. If you will not stand with me, I cannot let you stand with the Lightbringer."

Priest struggled to control his temper at hearing this. He approached Astolath to within a few feet and opened his arms wide to convey his despair.

"Are you deaf as well as ugly and stupid? I don't want any part of this and I care less about what Lucifer wants than I care for your ambitions. Why can't you just go somewhere and have it out between you?"

"There's no time like the present..." a voice came from behind Astolath.

The huge demon turned around to see where it came from and Priest in turn peered around his bulk for the same reason.

Sitting on a concrete block from the building site was Lucifer, still looking disheveled, as if he had spent several nights on the tiles. He was still in human form, wearing a long black coat, the collar of which he pulled up around his neck as if he were feeling cold, despite the warmth of the evening. He peered around Astolath to meet Priest's gaze.

"You may leave Priest. This is not your fight. We can talk later." He looked at Rose too, "Go with him."

Rose felt in that glance as if her veins had turned to ice. Had she just been addressed by The Devil himself, The Prince of Darkness... Satan? He looked so ordinary and yet there was a million years of evil in his eyes and his voice dripped with cruelty. She could feel it coming off him in waves of despair and, strangely enough, sadness that made her head swim. She'd become used to the presence of demons but this was something completely different and she had no desire to stay there any longer. Unsure of the etiquette for this sort of occasion she found herself quickly curtsying and walking away. She looked back once for Priest to make sure that he was following and then broke into a run and then flight for she knew not where – just anywhere away from Lucifer.

Priest joined her and took her by the hand.

"Don't worry about Lucifer. If he'd wished us harm we'd not be here now to have this conversation. I almost feel sorry for Astolath though… I wonder what he'll do to him?"

\*\*\*

Back at the crossroads, the devil stood up and approached Astolath.

"Have you nothing to say now that we're alone and you have no army or allies behind you?" he asked calmly, in almost a whisper.

Despite his thick headedness, Astolath knew that the writing was on the wall and he knew that he wasn't going to come out of this very well. He'd been well and truly played by Lucifer who had waited until the others had been taken out of the equation before making his move. What chance did he stand now against the Lightbringer? The only thing that he knew for certain was that he would go down fighting and would give Lucifer a few good scars to remember him by.

"I do not fear you Lucifer. Come, let us settle this," he uttered in contempt.

Lucifer turned his back on the demon and shrugged.

"What, do you think that there will be some epic clash of the titans here, that we'll battle it out in the hope that you may land a lucky blow and get the better of me?" He didn't give Astolath time to interject. "No, my misguided former Arch Demon. You will not have the opportunity for that. You will bow before me and if I tell you to, you will kiss my hind quarters. But there will be no battle. It's all over."

Astolath made to shout and to take a swing at Lucifer from behind but found himself rooted to the spot and unable to move or to make a sound.

"My only dilemma now," Lucifer continued, "Is whether to actually end your life now or whether to make this a lot more interesting – for me of course – and to bind you into bondage for a millennia or two until you either learn your lesson or I get bored of you and kill you. Either way, I need to return to Hell with you in order to make an example of you in front of its citizens."

Astolath was so angry now that his eyes actually filled with tears, as if the rage was trying to escape through his tear ducts. Death he could handle, but humiliation and ignominy would be unbearable and for the first time he actually felt sorry for himself. A day ago he'd been eating 'All-day Jumbo Breakfasts' and had been the Lord of Hell. Now it had all gone wrong and the tears of rage did in fact turn to ones of self-pity.

Back away from it all and unable to hear what was being said, the officers and gaping onlookers at the barriers and cordons around the crossroads had all breathed a collective sigh of relief when Rose and Priest had flown away. Surely all the chaos was now at an end?

Now they were left with the puzzling site of a strange man in a long coat talking to a blubbing demon. There was just no way to write all of this up in the police reports but yet again, the social networking sites were being given a constant feed of photographs, video files and Tweets conveying what had been occurring to the greedily devouring online masses.

The latest video online video sensation was even now being uploaded and streamed from a variety of points of view. It showed the strange blonde man turning around to face the hulking demon creature. He then reached up as if he was going to pat the demon on the head, but instead pressed downward, squashing him almost flat. The man then squeezed what was left from the sides until the demon was no longer visible. Reaching down to pick something up, they then saw the man moulding something in his hands as if he were rolling a ball of silly putty or cooking dough. He then tossed it into the air a couple of times before putting it in his pocket.

Having decided to keep a hold on Astolath for a while, and with him safely stowed away in the zipper pocket inside his coat, Lucifer then looked at the watching crowds. He turned to each set of people and gave them a flourish and a deep bow, like a magician soaking up non-existent applause.

Then, his work done, he promptly disappeared with a loud bang, a flash and a puff of red smoke.

## XXXVI
## Perchance to Dream

Priest decided that the best thing course of action was to repair to his loophole and then decide what to do next. He and Rose needed to talk and to work out how he was going to get his essence back. Yes, he had ingested the essences of other demons, but it felt a bit like walking around in clothes belonging to someone else and he still didn't feel quite himself.

Because Rose had helped him and since *he* had dragged her into the whole affair he had determined to do right by her and not leave her in limbo. He wanted his essence back but not so much that he was content to see her suffer. Why he felt this way he couldn't quite say. It should have made no odds to him whether she lived or died, but for some reason it did. And besides, he was actually starting to enjoy her company. It was something about her trusting acceptance of everything that had been put upon her. Her whole life had not just been flipped upside down; it had been shaken up, turned inside out and thrown into the washing machine on a fast spin cycle as well. She had taken it all on with good grace and a lack of the panic and hysteria normally present in specimens of her race when under duress.

After a short trans-dimensional hop through the in-between places of time and space, they arrived back at the loophole. Rose immediately threw herself onto the bed and let out a huge sigh.

"What a day!"

"You have a gift for understatement sometimes Rose," grinned Priest, sitting on the edge next to her.

"I feel like I could sleep for a hundred years…" and with that, her breathing started to deepen and she fell into a profound slumber.

Again, Priest marveled at her resilience. Twenty minutes ago she was in the presence of Lucifer and now all she wanted to do was to sleep. He guessed that he'd only been told a small fraction of what she'd been through in her life to be able to take such events in her stride. But it wasn't over yet for her: she was the custodian of his essence and he wanted it back. He tried to think back over how long he had been on the run from Astolath and how much time had passed since the ritual with Tris: four, five days?

So he had another three weeks in which to fulfill his obligations to do something about 'guiding men to wisdom'. He figured that he already made a good start in that direction – men now knew not to mess with demons. He was thinking about the carnage caused around London and was unaware of the exorcism that had been interrupted by Asmodeus and friends. Despite their differences though, had he known, it was something of which Priest would have approved and maybe even have done himself under the circumstances.

Perhaps, he thought, the only thing to do in the short term was to seek out Brutus and apologise for his behaviour. Epona was his only link to the psychopomps now that the Arcanum was in ruins. At least he assumed that he wouldn't be able to use the weathervane to contact them anymore - unless there was more than one conduit through which to reach them?

He reflected as well on the loss of Mulciber.

Mulciber had been his friend for as long as he could remember, but now he felt used and misled. It irked him that he couldn't be a bit more self-righteous about this, but having made a career out of these attributes himself, he felt a definitive landslide on the moral high ground. He was gone now and old Crowley would be left to rattle about the mansion on his own for a while. Perhaps he would pay him a visit to relay the news of his master's demise, just to see the look on his face. Or, maybe he'd take the butler on himself. His own palace was self-maintaining really, but something stuck in his craw – as it did for all demons – that Crowley had crowned himself 'To Mega Therion' while alive. He fully understood why Mulciber had wanted to take the pretender down a peg or two, and now that he was gone, perhaps Priest would adopt the mantle of master in honour of the better times that he had shared with his friend.

Priest laughed to himself at the realization that along with taking on the traits of his demonic enemies, he seemed to have also picked up a few human traits from his brief time as one of them. He had become, it seemed, slightly sentimental and forgiving: two more strange and unfamiliar feelings which he wouldn't quite understand or begin to identify until he explained them to Rose later on. For the moment though, he felt quite low and depressed at the thought of a future without Mulciber, no matter how duplicitous he had been.

He also had a little unfinished business with Eldredd to take care of as well. Perhaps he would be able to fill in the gaps in the story for him and to explain what the hell he had been playing at. Sinn too would probably be interested in all that had happened.

Once Rose awoke he would explain to her his plan about contacting Epona once more. For the moment they were both safe from unwanted attention and could direct all of their efforts at discovering what their quest really entailed. He needed no sleep himself now that he was back in demon form, but that didn't matter. He climbed gently onto the bed next to Rose, lay down and closed his eyes.

# XXXVII
## Happy Returns?

News hadn't yet reached the palace that Lucifer had exacted a humiliating and very public revenge upon Astolath. That morning Helnocker had even dared to sit on the Infernal Throne in the great hall, content for the first time in a long while that he had things under control. His lord and master would soon return triumphant (and hopefully in a good mood), to find that a tight ship had been run in his absence. Yes, things were going right for him at last. He might even end up with a promotion and he allowed himself a small grin at the idea.

Below him, creeping through the catacombs upon which the palace stood, a dusty and distraught Eldredd was making his way to visit Sinn. He'd not dared to try the front entrance again and had instead used the unsophisticated route of bribing a solitary guard at the rear of the palace to look the other way while he disappeared down the cellar steps. He'd promised the minor demon a step up and a place in the new administration in return for his help and the fool had been so gullible and ambitious that he went for it hook, line and sinker.

Of course, once he'd turned his back, Eldredd had fallen upon him with great gusto, taking out his frustration on the guard in a savage attack that left the dupe mounted on his own spear and with his head facing the wrong way. For the sake of prudence, Eldredd propped him up against a wall so that at a glance he would appear to still be on duty if anyone bothered to check on him. With Helnocker in charge, he gambled that things would still be a bit more lax than usual.

Emerging at last from the gloom of the catacombs, Eldredd quickly orientated himself toward a small servant's staircase and began his ascent into the palace proper. Once he was on the ground floor, it was a simple matter to make his way unseen into the library where he banked on Sinn being, still poring over the books.

Sinn was indeed still there. Not needing sleep, he'd been at it continuously and had amassed a large stack of weighty-looking tomes on the desk in front of him. They were piled so high that he didn't see Eldredd approach and sit down on a chair opposite.

"What are you still doing here, Sinn?" he said in a low tone.

Sinn jumped up, scattering books and papers all about the floor at his feet.

"Eldredd! Where did you spring from?" he gasped in surprise. Then, recovering his composure and not waiting for an answer he continued, "You'll never guess what I've found out…"

"Save it for later, we've got to go now. Take whatever you need, but we need to get out of here – quickly."

"What's happened?" asked Sinn indignantly.

"The long and the short of it is Lucifer 1, Astolath 0."

"What?"

"Yes, he was caught off guard and now Priest is an Arch Demon, that is, the only Arch Demon, and Lucifer is back in charge of things."

Eldredd had followed Priest and Rose back into the city and had seen the whole thing from afar. He'd seen the messy demise of Belial and realized that something similar had probably happened to Asmodeus when Priest emerged from the wreckage of a restaurant. Then, he'd witnessed the final humiliation of Astolath.

He quickly conveyed all the events to Sinn then explained finally that they were even shorter of time than they had been and that they now had to get moving.

Sinn picked up several volumes and tucked them under his arm.

"So we are to come out of all of this with nothing?" he complained, just about keeping the panic out of his voice.

"I wouldn't say that exactly," replied Eldredd, producing a golden trinket seemingly from thin air. "We have this."

"And what is it, a souvenir?"

"It's the Golden Ankh of Hermes Trismegistus," beamed Eldredd. "I took it from the body of Mulciber after Priest had dispatched him. Priest didn't know that he had it, but I'm sure that we can use it as a bargaining chip if Priest now decides to come after us. It's got something to do with what Priest was attempting to do on Earth and I suspect that he'll be anxious to get his hands on it."

"And Lucifer – does he know of our involvement with Astolath?"

"I can't be sure, but to be on the safe side, this is why I'm suggesting that we make a swift exit and lay low for a while." Eldredd pointed toward the door and nudged his head in its direction to convey the urgency of his request.

"Well, you're the one that's just been standing there talking,' returned Sinn. 'I'm ready when you are. Where shall we go?"

Eldredd was almost fit to burst with frustration.

"Can we just get outside and away from the palace first and then we can make plans. I don't want to be here when the Lightbringer gets home, do you?"

"I suppose not. Can I have a look at the Ankh?"

"NO, GET OUT NOW!" shouted Eldredd, allowing his temper to get the better of him before realizing that he might have just announced his presence to the whole garrison.

Peeking into the hallway before leaving the library, there seemed to be no one around and so Eldredd signaled the all-clear. The two demons headed quickly and quietly for the service stairway, neither saying a word until they reached the relative safety of the catacombs.

"Well?" Sinn whispered. "Where can we go to hide out in safety?"

"I'm thinking, I'm thinking!" hissed Eldredd in reply, looking about him left and right to make sure that they were alone.

"How about the Garden of Hesperides – I've heard that it's very nice at this time of year?" interrupted Sinn again.

"Will you shut up and let me think!"

"Or there's the City of the Caesars, or Meropis – I've always wanted to go there."

"Wherever it is, you'll end up going on your own if you don't shut that gaping hole!" threatened Eldredd in frustration.

"Well maybe I will go on my own if you're going to be like that."

"I should have stayed behind in London and let Astolath stave my head in," muttered Eldred in frustration. "It would have been a sweet mercy rather than a lifetime of having to listen to this!"

***

There was no fanfare when Lucifer arrived back at the palace, he just appeared at the gates and strolled by the terrified guards who competed among themselves to be first to fall to their feet and grovel for mercy and forgiveness – neither of which Lucifer was in the mood to grant. As he made his way across the courtyard and into the huge atrium, he left a trail of charred and smoking bodies behind him; each one had spontaneously combusted at the merest steely glance from the Lightbringer, their bodies burned and their souls consigned to endless oblivion in the blink of an eye.

At the sight of Lucifer entering the great hall, Helnocker broke into an instantaneous cold sweat while at the same time finding that his throat had dried completely and he was unable to make a noise. He just about found the strength to leap from the Infernal Throne before prostrating himself on the ground before the returning Lord of Hell. All around him, guards, servants and advisors were being reduced to the same blackened state that the others had been, leaving Helnocker awaiting the same fate.

"Get up Helnocker, you are safe for the moment and I have a task for you," commanded Lucifer, lowering himself into his throne and kicking off his shoes.

Helnocker did as he was bid and stood trembling, still unable to utter a syllable.

"I have something here that I want you to look after," said Lucifer reaching into his coat pocket. He pulled out a small green ball of something unidentifiable and tossed it onto the floor at Helnocker's feet.

The former second-in-command of the Arch Demon bent down to inspect what he had been given. It was mushy and leathery at the same time. There were teeth dotted about its surface and there was also definitely an eye peering up at him. As it lay there it pulsed as if it where breathing in and out.

He looked up and gave a 'what is it?' kind of look to Lucifer.

"This is your former master. I have made my displeasure known to him and this is the form that he will be occupying for the foreseeable future – at least 'til I finally decide upon what to do with him."

"W-where shall I keep him my lord?" asked Helnocker, finally finding his voice.

"That is entirely up to you. Now leave me."

"Yes my lord." Helnocker bowed low and went to pick Astolath up off the floor before thinking better of it and kicking him toward the door instead. As he did so, he fancied that he could hear a tiny noise of complaint from the round ball and so he kicked it again harder just to test whether it had been his imagination. But no, the ball definitely didn't like being kicked. And so he continued to hoof it along the corridor before deciding to take it to the top of the nearest staircase to see if it would bounce as well.

Back in the great hall, Lucifer stretched out his legs and wiggled his toes, sinking back into his throne. He was back in charge but it was ultimately an empty victory. He was still the ruler of a place that he didn't want to rule. He'd once told someone that it was better to reign in Hell than to serve in Heaven, but now he wasn't so sure of this. In a way he had even been grateful to Astolath for providing him with a distraction and allowing him an excuse to abandon the Infernal Throne for a time.

He sympathized entirely with Priest and his longing to escape. It's just that he was Lucifer and a permanent vacation wasn't an option. He had a role to fulfill and a part to play on the cosmic stage that didn't allow for alteration. Perhaps he could spend more time with Priest in the future to discuss how he felt? Maybe that would make him feel better.

He got up and crossed to a large window looking out across his realm and wondered - could the devil ever have a friend?

# Epilogue

Somewhere in the deepest English countryside, four figures stood in the middle of a stone circle. It was raining gently, darkening the tops of the megaliths and giving them an ominous look, as if they were frozen giants waiting to step backward and leave the hilltop on which they had stood for so many millennia. Far older than the stones, Anubis, Michael, Epona and Barnumbirr made for a strange sight among the fields and hedgerows but in the next field the sheep paid them scant attention and continued to graze as their young gamboled around them oblivious to the downpour.

"Trismegistus, The Thrice Great One, is dead," explained Epona to the others. "He was killed by a demon named Mulciber who also stole the Golden Ankh. This is all that I have been able to find out so far."

"And where is this Mulciber now?" asked Barnumbirr.

"He is dead too, but when I found what was left of him, he didn't have the Ankh."

Anubis attempted to summarize their position, "So we have Priest's essence for safekeeping, but this girl, Rose, has his powers and these are keeping her from crossing over. He has three more weeks in which to carry out our request or we get to keep his soul… and hers too presumably?"

"That would seem to be the position," confirmed Epona.

"But you helped him and attempted to take him to safety when he slipped away and went to confront Astolath," said Michael. "These don't seem to be the actions of someone who wants to aid mankind to fulfill its destiny."

"Well, if we're honest, Priest was coerced into that part of the bargain – it wasn't his choice," Epona corrected the Archangel.

"Yes, but the end will justify the means, and besides, I enjoyed the irony of tricking a demon out of his soul."

This brought smiles out on to the faces of the others but Epona felt the need to remind them of their responsibilities.

"Yes, but only temporarily. If Priest delivers the goods then we will have to release it to him again."

"Of course Epona, I meant nothing by it," Michael said reassuringly. "Demons are allowed to have a sense of humour, but it always takes people aback when angels display the same trait. I don't know why…"

"I've always had the same problem," lamented Anubis. "The last time I weighed a soul, I put a hand on the scale to tip the balance out of favour to the traveler. When I revealed to her that I had just been joking and that she had really been found worthy, she went crazy at me instead of being grateful. But you know how it is; when you do the same thing for millennia, you have to cheer yourself up and find a bit of variety in the job, don't you?"

The others nodded and sighed in sympathy and agreement at his predicament.

"But to matters more important," interjected Barnumbirr. "Priest's activities have also resulted in a change in the balance of power in Hell. Lucifer will either want to keep him on his side in an alliance, or he will want to get him out of the way. Either way, we'll lose out."

No one had really considered the far-reaching consequences of what had happened in the last few days. Developments at the top of Hell's hierarchy usually had a domino effect elsewhere as policies and allegiances shifted and cemented.

"We need to recover the Ankh somehow," chimed in Epona. "Once we have that, we have a bargaining tool with Priest and can make him see sense."

"But we don't know where it is," complained Michael. "And I don't have time to look for it."

Epona shot a look at him that would have translated in human understanding to "You useless bloody male!" but the meaning was lost on the Archangel.

"I'll try to make contact with Priest again," she replied to his lame protest. "I've helped him before and he'll trust me. I've also made the acquaintance of the woman as well. I'm sure that I can influence her, and between us I'm sure that we can influence him."

This elicited a look from Anubis that would have translated in human understanding to 'You typical manipulative female' and the meaning this time was fully appreciated by Epona who smiled in understanding.

"Very well," intoned Michael, who always liked to think that he was the senior psychopomp at these meetings. "Let us meet again a week hence and touch base on progress."

The other three gaped at him in disbelief.

"Really Michael – did you just say 'touch base'?" asked Epona looking around at the others for moral support.

"Yes, what if I did?" protested Michael.

"Oh, no reason. Let's park it there and see where we are going forward," she chuckled.

"Yes," added Anubis, "we can synergize our efforts and formulate a solution!"

The others cracked completely up at this suggestion before Barnumbirr finished things off by suggesting, "Perhaps they could find ways to incentivize Priest in order to maximize his output?"

Michael maintained a straight face and a look of haughty offence, which only served to heighten the contagious mirth within the group. Eventually though, the laughter tailed off and composure returned, each one remembering once more the weighty responsibility of their position.

"Yes Michael, you are quite right," said Epona brightly. "We'll come together in week and I'll report back on any progress that I've made."

With that, the four of them nodded to one another and took their leave. As each one left the stone circle, they faded from view leaving Epona standing there on her own.

# About Aiden Truss

Aiden Truss is a forty one year-old geek who still thinks that he's twenty-one. Despite never having grown up, he's now been married for twenty four years and has two sons who have grown up against all odds to be strangely well adjusted.

Aiden spends his time flitting between high and low culture: he holds an MA in Cultural and Critical Studies and can often be seen stalking the galleries and museums of London, but also likes watching WWE, listening to heavy metal music, collecting comic books and playing classic video games.

Aiden lives in Kent, England and Gape is his first novel.

Made in the USA
Charleston, SC
18 September 2013